Carlette Poussant:
Island Girl

Carlette Poussant: Island Girl

Leola Charles

URBAN BOOKS
www.urbanbooks.net

URBAN SOUL is published by

Urban Books
1199 Straight Path
West Babylon, NY 11704

ISBN-13: 978-1-59983-084-1
ISBN-10: 1-59983-084-1

First Printing: March 2010
10 9 8 7 6 5 4 3 2

Printed in the United States of America

Carlette Poussant:
Island Girl

PROLOGUE

Standing in the long line at the airport, seventeen-year-old Carlette peeked around the tall white man in front of her and counted the customers in front of him, then behind her. She was number fifteen and the last in line. She looked at all the other lines. Those were longer than the one she stood in. Before she could shift from her right foot to her left to balance the pressure of her weight and do a little pouting, she heard uproarious laughter and talking.

"Sadie Ann Ray! Where's your bags? You got 'em all?"

"Yes, I have them all. I'm not that helpless, Sandra Bernice Ray!"

"I was just asking you because I know how forgetful you are, always leaving something behind. And you don't have to git mad."

"I am not mad."

"Yes, you are, Sadie. You call me by my whole name only when you're mad or somethin's wrong."

"You called *me* by my full name—"

"That's different. I always call you by your full name and tease you like that, but you call me Bernice, never Sandra, unless you're mad or somethin' is serious." Bernice smiled playfully. As usual, she was purposely trying to get on her twin sister's nerves.

Almost everyone in the airport, including Carlette, focused their attention on the two neatly dressed older women, who had come bursting through the doors of the terminal in a disruptive manner and talking loudly, one in a blue suit with blue and white spectator pumps, the other in a red suit with red and white spectator pumps. Both were of average height and wore their graying hair short. The only difference between them was one was a little browner than the other.

Although Sadie seemed not to be annoyed with her sister's incessant pestering, she raised her voice slightly but remained calm as she responded, "Sandra Bernice Ray, if you don't stop fussin' at me . . ." She stopped walking and put her hand on her hip and stared Bernice down without saying another word.

The debate instantly ceased, and the two went on walking and talking loudly about something else.

Bernice ruthlessly teased Sadie at times, but she also knew when Sadie meant business, and the teasing would stop. She had never forgotten the knock-down, drag-out fight the two had had at twelve, when Sadie had given her the look and Bernice had continued to tease her just because Sadie had always been a little less fiery and a little sweeter.

Bernice had worn some visible battle scars that day and had learned that Sadie's shut-up look meant just that, so there was no need for her to feel her sister's furious, whirling fists a second time.

As the two sauntered through the airport, their eyes roamed for victims, anyone who would stand still long enough to listen to their endless chatter.

Suddenly Sadie tapped her sister's shoulder and pointed. "Bernice, you see that pretty baby over there?"

"That is one pretty child. His parents have to be proud."

As the two women headed off in the direction of the unsuspecting parents, Carlette continued to watch them. The two seemed to be making rounds in the airport, and she was hoping and praying that she would board the plane before they got in line and got the notion to set their sights on her.

No sooner did Carlette turn her head to see how far along the line had moved than there was someone's hot breath on the back of her neck.

"What's your name, suga?" Bernice asked loudly.

Afraid to turn, she spoke in a whisper, hoping to discourage the woman's loud tone. "Carlette."

"Baby, are you pregnant?" Bernice quizzed.

Embarrassed, Carlette looked down at the floor. *Surely the old bitty isn't so ancient that she can't remember what a pregnant woman looks like.* She answered politely, "Yes, ma'am, I am." *But it's none of your old ugly business,* Carlette wanted to say. She kept her back to the woman. Ignoring her might help get rid of her.

Bernice touched Carlette's shoulder. "Oh,

honey, don't feel shame. You didn't get that way all by yourself. A lot of people gotta take that blame."

Sadie crooked her mouth. "Hush up, Bernice. Don't you see you shaming this poor child?"

Carlette took in a deep breath and bit her lip to silence her thoughts.

"I ain't trying to shame her," Bernice insisted. "Just tell the truth, Sadie. You know for a fact that people don't tell you right. When you first start talkin', they try to keep you from cursing. They tell you that certain things are hot. They might even put your hand near the heat to prove it. When you start walking, they tell you that you can fall, and not to climb up and stand on certain stuff, and you learn real quick that what you've been told about falling and hot is true, because they put it in a form that you understand. But don't nobody get deep into what can happen if two naked bodies connect, and tell you not to get up under a naked man or a woman or not to climb up on top of one of them to keep from making babies. They just say, 'Don't come home with no babies,' and they believe that, just like animals, their children will automatically know all about sex. And the most ignorant part is, they still refuse to educate themselves or their children even after their children have prematurely interrupted their lives with sex, babies, and even disease. And, Carlette, after you have this child, remember that you, me, and everybody is responsible for what happens to any of our children, okay?"

Carlette nodded.

Sadie snickered at her sister's bizarre sex lesson.

"That was in our day, Bernice. They teach the young people about all that nowadays."

Bernice shook her head. "No, they don't. You know I work for the teen center and know what I'm talking about. They might tell them a little something, but I know for sure that many times they give those children pills, condoms, pamphlets, and very little educating, and most times that be the end of that." She put her fist on her hip and took a serious stance. "There is not much you can teach someone about sex from a little pamphlet, and with the little resources and time we have to inform people about their bodies and how important they are to them. And you'd be surprised at the number of girls who get abortions behind their parents' backs. Sometimes those girls don't get pregnant for years to come after that, and some of them contract diseases that their parents don't know nothing about. . . ."

It seemed like the entire airport was listening to the loud conversation along with Carlette, but she didn't care and turned to face the women and began listening intensely to the edgy discussion. Although she was shy, it piqued her interest, and she wanted to know more. This was one of the most exciting moments in her life, the dialogue was juicy, and she was learning some new things. She was also the center of attention, and for some strange reason, the weird situation made her feel important, like a celebrity.

Bernice continued. "Yes, honey, it is true, 'cause one of my nieces"—she pointed at Sadie, then at herself—"our brother's daughter, she got into that new stuff . . . the stuff God say is ugly. She's a pretty girl, so this man, who is older than she is, got hold of her that way, and now they're living in sin." She clutched her chest and closed her eyes like a dying woman.

Some listeners snickered; others laughed out loud.

Carlette blushed. She knew exactly what the new sinful stuff was. She and her aunt had just discussed it, and she still had questions about the strange intimacy.

"Come on up here," called a young, handsome black man, who was waving and beckoning, drawing Carlette's attention away from the conversation.

Carlette turned her head from side to side, looking for the person whose attention he was trying to capture.

The stranger pointed at her. "You. I'm talking to you. Come on up front."

Hesitating, Carlette used her finger to touch her chest and moved her lips. "Me?"

"Yes! Come on up here, honey. You shouldn't be way back there," he replied.

Carlette wasn't ready to leave the two women. She wanted to know more.

"Go ahead, honey," Bernice said, touching Carlette's shoulder. "You don't need to be standing in this line so long, anyway. There are at least eight people ahead of you."

Carlette looked down the line again. In a matter of minutes it had shortened. She thanked Bernice and moved forward.

Some of the customers who hadn't heard the Ray sisters' blunt announcement regarding Carlette's pregnancy frowned as she sauntered closer to the front. When they glimpsed her protruding stomach, their faces softened, and their lips curled into smiles.

The young man had much respect. He took Carlette's hand and gently patted it as she approached him. "Sorry, but I felt as though I needed to rescue you from that production of *Biology to the Fifth Power in a Crowded Airport,* and the two old ladies who featured themselves in the starring roles."

The two laughed almost hysterically.

"What's your name, young lady?" he asked.

"Carlette."

"I'm Harold Beacon. My wife is also with child, and I'm trying to get home to her before she delivers."

Carlette smiled at him shyly. "Were you visiting here on the island?"

"No, I'm here on business. If it wasn't for that, I would be home with the love of my life." Harold let out a breath of exasperation that made his body shudder with its release, causing him and Carlette to chuckle.

"Well, thanks, Harold, for letting me ahead of you. Oh, and the rescue . . . I was actually beginning to enjoy the crazy conversation."

"Really?"

Carlette grinned as she nodded.

"Well," Harold said, hunching his shoulders, "I think we all learned something from that production."

They both laughed again.

"Hope you make it home before your wife delivers."

"God, Carlette, me too. Are you meeting up with your spouse, too?"

"No, I'm going to visit my aunt's friend."

"Don't tell me you're on your way to Washington, too."

"No. Atlanta."

They both broke into laughter again as they said in unison, "It's hot there!"

"I hear a little accent in your voice." Harold rubbed his chin and smiled. "What part of the island are you from?"

"Tret. It's a small place, sort of a village."

"It must be beautiful."

"It's okay. They're putting in some new buildings for businesses, schools, things like that."

"Well, it sure did produce a beautiful young lady."

Carlette blushed. She didn't feel beautiful. Harold was only trying to be polite.

"You know, Carlette, it's too bad that you and I met at the airport and not on the island. I'm thinking about bringing my wife back here after she delivers. You could have shown us some of the sights."

"I know a few." Carlette gave a positive smile, not wanting Harold to detect her naiveté and unfamiliarity with anything outside her small village.

"Well, Carlette," Harold said, extending his hand, "it was nice meeting you. Maybe we will meet up on the island again someday."

After confirming their flights, Carlette and Harold gave each other comforting words and hugs, then parted.

Amazed at how good the stranger had made her feel about herself, Carlette watched him until he disappeared. She looked around for the two sex professors, and they, too, had disappeared. Carlette was only somewhat relieved. The women had seemed knowledgeable about a subject that had always confused her, but she was still thankful for the rescue. She'd met someone nice.

Tret, Tret, T-T-T-Tret. Carlette laughed as she thought about how she and others were constantly teased about the name and size of their village, how you had to stutter to make sure you said it right, and walk by it slowly so that you wouldn't miss it. The villagers also laughed at how the name sounded like a medical condition, but they loved it just the same. The little village had its own police department, a hospital, an emergency auto service, schools, a recreation center, two theaters, and more, including places where many out-of-towners and islanders went for their portion of hidden sin, and the water was clean and clear, just right for swimming.

On the plane a gentleman tried giving up his aisle seat to Carlette. He had seen someone be kind to her and had caught the bug. Carlette thanked him but let him know that she needed to sit in an aisle seat closer to the bathroom.

Before taking a seat next to a woman, Carlette clumsily struggled to store overhead the bag containing her meager belongings. Holding the strap of her zipperless, pouchlike purse tightly to secure its movement and contents, she slowly lowered herself in the seat. Her reflection stared back at her in the tinted window of the plane, causing her to plop down rapidly in the cushiony chair.

Feeling insecure about her appearance again,

Carlette looked at the woman sitting in the seat next to her to see if she, too, was appalled by her reflection. The woman was reading a magazine and hadn't as much as glanced up. But the pretty, thin, young blonde's features still caused Carlette discomfort.

Out of reflex Carlette took in a deep breath and subconsciously ran her hand over her stomach. *God, I feel ugly. Hope my figure comes back after I have my baby. Wish Aunt Genevee had had enough money to get back home from the airport. If she'd seen me off, then I wouldn't feel so alone and ugly.*

It had been a little short of four years ago when Carlette had met Ricky, but 1985 now felt like a lifetime away to her. Nineteen eighty nine had come so quickly, her sudden pregnancy seemed like a blur and made her feel old, out of place, and as though she had lived another life.

The movement of her baby made her forget how old and out of place she felt at seventeen. *Thank you, God. I can't wait until my baby arrives. He's going to be just as gorgeous as his father.*

Carlette was still unaware of her beauty and believed she needed to return to the time she secretly called "before the stomach." She glanced down into her pouchlike purse, and there it was, her savior and best friend, her personal journal, in which she wrote in the third person, because it made her life more purposeful. Just holding the journal lightened Carlette's heart, and thoughts of Harold's kindness filled her mind, causing her eyes to tear up with sentiment. Her encounter with Harold would definitely have to go into her journal, as would the encounter with the sex professors. Reflecting back on those two almost made her giggle out loud.

Carlette held the journal up to her breast and thought, *Part of my entry about Harold will read: Amazed at how good the stranger made her feel about herself, Carlette watched him until he disappeared.* It had definitely been one of the warmest feelings she had experienced in her life. She had watched him until he was out of sight, allowing the memory of his kindness to linger.

Carlette was one to remember pleasant encounters, because she had had so few. To her, they were as valuable as what she jotted down in her journal about herself, and the way she interpreted the entries. She would also find a positive way to include the two sisters she'd met, especially Bernice, who had told her some things she could have used before she got pregnant.

But now was the time for her to focus on her unborn child and caring for the baby. She would also mention this in her journal. Writing about her life as if she was describing someone else's existence helped Carlette to cheer herself on. It gave her hope for a brighter tomorrow whenever she was feeling low.

Allowing her mind to slip away from Harold and the sex professors, she flipped open her journal and began reading what she called her "beautiful beginning," the events that had led up to her plane ride.

CHAPTER 1

Carlette left her flute lesson, which she, like most children, hated but had to endure once a week as her aunt demanded. She would sigh with relief each time a lesson ended and would almost sprint to the bottom of the stairs of the small but somewhat modern two-story, redbrick building whenever she left the music room. The pleasant sounds of pianos, flutes, guitars, and other instruments made her feel free and tranquil and definitely conflicted with her negative feelings for her lessons. Why did she hate going to her lessons but want to sit on the steps and listen to the various sounds that escaped through the different doors in the music school? Carlette's reason was always the same. "Because the sounds are actually beautiful and pleasant." But as soon as her feet left the last step of the music school, she would forget about the sounds, look up at the bright tropical sun, close her eyes, take in a deep breath of the fresh island air, and allow her mind to wander to something she felt was even more pleasant. Ricky

Roxen. She had secretly admired him and would pretend to be with him whenever she thought about or saw him.

"Carlette! Carlette! Pretty Brown! Hey, Carlette!"

The deep-toned voice summoning Carlette from a distance interrupted her thoughts before she could round the corner to the next street. It caught up to her before she could turn around completely. There stood Ricky Roxen, the boy who lived in her dreams.

Ricky tugged Carlette's arm and proceeded to spin her around.

"Oh, hi, Ricky!" Carlette jerked away from him. Although her aunt wasn't around, she was afraid of a rumor getting back to her aunt.

"Girl! Don't you hear somebody call and see them chase you down just to say hi, Pretty Brown?" Ricky said casually, a smile showing his pretty white teeth.

"Yeah, Ricky. You never gave me a chance to turn. I was going to turn." Carlette was nervous.

"Were you, Carlette? Then why you snatch your arm from me, girl? You think I steal arms, Pretty Brown?" Ricky was smiling while he spoke the words in a teasing way.

A grin came across Carlette's face that made her look even prettier, enticing Ricky even more.

"You got a boyfriend?"

"No, Ricky. I—"

"Can I be your boyfriend, Carlette?"

"No!"

"Why not?"

"My aunt, Ricky, she um, um, my aunt . . . she doesn't allow it."

"But you're very pretty." Ricky took Carlette's hands and stood back to admire her. "You're wasting all of these good looks on nothing. It's time for you to have a boyfriend, or at least your first kiss."

Carlette eased her hands out of Ricky's. "I'm too young . . . still a little girl. I can't." Although Carlette had uttered those words, she was still daydreaming about kissing Ricky and wanted to return her hands to his. Before she could complete her thoughts, Ricky had taken her hands into his again.

"Girl, most girls, young or old, have done so much already, and you never been kissed or had a boyfriend? Not even secretly?"

"No, Ricky. Now, let go of my hands. I gotta go. Aunt Genevee will be upset if I'm late or if someone tells her that you were touching me." She snatched her hands from Ricky again.

"Okay, Pretty Brown, okay. Be like that. But you're going to be my girl someday."

With those words still humming in her ears, Carlette wrapped her arms around her flute case a little tighter and almost sprinted down the block, chanting to herself, "He likes me. He wants me to be his girlfriend."

The symptoms of light-headedness, weak knees, and butterflies in her stomach were foreign to Carlette, and so was Ricky noticing her and knowing her name. She didn't have any friends, and no one ever really talked to her, but Ricky thought of her as beautiful and wanted her for his own.

All the way home Carlette thought and daydreamed of Ricky and felt as though she were walking on pillows. As soon as she turned her key and crossed the threshold of her aunt's small house, the daydream stopped, and reality hit her across the back with an open hand.

"Girl, where you been? You're ten minutes late!" Then another hand across the back, and more yelling. "Get your sorry self in 'ere! Clean that filthy room and this kitchen! I wish your mother had never died! All I do is spend all my time . . . blah, blah, blah."

Carlette's mind shut down. Her aunt's speech about her being nothing but a burden had been delivered to her so many times, it sounded like a broken record. And Carlette was more than tired of hearing it. She had also wished many times that her mother and father had never died, that a nicer relative would come for her, or maybe she could just die and be with her parents.

She began remembering how nice her mother had been and wondered why she had to die when Carlette was only six; she had already lost her father at three. *This isn't fair, God! This isn't fair! I'm barely fourteen. I'm still a child. I should have someone who loves me.*

Carlette's silent pleading, as usual, remained silent. It seemed as though even God couldn't hear her. Little did Carlette know that time would change her life for the better, and that suffering had its rewards.

Carlette took a short pause to stretch.
"Ma'am, would you like something?"
Startled, Carlette wiped the tear away from her

left eye before it slid down her cheek. She looked up into the attractive face of the young black flight attendant, who was pushing a cart. "No, nothing for me." Again, she subconsciously ran her hand over her stomach as her eyes roamed the slender flight attendant's physique.

"Are you okay, Miss?"

"Yes, yes, I'm fine. I just don't need anything right now." The concern in the flight attendant's voice forced Carlette to perk up and smile. "Thank you for asking."

The flight attendant smiled back. "You're with child?"

"Yes," Carlette replied quickly.

"I have two girls." The flight attendant sighed. "Wish that I could take them on every plane ride with me. I miss them when I'm away."

"Does your husband watch them for you?"

"My husband? The only father my children know is mine. My parents watch my children. They encouraged me to continue with my life and let me know that it wasn't over just because I had twins by a man who didn't want to be responsible."

"He doesn't love his children, his girls?"

"He comes to get them, even pays child support, but when I was pregnant, he didn't want to have anything to do with me. And when I wasn't pregnant anymore, I chose not to deal with him ever again. What do I need with a man who can't hang during hard times?"

Carlette hunched her shoulders, looking sad.

"Are you married?" The flight attendant was still smiling.

"Yes, but me and my baby's father got separated. We still love each other."

"Was he in a war or something?"

"No. We're from a rural part of the island, and it's easy to lose a loved one with the wrong person involved in your life."

"Stewardess! Stewardess!" Another passenger was waving at the flight attendant, trying to get her attention.

"I'll be right there, sir. Anyway, ma'am—"

"My name's Carlette."

"Okay, Carlette, relax and enjoy the flight. Hope that you and your husband reunite. And you can call me Illia, okay? And don't hesitate to let me know if you need anything."

"Okay, Illia. Thank you."

As Illia scurried away to tend to the summoning passenger, Carlette opened her journal and continued to read.

CHAPTER 2

It was still early when Carlette finished her chores and lay across her small bed and fell asleep. When she awakened, it was dark, and she could hear her aunt snoring from her bedroom. That made her happy. More than those stupid flute lessons, she hated her aunt's pestering.

As Carlette grabbed her robe and headed for the bathroom, she heard something hit her window. When she looked out, she saw Ricky. Her heart began to race with fear. With shaky hands, she slowly and quietly lifted the window and whispered, "Get away from 'ere."

"Carlette, come down, or I'll come up," Ricky whispered loudly.

"No. My aunt will kill me if she catches you around my window, so go away."

Carlette wondered how he had found her. Then she thought again. Anyone could be found in her tiny hometown. It would be easy to find a timid mouse if you really wanted to.

Ricky walked away from Carlette's house with his head down, his hands in his pockets.

Carlette gently closed her bedroom window and immediately walked to her door to see if her aunt was still sleeping. She was snoring, with her usual roar of a lion, which was why a few years ago Carlette had dubbed her "the Lion Queen." Well, that was one of the reasons; her aunt's nasty disposition was the other.

Heading to the bathroom for her nightly bath, she placed her hand over her mouth to silence her giggles as she tiptoed past her aunt's bedroom. She turned on the water and poured a flowery-smelling solution into the tub. The sweet smell of bath salts filled her head with pleasantries and made her feet take on a mind of their own. First the left, then the right touched the warm, calming water. She closed her eyes and allowed her body to submerge in the relaxing spa.

Sitting in the bathtub, relaxed, with the warm water surrounding her, she hummed softly, touching the faucet playfully with her toes. "Boy, oh, boy," she said quietly. "It would be good if I could just live in this tub, in this beautiful silencc, forever."

Almost an hour had gone by when Carlette stepped out of the tub. She began drying her feet as she pulled the stopper out of the tub drain and continued to hum softly. As she stood up to wrap the towel around her, she caught the reflection of her face in the medicine cabinet mirror, mounted directly across from the tub. Suddenly she realized why Ricky had complimented her beauty. There it was, staring back at her. Smooth pecan-colored skin, round eyes as black as the night, and thick, perfectly arched eyebrows. They looked just like her aunt's after she had gotten hers shaped professionally, but Carlette's were definitely thicker and natural.

She touched her long, shiny hair as she noticed its dark brown color and wondered why she hadn't been aware of her looks before. She had spent many nights staring in this same mirror, pretending to be someone else so that she wouldn't be so miserable. Why hadn't she noticed her attractive features on those occasions? Was it because Ricky had just pointed them out, or was she at the age of vanity?

Carlette peeked out of the bathroom to make sure her aunt was still asleep. Still snoring like a roaring lion. She opened the side of the medicine cabinet where her aunt kept her makeup, body powder, and toiletries. She grabbed the dusting powder, let her towel drop to the floor, and stood on it to catch any flyaway particles. *The smell! Uh-oh, I can't. Aunt Genevee will definitely find out. No, she won't. She wears so much of this stuff and other perfumes that the scents remain in the house. It always smells like her, so she'll never know the difference.* Carlette was afraid of even a sleeping Aunt Genevee.

Standing in front of the full-length mirror that hung on the back of the bathroom door, she stepped back and proceeded to dust her body with the powder. A slight gasp escaped her lips when she saw that her body was still petite but seemed to have changed overnight. She thought loudly in her head, *My breasts, they are bigger. How long have they been like this? Are they what Ricky was looking at? I need a bra. Now I have to find a way to ask Aunt Genevee for a bra without her thinking that I've been fooling around with boys. She was really hard on me when I got my first period. What am I going to do? What do I say?*

She then stood back and looked at the rest of her body. The loud screaming in her head continued. *I'm getting a figure. How long have I looked like this? Can Ricky see my figure through that stupid school uniform? Can he see what my body looks like under that white blouse, dumb vest, and pleated skirt? Do I look dirty? Is that why he was so interested in me?*

Carlette was shaken. Tears welled up in her eyes. She took a cloth and removed all the excess powder, slipped on her robe, and immediately returned to her bedroom, shaking and almost crying loudly. She stood at the door of the dark room, trying to remember when she'd turned out the light. As she reached for the switch, a hand touched her wrist, and she let out a small scream.

Ricky put his hand over her mouth. "It's me, Carlette. It's Ricky."

Carlette trembled more, her heart pounding like a drum. "Ricky, please! Leave! My aunt is very mean. She'll beat me very badly if she catches you 'ere!" Carlette was hysterical by this time but knew enough to keep her voice low.

Ricky whispered, "All I want is to talk to you for a while . . . just a few minutes. She'll never know I was 'ere."

"How did you get into my room?"

"I climbed the tree and jumped onto the roof of your porch. I'm glad you forgot to lock your window."

"You have to go now!"

"Only if you let me talk to you for a while."

"Okay, but please make it quick."

"Let's sit on the bed."

"No! We'll stand. You have to get out of 'ere."

"Okay, but I can't think very well standing. I have many questions for you, and it's going to take me longer to think of them if we're standing. Come on. Let's sit for a moment. Your aunt will never awaken. You know she snores like a lion."

Carlette almost smiled again, but she didn't want to encourage Ricky's stay. Realizing Ricky might stay longer if she didn't sit, she reluctantly walked over to her bed, and Ricky followed like a child, still holding on to Carlette's wrist.

Ricky broke the silence. "Hey, nice room. One day I'm going to be a big, rich architect, you know, a building contractor, and—"

"I thought you wanted to ask me questions and then you would leave. You really have to get out of 'ere. You don't know my aunt. She's always angry. I think she hates me. Please, Ricky, please don't make more trouble for me."

"Carlette, what makes you cry so?"

"My aunt, Ricky, my aunt. Haven't you been listening?"

"Then why do you stay?"

"I'm only a child, Ricky. A little girl—"

"Oh, my beautiful Carlette, you're more than a little girl. You're special." Ricky kissed Carlette's forehead. "But you do need someone, someone to hold you and love you, but for now just let me wipe those tears."

Carlette didn't really want Ricky to touch her.

She was in fear of him noticing that she was wearing only her robe, and smelling the dusting powder might entice him the way it did her aunt's male friends. She remained silent and sat as still as possible while he wiped her tears. The attention felt good. She couldn't remember her aunt ever showing her affection of any sort.

Ricky clutched Carlette's hand tightly. "Do you feel better, Carlette? Are you more comfortable?"

"Yes, Ricky, but you still have to go."

Ricky agreed. He leaned over to kiss Carlette, but she backed away.

"You smell very pretty, Carlette."

"Thank you. Please leave . . . please."

Ricky stood up and, without another word, carefully and quietly exited through the window.

Relieved, Carlette slowly reclined and began thinking of the encounter. "I must be special. I must be better than my aunt thinks I am. Ricky likes me. He really, really likes me."

Carlette could still hear her aunt's snoring. She chuckled to herself. A man had entered her room without that lazy cow even knowing. "I hate 'er. She's always criticizing me, and she thinks I don't know how many men she's lain with. I hate 'er. I'll never lay with men the way she does. I'll never be like 'er."

Unlike most nights, Carlette drifted into a deep, relaxing sleep, which kept her from wishing she had never been born.

CHAPTER 3

Carlette jumped out of bed and ran to the window. The sunlight made her feel energetic. "Saturday morning! Freedom!" The words sounded like a song she'd just made up. On Saturdays she went to the center and stayed there all day. While her aunt worked, the center was her babysitter. She played all the games but barely said a word to anyone while there.

As Carlette walked down the street, Ricky caught up to her a block away from the center.

"Pretty Brown! Pretty Brown! What's going on, Pretty Brown?"

"N-n-nothing."

"Then, where you going?"

"To the center."

Ricky knew that. He also knew that Carlette liked him. Although she never knew it, he had caught her watching him many times, which was another reason for his attraction to her. He knew more about Carlette than she realized.

"So, Pretty Brown, why are you always at the center on Saturdays?"

The pounding in Carlette's heart sped up. "How do you know that?"

"When I want a womon, Carlette, I always watch 'er. Ain't no other mon gonna be botherin' with you. If you were my womon, I wouldn't let your aunt treat you so indifferent, either."

"Well, you ain't my mon, and I ain't old enough to date. So just leave me alone."

"But, Pretty Brown—"

Carlette raised her voice. "Ricky! My name ain't Pretty Brown! It's *Carlette!*" Carlette was using all she had to make Ricky lose interest in her, and to slow her heart down.

"Carlette, I'm in love with you, girl."

Carlette's heart started beating fast again. She was at a loss for words.

Ricky continued the conversation. "Carlette. I've really gone out of my way to see you, girl. Why can't you just talk to me?"

"I tol' you, my aunt don't let me see no one yet."

"You can see me, and your aunt don't have to know. Or you can stay lonely without any friends. Think about it." Ricky started to walk away.

Carlette knew he was the only person she sort of liked in that town, and he wasn't lying about her being lonely. After all, he only wanted to talk. "Ricky! Wait!"

A big grin appeared on Ricky's face, one that quickly diminished before he turned to face her. He tried to remain humble.

"Ricky. We can talk, I guess."

"Do you guess, little pretty one, or do you know?"

"We can talk. That's if you still want to be friends."

"What if I want to be your mon?"

"Ricky!"

"Okay, let's talk. But what if they miss you at the center?"

"They won't. Nobody special takes care of me. My aunt just instructs me to go there while she works at the library."

"Then can you come to my house?"

"No. We gotta talk 'ere!"

"I'm sorry. I just didn't want anyone to see us and go back and tell your aunt they saw you talking to some ol' mon or something."

"You're not that ol'. I mean, not really. But do you really think someone will go back and tell 'er?"

"It's a small town, Carlette. They might."

"Oh. I didn't think of that."

"I live a block away."

"Suppose someone sees us together? Won't they get the wrong idea?"

"If someone asks, I'll pretend you're my little sister. Come on. We've spent too much time already in a place where people can make up stories and gossip. Come on, Pretty Brown. I mean Carlette. I'm going to treat you nice at my house. I'm going to treat you the way that mean aunt of yours should."

Ricky led Carlette by the hand to where he lived to make it appear as though she was really his little sister and that no one gave them a second glance.

Carlette entered Ricky's apartment. She had never seen such a beautiful place. "Do you live with your mother, Ricky?"

"No."

"Then who do you live with?"

"I live alone."

"I never see you go to work."

"What's that suppose to mean?"

"I've only seen you standing on corners before I go to school and after I get out."

"Does that mean I don't have a job?"

"No. I was just wondering. What time do you go?"

"I'm on shift work at the Basin."

Carlette's eyes and mouth opened wide. "The naked lady club?"

Ricky laughed. "Yeah. Is something wrong with that?"

"No. I guess you're old enough."

"You want something to eat? And can I call you Pretty Brown? It's hard not to."

"Yeah. I guess it's okay."

"Then what do you want to eat, Pretty Brown? I have fried bananas, beef patties, leftover oxtail soup—"

"Oxtail soup! It's my favorite!"

"Okay. I'll warm it up. Hey, Pretty Brown, is your aunt as mean as you say?"

"She worse. A lot worse."

"You must live in fear."

"Most of the time. Saturdays are my best days, and when she's asleep is the best part of my nights. She's gone most of the day on Saturday, and at night I don't have to hear anything but 'er roaring snore."

Just then the phone rang.

"You're funny, Pretty Brown. Hold that thought." Ricky answered the phone. "Hello?" He covered the receiver and began to whisper. "Taylor, girl, stop calling 'ere. It's over."

"But you promised we would be together forever, Ricky."

"Taylor, you knew I couldn't keep that promise! Forever is a long, long time, girl. Now I've gotta go. My little sister's 'ere. She don't need to be hearing me talk to no womon this way."

"Okay, Ricky, okay. But I still love you."

"Taylor, forget me. Go find yourself another mon. I'm leaving the island soon, anyway." Ricky hung up the phone, poured soup in a bowl, then called Carlette to the table in a fatherly manner.

Carlette ate only a small portion. Not only was she a picky eater, but she was shy around Ricky.

"Is that all you're going to eat, Pretty Brown?"

"Yeah. I'm full. I don't ever eat much."

Ricky removed Carlette's bowl from the table and escorted her back over to the sofa to watch television. "So what do you like to watch? Cartoons?"

"I don't really get a chance to watch much television, but when I do, I like watching movies."

Ricky could hear irritation in her voice. "You have a temper. I'm sorry to offend you, Carlette. It was just a joke, Pretty Brown. Okay?"

"My aunt picks on me enough. You said you would be my friend and treat me nicer."

"Sometimes friends tease. Are you angry? Do you want me to take you home?"

"No. I'm okay."

"Good. Here's the remote. Watch whatever you want."

"I wish we had a television this big. I guess that I'm just lucky to have a place to stay."

"Don't feel that way, Carlette. Everyone deserves to live the best life."

"I'll never have it."

"Then why do you practice that flute so much?"

"My aunt makes me."

"Well, I think it's stupid to make a person do things they don't like. That's why I didn't kiss you." Ricky was still trying to bring up the idea of being intimate.

"You can kiss me."

Ricky was shocked to hear Carlette say those words. He tried to act humble. "Do you mean it?"

"Yeah. I guess I do."

"I don't want you to do anything that's not right for you."

"What will a kiss do to me, Ricky?" Carlette wasn't playing stupid; she was really that innocent.

"Nothing, Pretty Brown. Nothing but make us closer. Do you know how to kiss?"

"I've seen them do it on television." Carlette closed her eyes, urging Ricky to kiss her.

Ricky leaned in and gently kissed Carlette's lips.

"Is that all there is to it?"

To Ricky, Carlette seemed disappointed, but he gave her a response that he hoped would make her more curious. "For a little girl like you, yeah, that's all there is to it."

"You really think of me as a child?"

"Well, yeah. Even you said you are just a little girl."

"Oh, yeah, right."

"Are you ready to go home now?"

"No. My aunt won't be home until six thirty. I can stay at least three more hours. That's if you want me to. But I can go home if you want me to."

"No. I don't want you to go home. I enjoy your company. You're very mature for a little girl. You talk very grown up. You have lots to say. Important things. Do you want to try the kiss again?"

Carlette didn't say a word. She just closed her eyes and waited. Ricky gently brushed his tongue across her lips, which made her sort of tingle.

"Mmm, Carlette . . . sweet." Ricky could hear and feel her breathing hard. He kissed her neck, and Carlette made a sound that he recognized from the others he'd touched that way. "What's the matter, Carlette? Am I doing something wrong?"

"No. It's just time for me to leave."

"But you said you could stay three hours. Did I frighten you? Are you afraid of me?" Ricky knew Carlette would never admit it.

"No, Ricky. I just should be getting home. Maybe my aunt will come home early and go to the center to look for me."

"Okay. I'll take you back. I don't want something to happen to my favorite girl."

On the way back to the center, Ricky talked and asked questions. He seemed to want to know all about Carlette. She had felt so lonely and rejected before she had met him, and she gave him all the information he asked for. Ricky left Carlette standing in front of the center. That was the way she wanted it. She hadn't planned on going inside. Instead, she headed straight home.

By the time she got there, she felt so guilty about deceiving her aunt, she cleaned and did extra chores that weren't required of her. And all the work caused her to fall across her bed, exhausted and worn out.

CHAPTER 4

"Carlette! Carlette!"

Carlette woke up in what seemed like a state of crazy drunkenness. It was the snoring Lion Queen.

"Auntie Genevee—"

"Why aren't you at the center?" Genevee was furious. She had brought a date home with her. Carlette was in the way.

"I cleaned for you, Aunt Genevee. You work hard—"

"Shut up! Just stay in this room and out of my way!"

Carlette could hear a male voice coming from the kitchen. "Genevee, you too hard on the girl. She just a chile."

"Do you want 'er or something, Frank?" called Genevee.

Frank, or Francis Quarterly, one of the most prominent meat-store owners on the island, knew how to handle Genevee and would not back down from her accusation. "Genevee, don't be silly."

"I'm not being silly. She pretty, and she getting

a figure, too. Two women in a household ain't no good, or maybe you interested in removin' one."

"Genevee, you jealous of that chile? But she your niece!"

"I don't care, Frank. She still a female!" Genevee replied as she walked into the kitchen.

Carlette was heartbroken. How could a woman be filled with so much hate and jealousy for her? How could her own aunt feel that way about her? How could she believe that Carlette would want to lie with one of her old boyfriends? Carlette wanted to pack all her things and leave right then and there, but she had no place to go. "I should go stay with Ricky. He loves me," Carlette said to herself in a low tone. "But then I'd have to go get a job. I'm not old enough. . . ."

"Carlette! Get in 'ere!" called Genevee.

"Yes, ma'am, Auntie Genevee?" said Carlette as she ran to the kitchen.

"Francis wants you!" Genevee grunted.

"Yes, Frank?" asked Cartette.

Frank shook his head. "Genevee! How dare you! Go back to your room, little one."

Carlette left the kitchen, but she listened intently to the fiery conversation that was going on in it.

"Genevee! It's over! You need help, womon! You sick!"

"Then get out, Frank! I don't need no mon who don't want no grown womon no way!"

"What grown womon? You act more like a chile than your niece do. No wonder you a pretty womon and you can't keep no mon! You stupid, and I don't want me no stupid womon. And I

don't want you no more, neither! Even if you do
have a lovely ass! You just two seconds from
stupid!"

Carlette's eyes bulged as she held her mouth
and tried stifling her laughter.

Before Genevee could respond, Frank stormed
out of the small cottage and slammed the flimsy
screen door behind him with as much force as
possible, making it shake hard enough to come
off its rusty hinges.

Genevee ran to the door, shaking her fist at
Frank and yelling, "Stupid mon! You gonna fix
my door if it's broken!"

Genevee's words were useless. Frank was already halfway down the block.

"You stay in that room, you 'ear! You just stay
in that room!"

Genevee was seething.

CHAPTER 5

For the rest of the week, television and radio were out of the question. Carlette was only allowed to eat, go to school and to the center on Saturday, clean, and go to her flute lesson.

"Pretty Brown!" Ricky was calling out and waving to Carlette as he walked toward her.

"Oh, hi, Ricky." Carlette's head dropped.

"You so down again. Your aunt bothering you again?"

"She accused her boyfriend of wanting me."

"Well, I can see how she could think that. You beautiful."

Carlette instantly burst into tears.

"Pretty Brown, Pretty Brown, come on now." Ricky tried hard to ease Carlette's tears, but she was crying uncontrollably. He held her close and hugged her until she quieted down some. "Do you want to go to my house, Pretty Brown?"

Carlette nodded her head, and Ricky led the way, again holding her hand like she was a little sister until they were safe inside his apartment.

"She only wants me to take flute lessons to get me out of the way," Carlette moaned.

Ricky held her hand as they both reclined on his sofa. "Out of the way of what, Carlette?"

"Her stupid boyfriends."

"She has many?"

"A few."

"Whoa! She doesn't look the type."

"I know. She looks too stupid for any man to like 'er."

Ricky laughed.

"No! I mean it! She stupid and I hate 'er! And how do you know how my auntie Genevee looks?" As soon as Carlette spoke those words, she began to cry again.

Ricky held her in his arms, close to his chest, until they both fell asleep on his sofa.

"What time is it? It's dark! Oh, my God! Is your clock right? Is it after eight thirty? My aunt's going to kill me!" Carlette shrieked when they awoke some time later.

"Carlette, I'm sorry. I fell asleep, too."

"Well, I don't care, anyway. I'm not going home when I leave here. I'm not going back home. My aunt probably won't care that I'm gone, anyway! Nobody in this little place cares about me, not even the police."

"Carlette, it's not safe on the streets for a girl like you. You can stay here with me for as long as you like . . . that's if you want to."

"I don't have a job. You must spend a lot for this apartment."

"You'll be my girl. You won't have to pay anything."

"I can clean." Carlette didn't want to owe Ricky anything.

"Okay, Carlette, okay. You clean. I'll work."

Carlette took off her shoes and put her feet up on Ricky's sofa and was off to slumber again.

Ricky looked down at her and smiled. He gently slid out from under her and headed for his bedroom, mumbling under his breath, "I told 'er she would be mine." He turned off the light so Carlette could get the rest she desperately needed.

CHAPTER 6

When Carlette awakened in the morning, she called out for Ricky, but he didn't answer. She went through the house, looking for him, and realized she was alone. She found something to eat and proceeded to fulfill her part of the arrangement. She cleaned the house thoroughly, changed some things around, and then took a bath.

When Ricky walked through the door, he almost didn't recognize his apartment. "Carlette, you're good at cleaning. I thought I was in the wrong apartment."

Carlette blushed and grinned broadly.

"Here. I brought you something." Ricky handed her a large bag.

"What? What is it?"

"Look in the bag, Brown."

"Clothes? You bought me clothes?"

"Well, were you going to wear those clothes forever?"

"I could wash them."

"No. You're sorta my girl now. You don't have to wear the same thing all the time."

"I'm not your girl, Ricky, and I can wash my clothes. I don't mind. I don't need you to buy me anything."

"Okay. Then I'll take the clothes back if you don't want them. You don't want them?"

Carlette remained silent.

"Here . . . just take them. You need them. I want you to have them."

Carlette felt uncomfortable but took the clothes.

"When you're all changed, we'll go out to eat."

"But my aunt—"

"We're driving. I have a car. She won't see us."

Carlette went to change and returned wearing the pink, puffy, short-sleeved fitted blouse, black jeans, and black ballerina-looking flats that Ricky had bought her and that he loved to see on his women.

"Sit down on the sofa, Carlette. I have a way to fix your hair that I know you'll like." Ricky unbraided her hair and brushed it back so that the waves would flow freely down her back. "Look in the mirror. See if you like it."

Carlette was pleased. She thought the style made her look even prettier, and so did Ricky.

They left for dinner and stayed out late playing at the arcade. Ricky drank wine, and Carlette asked to taste it, but he would only allow her to have soda.

Almost every day after that, when Ricky came home, he would have something for Carlette and would take her out. As time went on, Carlette grew closer and closer to him, and she felt happier than ever.

CHAPTER 7

Ricky and Carlette had been living together for three years.

Only Ricky knew why Genevee was Carlette's guardian. When Genevee received notices from the school regarding Carlette's absences, it was easy for her to lie, but she continued looking for her niece. Ricky heard the rumor and told Carlette, but Carlette announced boldly to him that she wasn't ready to face her aunt. She was still afraid of what her aunt might do to her for being gone so long, so he kept Carlette's secret.

As the two sat and watched television, Carlette noticed how Ricky's demeanor had suddenly changed. She wondered if it was because he had spent so much money on her for her birthday last weekend. She needed to get a job. Then she would feel more secure. The way things were now, she felt as if she was taking advantage of Ricky, and his restless mood only added to the way she felt. Carlette kept waiting on him hand and foot, trying to get him to change his attitude. She had already served him three or four glasses of wine, and he had smoked a half pack of cigarettes, but nothing seemed to help.

"Can I have a kiss?"

Carlette jumped. Ricky's sudden words startled her. She didn't know how to react.

"Well, can I?"

He sounded a bit cool but sexy, and she couldn't say no. It wasn't only Ricky's voice that made her agree. She couldn't help but think of how nice he was being to her, giving her things and taking her out. They had been together since before she had turned fifteen, and every year he had taken her out for her birthday. She also remembered that he hadn't asked her to kiss him since that time he had run his tongue across her lips, so she felt somewhat obligated to honor his request.

She looked at him sweetly. "Yes, Ricky, you can have a kiss."

Ricky leaned in to kiss her. She could smell the wine, cigarettes, and his cologne. The mixture made her feel at home. She liked it and relaxed for him to kiss her. Again, he brushed his tongue across her lips, making her shiver.

When Ricky felt the small bumps rise on her arms, he kissed her neck again. She tried to pull away, but Ricky was holding her shoulders and drawing her to him.

"Ricky!"

"What?"

"You said a kiss."

"And that's what I'm doing. Am I 'urting you, Carlette? Am I 'urting you?" His accent became stronger. "You know I'm not 'urting you, girl! 'Ow can I 'urt you by kissing your neck?"

Carlette remained quiet, and Ricky continued kissing and gently biting her neck. She opted to keep her eyes and mouth shut tightly until it was over. Ricky moved his mouth down lower and touched her breast with his lips.

"No, Ricky!"

"Hush, Carlette. I won't be going far. Just sit still and hush."

Carlette was frightened but sat still. Ricky began again, without removing Carlette's blouse. His movements made Carlette's small body tilt and rock. She liked what Ricky was making her feel, but wouldn't submit. Instead, she let her small arms flail out to the sides. Ricky would never think of her as a whore.

She could feel the dampness and cold from Ricky's saliva through her blouse, and she smelled the scent of wine and cigarettes it left. Tears of pleasure began to roll down her cheeks as she cried in silence. Ricky removed Carlette's blouse over her head and tossed it to the floor.

"Ri-cky!" Carlette was all tears, still pretending not to enjoy or want the feelings she was experiencing for the first time.

"Hush, girl." Ricky's words were firm. He leaned over and gently pulled on Carlette's throat with his lips to make her more excited. He knew that she wanted him as much as he wanted her.

CHAPTER 8

Ricky finally emerged, allowing Carlette to sit up.

"See, Carlette, that wasn't so bad."

Carlette just sat there in a daze, not saying a word.

"Go ahead. Take your bath. You been a good girl. You sleepin' in my bed tonight."

Carlette covered her chest with her arms and went into the bathroom, and Ricky watched her small, curvy body until she was out of sight.

After bathing, she took the gown and robe that Ricky had bought her and put them on. She headed back to the living room.

"No, no, Pretty Brown. You've had a hard day. Go on to bed."

Carlette wanted to say, "I'm not sleepy," but was afraid of disappointing Ricky. She turned and went into the bedroom.

Carlette had almost fallen asleep when she felt the bed move. Ricky was climbing into bed with her. She panicked. "Ricky!"

"Hush, Pretty Brown, hush. I'm tired too. Lie

back down." Ricky had no intentions of going to sleep or letting Carlette get any rest. He slid under the covers and began to tease Carlette. "Pretty Brown, Pretty Brown, Pretty Brown, you angry?"

Carlette wouldn't answer.

Ricky tickled her. When she began to laugh, he ducked his head playfully under the covers. Carlette called out to him playfully. He grabbed her tightly by both legs, wiggled his way up, and stuck his tongue in her navel.

She laughed, thinking he was just being silly.

He slid down and pulled her gown up and kissed her in the pelvic region.

"Ricky, no! Don't!"

"Pretty Brown, calm yourself now. If you don't like it, I will stop."

Carlette relaxed a little but was still a little fearful. No man had ever touched her before in any way. Ricky kissed her gently in the pelvic area again, then covered her sex with his mouth, and Carlette moaned as if she was in agony.

Ricky climbed on top of her and whispered in her ear, "I love you, Pretty Brown. I love you more than any womon I ever know. I want you to be my wife, have my babies. Please love me enough to do dis thing for me."

Carlette wanted to fight Ricky off, tell him no, but she had loved him from the very beginning. To her, sex with him would be like a fairy tale. She nodded in agreement, closed her eyes, and held her tightly clenched fists next to her head.

Ricky grabbed them and held them down at her sides. Then he slowly and gently penetrated her.

Carlette began making sounds again, but from

real pain. A ripping, burning pain that made her feel as though she was having severe cramps. She felt as though she was living a nightmare that she couldn't wake up from. What she was allowing to happen to her couldn't be true.

Ricky wanted to feel sympathetic, but his manhood and hormones were calling out to him. For most of the three years they'd been together, he had been saving himself for her. He couldn't help but writhe, bounce, grind, and clutch her body, while she screamed, moaned, and felt the air being knocked out of her with each movement he made, until he finally stiffened up and let out a noise that sounded like he was in pain, too.

He rolled off Carlette to catch his breath.

Carlette lay on her back, staring at the ceiling, while tears ran down her face. *Why? Why?* was all she could ask herself. If only she'd known that sex felt this way, she might have refused him.

When Ricky went to the bathroom, Carlette got on her knees to relieve the pain. She felt as though she was soaking wet and lifted the covers. There was blood on the sheets and her gown. "My period! My period! How can it be on again? It just went off two weeks ago."

While he was in the bathroom, Carlette changed everything and lay on her side, crying silently.

Ricky climbed back into bed. "So, Pretty Brown, talk to Ricky."

Carlette just lay still on her side and wouldn't say a word. She wouldn't even face him.

"Do you want us to do it again, Pretty Brown?"

"No! No! No!" Carlette was hysterical.

"Come on now, Pretty Brown. I didn't mean it. I just wanted to make you talk to me."

"I don't want to talk to you, Ricky! I just want you to leave me alone!"

"You're in my house, Carlette."

"I don't have to be 'ere. I could have left. If you had just tol' me what you wanted from me, I would have left. I mean, you tol' me. You asked me, and I said yes, but I didn't know it would be like that. I would have left if you had let me know."

Ricky felt pity for Carlette, but he didn't want to seem frightened. He took control of his voice. "And go where, Pretty Brown? The streets? Men out there would have done worse, much worse, by you. At least you know me. Think about that, Pretty Brown. You say you really like me. You say you want me to have you. I'm sorry for 'urting you in any way. If you want to leave 'ere, I will take you, because I love you. I don't want you to think I wanted to trick you. Do you want to go home?"

Carlette wouldn't answer.

Ricky could hear Carlette crying. He put his arm around her waist and pulled her close to him. He could hear his own sorrowful tears tapping the linen. Ricky fell asleep thinking, *Why do I love this little girl so much? Why can't I just put her out and get her off my mind like all the others?*

Carlette lay on her side, her back to him, wondering what had happened to her body during and after sex. She felt an unquenchable love for him, but she was hoping that he would sleep through the night or even forever. She didn't ever want to go through that ordeal again.

CHAPTER 9

After thinking back to when she didn't know Ricky, to when he'd taken her to his apartment for the first time, to when they'd shared their first kiss, to when he'd taken her in and bought her pretty things, and about how she'd lost her virginity, Carlette finally drifted off to sleep.

When she woke up, Ricky wasn't next to her. She could hear him moving around in the kitchen and could smell the good food he was preparing. At one time this had been fun. Now she no longer desired to eat, play with Ricky, or be at his house. It all made her sick now. It was all too real. She had lost her virginity to a man who wasn't her husband.

Surely, Aunt Genevee would never let her back in the house once she found out. And she did, since Ricky was bullheaded enough to tell her aunt about their love and their plans to marry.

"Carlette! Carlette! Come and eat!"

"How can he call me to eat with him after what he's done?" Carlette felt sick. What Ricky had done to her made her feel sick, and she lay in bed until he came to the door, trying to coax her to the kitchen.

"Carlette, aren't you going to eat with me?"

"I'm not hungry."

"Do you feel sick?"

"Yes."

Ricky went over to her and sat down on the bed. "Carlette, I know you're angry right now, but you'll understand someday how I felt and why I had to be with you so bad."

Carlette couldn't understand anything at the moment. She just wanted him to leave her alone.

Ricky saw things differently. It was his duty to take care of her and make her happy. He pulled the covers back to carry her into the kitchen. He would coax her into eating and hand-feed her if he had to. When he realized she had changed her nightgown, his facial expression changed.

"Why'd you change, Pretty Brown? This isn't the gown you wore to bed."

Carlette didn't respond and tried to grab the covers, but Ricky saw the results of his aggressiveness.

"Carlette, you bleeding? Is that why you so upset? Don't worry. You a virgin, and I'm large. That happens to a lot of girls I've touched the first time. We just won't touch for several days."

Carlette almost laughed. She wondered how many girls he had been with. She also wanted to beg him not to touch her ever again, but remained quiet.

"Carlette, you 'ear me?"

"Yes, I 'ear you. Now leave me alone."

Ricky got up off the bed. "Carlette, I'm going to work now."

Carlette still didn't budge, and Ricky left.

Carlette got out of bed and went into the bathroom. She soaked in the hottest water she could stand and scrubbed her body until it was sore, then continued soaking. The scent that had once made her feel comfortable now made her want to hate him, and she sat there, resentful, hoping the water would remove his scent from her nostrils and make her body go back to the way it was.

She thought over and over of ways to leave. She really wanted to leave. Away from her aunt for three years, she wondered if her aunt missed her. She was ready to go home after what Ricky had done to her, and was willing to face the consequences, although she felt that her aunt didn't want her there. That thought made Carlette cry again. She put her face in her wet, soapy palms as she cried some more and murmured, "She'll probably just put me out. She'll probably even hate me more."

Carlette felt trapped and hopeless. She cried all day, until she fell asleep again in Ricky's bed.

CHAPTER 10

Ricky came home early. Not only was he worried about what he had done to Carlette, but he'd received some news to give her. He went to the bedroom and saw that she was asleep. He sat down on the bed quietly and gently caressed her hair.

She jumped up out of her sleep and pushed his hand away. "No! No! Ricky! Please."

"I'm not going to 'urt you. I was worried about you and came home early. I'm sorry for what I did to you last night. I was drinking. You're lovely. It will never happen again, Carlette. I—"

"Leave me alone! Just leave me alone, Ricky!" Carlette was trembling.

Ricky put up the palms of his hands. "Okay, Carlette, okay." He got up off the bed and backed away. "But I have something to tell you. Your aunt is still looking for you. She's really worried about you."

"I don't care! I hate 'er, and now I hate you just as much. You can apologize a hundred times, Ricky. I'll still hate you!"

Ricky's expression turned into sorrow, and his shoulders, head, and the tone of his voice dropped. "Carlette."

"Shut up! Don't talk to me! You're no longer my friend, Ricky! You're no longer my friend!"

Ricky ran over to the bed, grabbed both her wrists, and tried shaking her to calm her down.

"Hit me! Go ahead! Do it!"

"I'm not going to hit you!"

"Then get out of 'ere, and leave me alone! Get out!"

"Carlette, this is *my* room."

"Then I'll leave!"

"No. Stay. I won't bother you again."

"Then leave!"

Ricky walked out of the room with his head lowered, worried that Carlette would turn him in to the authorities, although she'd agreed to have sex with him.

He'd had females, plenty of them, and some very young. Those who didn't have jobs or some type of assistance had sold their bodies to him, but Carlette was the youngest he had ever taken in, and by far the prettiest. She was even smart, genuinely innocent, and sweet. Things were different with her. He had really fallen in love with her and enjoyed taking care of her. He was even jealous of her. Whenever they were out, he made it a point to have her sit close to him and wouldn't let anyone, not even his friends, talk to her for fear of losing her.

But now Ricky had new fears regarding Carlette. Her aunt was looking for her, and he was sure his behavior would eventually get him into trouble. Carlette was angry enough to make sure that it would, and that he would spend the rest of his life in jail. One of the last things he wanted was to be like some of the men he had seen on those daytime shows, still strung out over the women who had put them away.

Ricky's paranoia had him constantly calling Carlette when he was away and remaining exceptionally close to home, making sure she wasn't in need of anything or hadn't gotten too bored. He still took her out and bought her nice things, cooked for her, and avoided various phone calls, although they barely spoke more than two words at a time most days.

When Carlette became ill, Ricky took her to the doctor three times, using his hard-earned dollars. He found out that he would soon be a father. The thought made him smile.

Carlette was bitter. "I'll keep this baby, Ricky, but I'll never forgive you for destroying my life."

"Carlette, I know that you won't, and I don't blame you. But I love you so much that, no matter how much you hate me, you and my baby will never have anything to worry about. I'll always be there for both of you."

Carlette ignored Ricky's comment and headed straight for the bedroom and shut the door. She lay across the bed and thought back to the time she'd spent with her young cousin, Keith Eric, her father's brother's son. He had lived with her and her aunt Genevee while his mother and sister moved. He was too small at the time to help and was in the way, so his mother promised to come get him as soon as she was settled.

Things weren't so bad then. Genevee ignored her and pampered Keith Eric, even treated him like royalty. Her mind spun off to his sister, Kellen, who was four years older than her. Kellen had gone off to college that year, at sixteen, because she was so smart.

The following summer, when they returned to pick up little Keith Eric, the entire family stayed with Genevee for two days. Keith Eric continued to sleep in the guest room, his parents slept on the pullout sofa, and Kellen bunked with Carlette. The two stayed up giggling quietly and talked most of the night. Kellen wanted to tell Carlette all about her college experience. There was great respect between the two girls, but Carlette thought Kellen was stupid for allowing her three college room-mates to initiate her into their sorority by having a ménage à trois.

Kellen told Carlette it had happened the week after her birthday and had started while she slept. When she'd awakened to the experience, she had accepted it, liked it, and couldn't wait to tell about it and do it again. Hoping that Kellen wouldn't notice the look of disgust on her face, Carlette tried to laugh it off and keep the conversation going. But both nights she slept on the floor and tried staying awake so her cousin wouldn't try any of that freaky college stuff on her.

The flashback of the almost forgotten incident caused Carlette to spontaneously drop her journal on her lap and grab her stomach. With beads of sweat on her forehead, she looked around the plane to see if anyone had noticed, but no one had looked her way.

Carlette sighed. *I was innocent way back then, very innocent and pure. Look at me now. Kellen never got pregnant from her indiscretion, but what I did with Ricky is very apparent. I wonder what people are thinking of me and my stomach. What would Kellen think? Would she still be so open-minded? Oh, I don't care. I just hope none of that funny roommate stuff goes on at Cora's house.*

Carlette quickly shook the thoughts out of her head and picked up her journal. *Aunt Genevee would never send me to a place where someone would purposely harm me.* And she went to the next chapter in her journal.

CHAPTER 11

As time went on, Carlette began to think about the life she carried inside of her and about its father, especially when the baby moved. She realized that she had feelings for Ricky even though she felt he had taken advantage of her. Slowly, she began to realize that she'd been a part of what had happened. Ricky had given her an option, and she had made the ultimate decision to go all the way with him.

She began to make small conversation with Ricky but pretended to be somewhat cool whenever she did. She would sit next to him on the sofa, hoping that he would put his arm around her, and when he did, she would wiggle away from him. She would allow him to kiss her on the cheek on mornings when he left for work so he wouldn't lose too much interest, but she didn't want him to know how she really felt about him. Carlette was in love.

"Pretty Brown, how long you gonna stay mad?"

Carlette wouldn't answer.

"Do you miss your snoring aunt?"

Carlette laughed.

"See, Pretty Brown, you don't need to frown forever. Now, come sit next to me."

Carlette lazily went to Ricky's side and plopped down on the sofa.

"Carlette, please forgive me," Ricky said, his words warm and sincere. "If you hadn't been so beautiful and so much the woman I wanted, I would have never wanted to touch you so bad. I kept thinking of you day and night, Carlette. Having you here every day with me and watching your beauty made me lose myself when I got drunk on the wine, and I couldn't control my feelings. At first, I wasn't going to go all the way with you, no matter what you said. All I was going to do was kiss and touch you privately, to make you want me. But the wine told me to go further, and that you wanted me. Then you consented. I'm truly, truly sorry, Carlette. I'll do everything that I can to make it up to you. Will you let me do that?"

"In time, Ricky. Having a baby at my age is the last thing I thought would happen to me. I need some time. I still can't believe this has happened to me." Tears welled up in Carlette's eyes.

Ricky put his arm around her, pulled her close to him, and laid his face on her head. He could feel the pain he'd cast on her and couldn't figure out why she made him feel this way, why he'd asked for forgiveness but couldn't forgive himself. Was it because her hair and body always smelled so good? Was it her looks? Ricky couldn't figure it out.

I've been with many women, and I've never felt hungry for any of them. Most of them have done whatever I wanted, and none of them have made me feel this way. What is it about this little girl that makes me so foolish, so crazy? Why can't I just take her to get an abortion, like I've done with many others, and let her go? Why is my mind on her so much? I know that I said I love her. I've said those words to many women, but why do I mean them now? Why am I so regretful about what I did to her but still want her to have my child? I didn't intend to be tied down to one woman so soon or to be a father.

CHAPTER 12

Carlette woke up to Ricky kissing and rubbing her stomach.

"My baby's in here, in the womon I love. You will be birthing my child."

Carlette tried to sit up abruptly, but her growing stomach now interfered with her previous agility. "Ricky!"

"No, Carlette, please don't stop me from touching you and my child. Maybe I'll never see either one of you ever again."

The words and serious tone in Ricky's voice made Carlette lie still.

While Ricky massaged and kissed her stomach and talked to his baby, Carlette talked to herself. *I love him, but I want my childhood back. I didn't want this to happen. All I wanted was a friend, and for my aunt to stop being so mean to me.* Her thoughts were broken when she felt Ricky kiss her thigh.

"Ricky!"

"Carlette, I won't hurt you like before. I promise."

Carlette closed her eyes and held her stomach

when she felt Ricky's breath on her lower body. The feeling that made her tremble and squeal came again. She grabbed Ricky's full head of hair and yelled, "I'm having the baby, Ricky! I'm having the baby!"

Ricky wanted to burst into laughter. He knew Carlette was feeling passion, and that it would subside.

Carlette squealed, trembled, and collapsed again. She was drained, like the first time he'd touched her.

Ricky crawled up to her and hugged her tightly. "Don't hate me for that, Carlette, and don't be afraid of me. I'm not going to lie on top of you again. I might hurt you and my baby." He rubbed Carlette's stomach. "I'll never touch you that way again unless you want me to. All I wanted was to show you how much I love you. That was all I really wanted to do in the beginning, Carlette. I never meant for this to happen." Ricky cried silently.

Carlette wanted to be with Ricky intimately, and to marry him, but shyness kept her silent. She lay in his arms and fell asleep.

CHAPTER 13

Ricky pulled the window shade up until it snapped, and the bright sunlight hit Carlette directly in the face.

"Ricky," Carlette said in a sleepy voice.

"Come on, Carlette," Ricky said, sounding excited. "We're going to do it."

"Do what?"

"We're going to get married. And stop acting so cranky."

"We can't get married. There's no rings or papers."

"Look, Carlette."

Carlette's eyes widened when she saw the big diamond.

Ricky slipped it on her finger.

"Oh, Ricky, it's beautiful. I love this ring. It's so pretty."

"Then you'll marry me, Carlette?"

"How, Ricky? I'm too young."

"I have a place where we can go. It's a small village—"

"Smaller than this one?"

"Yes. Very small, Carlette. I know people there. They'll do whatever it takes to get us married. Will you marry me if I take you there?"

"Yes, but what about my aunt? I really don't want to leave her. Even though she don't love me, I love her."

"I'll take you to your aunt if you want me to."

"Are you angry because I still love my aunt Genevee?"

"No, Carlette. I just love you enough to do that."

"No, no, don't take me to 'er. Let's just get married."

"Are you sure?"

"Yes, I really mean it."

Ricky borrowed his boss's car, which was more faithful than his, and he and Carlette packed lightly and left quietly. After the small, discreet wedding, they stayed in a very clean, quiet, and modest wooden cabin, furnished with a sofa bed, a stove, and an apartment-sized refrigerator loaded with food.

Carlette looked out the back window and saw a rock formation with a waterfall, colorful flowers, and trees. It was beautiful. "Come here, Ricky. You gotta see this."

"Yeah, I know. Isn't it pretty?"

"Yeah. You come here a lot?"

"No, Pretty Brown. I found it while doing business for the club. Come on, let's take a tour. You look too pretty to stay inside."

Carlette did look exceptionally pretty, even though she was pregnant. The white satin dress, the large white hanging bow that was pinned perfectly to the back of her head, and the white satin ballet-like slippers made her look like an angel. Ricky felt in his heart that he'd never get enough of her, and never leave her. All he could do was stare at her as they walked along, enjoying the gorgeous landscape, which brought out her beauty even more.

Carlette broke the silence without looking up at him. "Ricky?"

"Hmm? What's wrong, Pretty Brown?"

"Nothing. I mean, since we're married now, will we be having sex tonight?"

Ricky couldn't figure out why, but the question embarrassed him, and his face turned red. Carlette was too naive to notice. Ricky was glad about that and answered, "Yes, Pretty Brown, if you want to."

"Ricky, I do. I love you, Ricky."

"Do you really, Pretty Brown?"

"Yes. I always have, but I didn't think things would turn out this way. I didn't want to have a child so soon. It makes me feel dirty."

"Please, Pretty Brown, try not to feel that way. I'm going to do whatever I can to make you not feel that way."

"Is that the only reason why you married me?"

"No, Pretty Brown. I'm really in love with you. Let me tell you something. You may not like this, but I'm going to tell you. I've had my share of women. Many of them have gotten pregnant—"

"You have other children?"

"No. They all got abortions. Some I made do it. Some wanted to. When you started staying with me, I made them stop calling my house. Carlette, I really love you. It probably sounds bad, but you the only womon that make me feel the way I did the night I took you. I want us to be together forever."

When it began to grow dark, Ricky escorted Carlette back to the cabin, where he drank wine, beer, and smoked marijuana to celebrate. Carlette ate and had a glass of milk. After their stomachs settled, they headed off to the bathroom.

While showering together, Ricky massaged Carlette's stomach and bathed her, then led her to the bed. He was still feeling good and happy. He kissed her stomach and thighs.

During their intervals of lovemaking, Ricky told Carlette how much he loved her. Long after it was over, she was still trembling, and tears flowed down her face. When Ricky held her in his arms, she couldn't help but wrap her small arms around his neck and accept the comfort.

Ricky and Carlette began to pack. Carlette was feeling shy and wouldn't look at him. She had really enjoyed making love with him the day before, and the new experience had put her in a different place. She got chills whenever she thought about it, and she was light-headed just thinking about Ricky and the fact that they were now husband and wife.

During the entire drive back home, Ricky held Carlette's hand. "I love you, Carlette. I love you with all my heart."

Carlette didn't know exactly how to respond, but she took a chance. "I love you, too, Ricky." She refocused her stare on the dashboard as they traveled the rest of the way in silence.

CHAPTER 14

Three weeks had gone by since the honeymoon. Carlette woke up looking for Ricky. Instead, she found a note.

Pretty Brown:
 I had to leave suddenly. They're after me, the police are after me, and I have to leave town for a while. As soon as I'm settled, I'll send for you. I left enough money for rent and food for two months. I should be able to sneak back and get you before you run out of money.

"Oh, no! He can't just leave me like this." Carlette was scared and incoherent. She ran through the apartment, calling and looking for Ricky, but he was nowhere to be found. Her heart was pounding so hard and fast, she thought it was going to give out. "No, Ricky! No! What am I going to do without you?"

Carlette cried over and over all day. By the time she finally accepted that Ricky wasn't coming back, it was dark. She ate to make sure that the baby would be okay, like Ricky had told her, took a bath, and went to bed, hoping that he would be lying next to her when she woke up.

CHAPTER 15

Two months passed, and Ricky hadn't yet returned to Carlette, who was almost five months pregnant, had very little food, and had no money left for rent, which was a week past due. She lay in bed, thinking of ways to get money for rent and food, but she didn't know anyone, didn't know how to look for work, and she knew that no one would hire her in her present condition.

The sound of pounding on the door brought Carlette back to the present. She jumped out of bed and ran to the door, hoping that Ricky was standing on the other side of it. Out of breath, she anxiously put her hand on the knob and began to turn it. *Maybe it's not Ricky.* She cleared her throat. "Who is it?"

"The police!"

Carlette's heart began to beat rapidly. She touched her stomach in a calming manner before cracking the door and looking out. Two police officers with brown complexions stared down at her.

The one standing in the back licked his lips, his eyes wide. "How old you, girl?"

The officer that stood in front nudged his partner in the stomach with his elbow. "You see dis a mere chile 'ere, KC. And you know we ain't 'ere for none of dat. Dis business."

Officer KC held his stomach, his cheeks and eyes still bulging from the hit.

The lead officer smiled at Carlette. "Sorry he so stupid. My name is Officer Hixson." Hixson pointed over his shoulder with his right thumb without looking back. "This here is Officer KC, like the letters *KC*. Can we come in please?"

Carlette reluctantly stepped aside, and the two officers entered and removed their hats. Inside, she could see them more clearly and gave them a once-over. The scars on KC's face made him look like a brindle puppy. She instantly knew that he wasn't originally from the island. He had to have come from an African tribe or something, one that used scars and dyes to designate their tribe, status, or something of that nature.

Officer Hixson broke the silence. "What is your name, ma'am, if you don't mind us asking?"

Carlette spoke softly. "Carlette."

"And your last name?" asked Officer Hixon.

"Poussant." She had forgotten in that instant that her name was now Roxen.

Officer Hixson frowned inquisitively.

The look on his face made Carlette nervous. Why hadn't she remembered to use her married name? She could have lied and said that Ricky Roxen was her brother. Surely they would arrest him now, if they hadn't already done so, and take her back to her aunt. She wasn't ready to go back to the Lion Queen.

Officer Hixson looked at Carlette's stomach. "Ricky Roxen live 'ere?"

"Yes."

"Is that his baby you carrying?"

Carlette lowered her eyes. "No."

"Then why you 'ere?"

"Um . . . just staying 'ere with my brother."

"So Ricky your brother?"

Carlette nodded.

"Where duh man responsible for getting you with chile?"

Carlette hunched her shoulders. "I don't know." She wiped the tears that had begun to fall from her eyes. "You won't be arresting Ricky, will you? He all I got right now to look after me and the baby."

Officer Hixson gently put a comforting hand on Carlette's shoulder. "Don't you worry about Ricky or the father of your chile. A man who would leave a woman as beautiful as you is crazy, and the other just silly to be doing what he doing, knowing that he got a sister who needs him. 'Ere's my card, Carlette. If Ricky come back, call us, okay? Maybe we can work something out with him so that he can help you and your baby."

Carlette took the card and quickly locked the door behind the officers. When or if Ricky came back, she would tell him about the officers, but they would never catch him if they wanted her to be the one to turn him in. She was positive that the two of them would run off together.

Although everyone knew that Ricky sold drugs, nothing was done about it until the police received a tip-off and came looking for him. He had left town suddenly after one of his boys clued him in, and he hadn't had the time to explain the details to Carlette.

There was banging on the door again.

"Who is it?" Carlette was irritated.

"It's the landlord!"

This frightened Carlette more than the police. She instantly panicked. *Oh, my God! What am I going to do? I don't have his money!*

"Come on! Open duh door! Ricky didn't bring me my rent dis mont! Open up!"

Carlette slowly opened the door. Mr. Coles stood in the doorway, looking angry. He always leered at her whenever she and Ricky were around him or when she dropped off his rent. But now that she was alone, the short, thick, black, bald, greasy, round, yellow-eyed figure looked more frightening than ever. Carlette just stared at him.

"My *rent*, girl! My rent!" Mr. Coles shouted. He could see her fear. He wanted the shouting to finish unraveling her.

"I don't have it." Carlette was trembling, and Mr. Coles could see that, too.

"Then you're out on the streets, girl!"

"Mr. Coles, please—"

"Girl! If you tryin' tuh beg me for free lodging, forget it! I need my money!"

"But I don't have anywhere else to go."

"Then give me my money!"

"But—"

"But nothing! I need my money, girl! Or something round dis apartment that will be equal payment!"

Carlette looked around. She would have to empty the apartment. "That would be all the furniture, Mr. Coles."

"Then you lay wit' me."

Carlette wasn't sure she'd heard right. "What?"

"You heard what I said, girl! Either you lay wit' me, or you're out. Tonight!"

"But I'm pregnant, Mr. Coles, and—"

"I can see dat!"

Mr. Coles was almost drooling. Ricky had allowed him to sleep with his women in the past, but he'd never offered him Carlette, something Mr. Coles had been waiting too long for, as far as he was concerned.

"Come on, girl! What's it going to be?"

Carlette stared at him for a moment with teary eyes. "Okay, okay, but—"

"Come on, den!" Mr. Coles grabbed Carlette's wrist and pulled her into the bedroom.

"Mr. Coles, wait a minute."

"Do you want to go out on duh streets?"

"No."

"Then you'll do dis and shut up! Now crawl upon the bed and lie down."

Carlette did as Mr. Coles commanded. She heard the zipper of his pants and wanted to run, but she just lay there, crying and thinking about how much she didn't want him to touch her, especially with her baby inside of her, but she felt she didn't have much choice.

Noticing that he was taking a long time, she lifted her head to see why. *Impotent! That's what Ricky meant when he said Mr. Coles is impotent and*

*can't do a girl with his thing. He can't make himself
erect like Ricky can.*

As much as Mr. Coles claimed to want Carlette
and was desperate for her, he was unable to get
an erection.

When he stirred and the bed moved, Carlette
thought he'd finally prepared himself. She shut
her eyes tight and waited in disgust. *Ricky, help
me. Ricky, help me.*

Mr. Coles removed Carlette's robe and nightgown and began to have his way with her. She
shrieked from the thought of that drooling, white-
cornered mouth touching her body. It felt slimy,
and Carlette almost threw up. She thought he was
going to lie on her baby, so she tried to roll away
from him as he moved his heavy body closer to
hers. Carlette put her hand over her mouth so
that she wouldn't scream. She thought of Ricky
while Mr. Coles snorted with desire.

Mr. Coles could feel Carlette squirming. He
loved the way the girls would scream, squirm, and
wrench, trying to get away from him, and when
he liked one of them, he'd make sure it was
lengthy. It made him feel masculine and whole
again. He knew that was the only way he'd ever be
able to have Carlette and took total advantage.
He ordered her to do things and rubbed her
stomach with his rough, rusty hands.

Afraid to move, Carlette lay still, gagging and
flinching from his prolonged touching and coer-
cion. She didn't want him yelling at her again,
like he'd done several times during the course of
his lust, and just waited for his next command.

"You can get up now. Walk me to the door," he barked.

Carlette, her legs weak and trembling, slid off the bed and reached for her robe.

"No! I like looking at your brown skin and your smooth, round belly, which looks so much like mine."

That made Carlette angry, but she remained quiet. She was more interested in getting rid of him than starting a fight.

At the door he tried to touch her breasts and kiss her, but she threw up on his shoes.

Mr. Coles screamed, "Ah! You've got to clean that up!" He backed out the door and snatched his handkerchief out of his front pocket. He wiped at the vile-looking substance and mumbled angrily under his breath so that Carlette wouldn't hear. "This the pleasure I get for going through all the trouble of setting up that simpleminded little boyfriend of hers so that I could be alone with dis girl and have her?" Then he shouted, "Like I said, same ting next mont' if you want to live 'ere!"

Carlette dropped her head.

After Mr. Coles left, Carlette quickly shut the door, cleaned up everything, and scrubbed her body extra hard. Mr. Coles had made her feel filthy, but she loved Ricky and didn't want him to come back to nothing. She kept telling herself that everything was okay, that she hadn't really done anything wrong with Mr. Coles. "It's okay. It's okay," she repeated. "At least he didn't put it in me." Then she got into bed and drifted off to sleep.

Chapter 16

Mr. Coles was at the door. Rent was due again. Carlette quietly sat in the apartment until he went away. She refused to go through his torturous regimen again.

It was pouring outside, but Carlette was determined to leave, something she thought she should have done before Mr. Coles or Ricky had touched her. She abruptly packed her belongings, left the apartment, and began walking in the rain.

By the time she reached her aunt's house, she was soaked. Her long braids were dripping wet, and her clothes were plastered to her body, accentuating the outline of her stomach. As she passed the kitchen window of her aunt's house, she could see the light under the partially drawn shade. She could also see her aunt sitting at the kitchen table, drinking something from a cup she was holding tight with both hands. She was shaking her head and seemed to be crying, which made Carlette reluctant to go inside.

Carlette backed away from the door, but a flash

of Mr. Coles came back to her. She gently knocked on the door.

"Who is it?"

Carlette didn't answer. She wanted her aunt to just open the door. She figured, that way, if her aunt was too furious, she could run away before she got hold of her and made her lose her baby, the only person she knew would love her back, and which belonged to the only person she believed still loved her now.

The strong voice repeated itself. "Who is it?"

Carlette still didn't answer.

Genevee got up from the table and went to the door. She was sure it was the neighborhood children playing and snatched open the door with the intent of cussing them out. "What the . . . eeye! Carlette! Carlette! Baby!"

Carlette backed away. She thought her aunt was referring to her stomach when she said the word *baby*.

Genevee grabbed her chest, fell to her knees, and began to cry.

Carlette dropped her bags and ran to her aunt's side and tried helping her to her feet. "Aunt Genevee! Aunt Genevee! You okay?"

Genevee slowly stood up. "Carlette, I thought you were dead or working on Rockway."

Rockway was a small strip where girls turned tricks for money.

"Come in! Come in, baby! You soaked!" Genevee was so excited to see Carlette, she hadn't noticed her stomach. "Carlette, I'm so sorry for what I said to you when you left. The house was so empty without you. I've missed you. Let Auntie Genevee fix your hair. It's so wet. Oh, my God!"

Carlette was already crying uncontrollably and was almost convulsing by the time Genevee noticed her stomach.

Genevee didn't argue; she spoke gently. "Carlette, Carlette, it's okay, baby. We'll talk. We'll work something out."

Genevee put her arm around Carlette's shoulders and led her to the bathroom. She knew that Carlette loved long, hot baths, singing and humming in the tub, and using her powders and fragrances. She prepared a bath and undressed Carlette. She bathed her and gently washed her stomach, all the while talking to her unborn child.

Carlette, embarrassed by what had happened to her while she was away, was still crying, but the tears lessened with the attention she was getting from her aunt.

"Carlette, don't cry so much. The baby will cry much."

Carlette continued to cry.

"You want to tell Auntie Genevee what happened? Was you raped?"

When Carlette cried even harder, Genevee knew that she had hit the nail on the head or was close to the nail's head.

"Aunt Genevee, I'm married."

Genevee tried to keep her composure. "Married?"

"Yes."

"But how? You're barely seventeen."

"We went away to a small village and got married there. Rules are different."

"And you got pregnant after the wedding?"

"No."

"Is that why he married you . . . because you two had been together and—"

"No!" Carlette became frightened and backed away. This was Aunt Genevee she had snapped at, and her aunt didn't take to this type of attitude.

"Don't be afraid, baby. I'm not angry. I know you pregnant. Tell me what happened."

"I liked him, Aunt Genevee, and I'd seen him and daydreamed about him. I'd even pretended to kiss him, but it wasn't like I'd ever really talked to him at all, or anything. I'd never let a man touch me, Auntie Genevee, never!" Carlette began to cry again.

"Come on now, Carlette. Finish telling Aunt Genevee what happened to you."

"He'd been watching me as well. He talked to me on different occasions, and we became friends. One Saturday he met me on the steps at the center. He talked to me a long time, and I went to his house, but he never did anything to me. But the time you cursed me out in front of Frank, that was the weekend it all started. I went to my friend's house and fell asleep. When I woke up, it was late, and I was afraid to come home, and my friend let me stay with him. I thought you would kill me or just would not let me come back in, and I lived with him. He bought me nice things and fed me well for a long time. He got drunk one night and did things to me."

"He had sex with you?"

"Not at first. He just put his mouth on my breasts." Carlette lowered her head because she knew she had enjoyed it. "I became afraid. I felt as though I owed him for taking care of me. He told me to go take my bath and go to bed. When I returned to the living room, where I usually slept, he told me that I'd be sleeping in the bedroom, and that's where I went. He came into the room later and began teasing and playing with me. I thought he was trying to be funny and make me laugh because he thought I was angry with him for what had happened between us on the sofa, but instead, he ducked his head under the covers, and the next thing I knew, he was sticking his tongue in my navel. I still thought he was playing, Aunt Genevee. I knew nothing at all about, about, you know, all that, and I lay there, giggling, until he made a straight line down with his tongue and covered me with his mouth."

Not knowing that Carlette had enjoyed that, too, Genevee cupped Carlette's head and rested it on her chest and rocked her back and forth. Her niece's openness and naïveté had caused her to blush. How did her poor little baby, whom she had secretly loved so deeply inwardly but had disrespected outwardly, get into this position? She knew the girl was green, but thought she would know better than to tell her auntie certain things.

Genevee took a deep breath. "Oh, Carlette, baby!"

"I know it's shameful, Auntie, but I wanted him. I wanted to see what made people get all those feelings I hear them whispering about, all the stuff that's supposed to be bad and kept quiet but, I hear, feels so good when it happens. So when he asked me if he could go further, I said yes because

I could feel how much I loved him. And, like I had heard out in the streets, I believed having sex with him would make us love each other better. But it hurt, and I got angry. I wanted to hate him, but my heart wouldn't let me." Carlette looked up into her aunt's face. "Why is it that we have to keep all that so quiet? Why can't we talk about it openly? Is it better to just do those things in secret and let girls get pregnant, like I did? I heard that my friend Verma even got a disease. I'm just so scared, Auntie, so scared. Why is the truth hidden?"

"Sh, sh, sh, Carlette. Think about the baby. We don't want an upset child."

"But I am upset about this."

"Okay, Carlette, this is what I believe. I believe a lot of people aren't ready to talk about sex and sexually transmitted diseases, which is why so many of us remain silent about it. They don't want to talk or admit that there are incurable diseases that can kill us off. Young girls get pregnant and are looked down upon, but people fail to realize it's because of our carelessness and unwillingness to educate and be educated that a lot of that happens. But you, Carlette, this will not happen to you again, because I won't allow it. I love you too much for that."

Carlette wrapped her wet arms around Genevee's waist and cried some more. This was the first time she had heard those words coming from her aunt's lips.

Genevee stroked Carlette's head.

"I swear to you, Auntie, I didn't do this out of spite. I love him. He took care of me because I was afraid to come home to you in the beginning and didn't want to leave him once we'd done that. He kept on saying he loved me, that he wanted to marry me, that he'd take care of me and the baby, so I married him. I needed him, Auntie. I needed someone to love me, to help me to take care of me. You'd said many times that you wished I'd never been put in your life, so I thought I didn't have a choice. Then I woke up one morning, and he was gone. He left me a note telling me that he was coming back, but he never did."

Carlette was crying so hard, her nose was now red and running.

"When I came to your door, if you'd tried to harm me or my baby in any way, I was prepared to run away again. But I love you, Auntie Genevee, no matter how you feel about me or how many times I've tried to deny it. I love you."

Genevee was now crying with Carlette and was filled with shame. "I love you, too, Carlette. I'm sorry about being so mean to you. It's just that I thought I needed some ol' mon to make me feel happy and secure, but after you left 'ere, I never felt so alone and lonely in all my life. I'm sorry for all that I have done to you, Carlette. I'm going to do better by you. I'm going to show you how happy I am to have you back. Are you keeping the baby?"

"Yes, yes. I have to keep the baby. It belongs to my husband, Auntie Genevee."

"Okay, we'll work it out."

Genevee got up from the side of the tub and went into the kitchen, and made them some hot tea. Shortly after she poured the tea into cups, Carlette climbed out of the tub, threw on her robe, and joined her aunt at the small, blue Formica table that sat in the middle of their kitchen floor.

"Carlette, I've been thinking . . . How would you like to go live with my girlfriend in the States? Her name's Cora. We met at the library when I first started. We had plenty to talk about, went to lunch a lot, and drank lots of beverages. Her husband has passed on now, but he was based near the island."

"You don't want me 'ere, Auntie Genevee? You ashamed of me?"

"No, Carlette, no. I told you the truth. While you were away, I was more lonely than ever. I never knew how much I loved you and how much you meant to me until you left and I thought I'd never see you again. You were all I had to call my own. But I also love you enough to want the best for you. You see, Cora runs this house in Georgia for special girls, and there's an extraordinary school she sends them to. You still need your education and something other than just a high school or college background to help you make it. If you don't like the flute, maybe you can dance or sing, maybe even model. You are very talented and beautiful."

Carlette was stunned. What her aunt thought of her meant a lot. She had actually called her beautiful. She lowered her head. "Did you always think that I hated the flute?"

Genevee smiled. She sat up as straight as she could, stuck out her chest, and held her fists out in front of her and shook them. "Well, I always wanted you to play it because I felt that it was a sophisticated instrument. I knew that if you were to choose an instrument, it would not be the flute." She brushed a strand of hair out of Carlette's face, then took another sip of tea.

Carlette sat quietly for a moment. "Do you really mean it, Aunt Genevee? Do you really think that I'm pretty . . . beautiful?"

"Girl, if I had your look, I'd be long gone from 'ere. You got to be the most beautiful girl on this island. Them other girls just ain't notice it yet, 'cause you still young."

Carlette smiled. "But how can I model the way I am now, Aunt Genevee?"

"Pregnancy doesn't last forever, Carlette. Besides, pregnant women are used quite often for modeling. How do you think maternity clothes are sold?"

"I don't know, Auntie. I don't have any. I didn't know people wore those."

"Well, they do. You're just thin enough to get away with wearing regular clothes, right now, anyway, and if you hadn't gotten wet, I wouldn't have been able to tell that you're pregnant at all. That mon must have taken good care of you, Carlette. You look very nice, you know."

"Oh. Thank you, Auntie Genevee. He did take good care of me."

"So what do you think? Would you like to go to the States?"

"Yeah, I guess."

"I promise, if you don't like it, I won't make you stay. I'll send for you promptly."

"When will I leave, Auntie?"

"Cora likes taking girls when they're at least six months pregnant. How far along are you?"

"Just about six months now."

"Okay, let's set a date for four weeks from now."

"Okay, Auntie Genevee. May I go to bed now?"

"You don't ever have to ask me questions like that again, Carlette. This house is just as much yours as it is mine. Your mother left money to help me pay for it."

"Really? Then why do you hate her so?"

"Oh, no, Carlette, oh, no. I could never hate my baby sister. It was all jealousy, including the way I treated you. She married your father, the man I'd tricked into sleeping with me in the beginning, and then I became ashamed after he told your mother and married her, anyway. It was all shame, jealousy, and guilt."

"You were with my father first?"

"No, not really. I loved him first. Your mother was like you. She hadn't even noticed boys, but McArthur Poussant noticed her, and every time I'd call myself, trying to get close to him, he'd ask about her. Daddy didn't allow us to date, so randomly, after hours, McArthur would come around to Deltra's bedroom window and talk with her. He was only trying to hang around until my father finally allowed her to date. He wanted to be the first in line, and that burned me up. And when I'd hear them giggling and whispering, I'd lie in bed, feeling so jealous, I couldn't sleep most of the night. I'd be too tired for school or anything else the next day.

"I got tired of that and asked Deltra if she would switch rooms with me. My excuse was, I needed more air. She was always nice and easygoing, just like you, so she let me. We had the same hair texture, were just about the same size. Well, I always had a larger butt and hips and breasts, but I knew that my plan would work. He'd never slept with Deltra or seen her naked, so he wouldn't be able to tell the difference between us once I was naked and in the dark. So earlier that day I told McArthur she would be waiting for him, that she was leaving her bedroom window open for him to climb through, and I advised him to be very quiet and just get in bed with her and not say a word.

"I made very sure that he was very aroused before we got started. He was like your friend, deeply passionate, and he made me moan his name. When I did, that's when he found out it was me. He was so angry, he got up before we were done and later told Deltra everything. It hurt me so bad to know that he wanted my sister more than me, and she hadn't given him a second thought in that way. I'd done things that night for him that not many people did or talked about back then. I even had him calling me by my sister's name. So, the idea of him brushing me off and telling her really hurt me deep. And I purposely tried to hate him, Carlette."

"You've been that way to a man, Auntie Genevee?"

"Yes, but that was the last time, and I've never been nice to a man since then, neither. That's why I never married or had children."

"You allowed my father to turn you bitter?"

"Actually, it was my own stupidity that did it. He never even pretended to want me. After you left, I had a lot of free time to think about that and how stupid I was to try to trap your father that way, do all those passionate things, then be angry because of it."

"How do women learn things like that, Auntie?"

"Back in my day, not from their parents. Mostly, they watched other people, sneaked around and read books, watched movies, then tried them out."

"Does doing something like that make you feel good, too?"

"Why? Are you thinking about doing it?"

"No! No!"

"I can tell by your red face that it embarrasses you."

"It does. Mr. Coles did that to me for the rent last month. That's why I left. I couldn't let him do that to me again. He's disgusting."

"Why was he doing that to a pregnant chile?"

"He's what I heard my husband, Ricky, call an *impotent*."

Genevee snickered, but hurtful tears also formed in her eyes at how innocent Carlette still was after the ordeal she had been through, the ordeal she believed she had caused Carlette to endure. Why hadn't she discussed sex with her perfect, beautiful child before this all happened? Why hadn't she let her mind see the light sooner?

Genevee quickly changed the subject. "Ricky is the one you call your husband?"

"Yes, Auntie."

"Is it that Ricky Roxen?"

"Yes, Auntie Genevee."

"He's very handsome, Carlette, and your baby's going to be beautiful. But Ricky's a street hustler, and I heard he has some girls."

"He did. But he gave them up and just worked at the Basin."

"The strip club?"

"Yes, Auntie Genevee."

"That boy loves working around sin, huh?"

Carlette smiled bashfully and put her head down.

Genevee snickered again. "I don't know where he went, but he must have intended to come back. He's given up a lot for you already. He must really love you."

"He does, Auntie. I know he does. How did you know that I was talking about Ricky Roxen, Auntie?"

"Only a boy like him could capture a girl as beautiful and as smart as you." Genevee smiled.

Carlette stared down into her cup and became quiet. Genevee allowed her the silence and then changed the subject. When the conversation ended, Carlette was hungry, and Genevee fixed her something to eat before she went to bed.

While washing dishes, Genevee thought to herself, *I can't believe what I've done. I'm Carlette's only living relative, and I let her down. If I had left my stupid jealousy out of all this, that child would not be in this predicament. Her mother and father must be turning in their graves because of what I made happen to her. All I had to do was talk to her and her parents the way I did tonight. A little talk can go a long way, and so can a lot of forgiveness, but I didn't even allow McArthur in my house after what I'd done. And I continued to take my feelings out on Carlette, because she looks so much like him. I should have let that stuff with*

McArthur go a long time ago. That man never wanted me, anyway. Why couldn't I accept that until now?

Genevee shook her head, trying to shake away all that had happened. Yet she had never felt so good before, so happy. Her confession and Carlétte's safe return made her feel somewhat unburdened. She was even ready to be a grandparent.

CHAPTER 17

Sirens blared at a distance, and loud yelling and screams coursed the air.

"Let him go, Ricky! Let him go! You're going to kill him!"

Ricky, who had secretly returned to town, was crying and beating Mr. Coles to a pulp. He had gone home, and Carlette hadn't been there. When he asked Mr. Coles if he knew what had happened to her, Mr. Coles told him what he'd done to her. Ricky had paid him handsomely to watch over her until he came back to get her, knowing that Carlette wasn't really old enough or capable enough to take care of herself for so long. Mr. Coles had spoiled their relationship by running his young wife and unborn child away before he could return home and reclaim them.

"I didn't know she was your wife! I swear! I didn't know!" Mr. Coles was lying on the ground, crying gutturally, holding his stomach, and pleading, hoping to get some pity.

Manson, one of Ricky's close friends, was

holding Ricky, but Ricky got away from him and kicked Mr. Coles in the stomach again.

"Ahhh! Boy! You're going to kill me, mon!" Mr. Coles screamed.

"I intend to! All you tink about is that ting of yours that don't work, you greasy, crazy, immoral, limp bull!" Ricky yelled.

Manson grabbed Ricky and attempted to hold him off again, but Ricky was too wild for him. Ricky's other good friend, Grandell, had to help hold him back.

"Let me go! Let me go! Bot' of you, let me go!" Ricky ordered.

"No, mon! You got yo'self a wife and baby on da way." Grandell lowered his voice for emphasis. "You out of that trouble, too. When you find your wife and kid, you can be wit' dem. That's all you need to worry 'bout."

Ricky quieted down and assured them that they could let him go. He would not attack Mr. Coles. When they released him, he ran toward Mr. Coles as if he was going to kick him again.

Mr. Coles flinched. "Ahhhhhhhh! Don't kick me no more, Ricky!"

Ricky laughed, then spat on him before he walked toward Grandell and Manson. The three friends huddled together and talked quietly as they made plans on how to take care of Mr. Coles. Grandell and Manson agreed to do what Ricky asked. Mr. Coles had violated a friend's wife and trust, and that wasn't something their ring of acquaintances did to each other.

Ricky leered at Mr. Coles, who lay on the

ground, holding his gut, pretending to hurt more than he did, afraid of being beaten some more.

Ricky yelled out, "You like my product—my women! I'm going to fix you up, mon! I'm going to fix you up real good! Give you something just for you!" With that comment, Ricky walked away, calm and cool.

CHAPTER 18

The story on the island was that Ricky's last comment was a threat.

Mr. Coles went home to sit in front of his television, the way he did each night. There he met two large men he'd never seen before. They were standing in his living room, waiting for him.

When he tried leaving, one of the men grabbed the back of his collar. "Where you running to, fat mon?"

"Just let me go. I have money." Mr. Coles trembled as he stood there, his face to the door.

"So where's duh money, fat mon?" asked the same man.

Mr. Coles sidestepped them and led them to his bedroom. He opened his top dresser drawer, where he kept his gun and some of his money. His hands shook nervously as he moved the underwear that covered his valuable items.

"Whatchoo looking for, fat mon?"

"I'm looking for duh money! Duh money!" Mr. Coles was terrified. The gun was gone.

Ricky knew that Mr. Coles always went for that gun when anything got too hot for him, so he'd tipped off the intruders.

"You mean dis money, or maybe dis gun?" One of the men held the items up in the air and dangled them. "I 'ear you like variety sex, mon."

Both men laughed.

Mr. Coles panicked. "You got my money and everyting! Just take it and leave!"

"We don't got everyting, greasy ball. Cock bull!" said the man who had spoken first. He walked over to Mr. Coles and lifted his sleeveless T-shirt. He asked his friend, "Hey, you think he's pregnant?"

Mr. Coles snatched his shirt down. "You'd better get out of 'ere! Now!"

"Oh, did you 'ear dat?" replied the other man. "We better get out of 'ere! Now! We bot' scared, mon! We bot' scared of the soon-to-be batty boy!"

Mr. Coles's eyes grew so large, they appeared to be completely white. He tried to walk past the men, but one tripped him, and all three began to struggle. Mr. Coles lost to the intruders and was whipped with his own pistol.

"Pull his pants down! 'Urry up! We got to get out of 'ere! Come on, 'urry!" cried one of the men.

Mr. Coles was pleading with the two men intensely. He knew what they were up to. In his glory days, he'd done these same things to people who either owed him money or were presented to him as payment by someone else, or when he was allowed to have a good time with someone. Sometimes they were willing; sometimes they were not. Now he was the victim.

The sounds that came from him were signs of accomplishment to his intruders. They would deliver a good report.

CHAPTER 19

Mr. Coles woke up swinging but was only fighting air. He tried to stand up but couldn't. He tried to crawl but couldn't. All he could do was drag himself to the bathroom, using his arms. As soon as he entered the doorway, he began to vomit. "Ah, ah, ah. Urgh . . . those nasty bastards, they mess me up but good. I can't even walk. I've gotta get help."

When the ambulance arrived, the EMTs immediately detected what had happened to Mr. Coles. They'd been in this area many times before to aid people who'd been attacked the same way. All the victims suffered from the same physical complaints. The EMTs knew that it was some sort of punishment, and that the victim must have known his attacker or attackers, but they couldn't figure out why the person who'd been attacked didn't leave before it happened, and why the police never did anything about it when it did.

One of the EMTs recognized Mr. Coles. He didn't particularly care for him. He had bought some lottery tickets, coffee, and a paper at Mr.

Coles' newsstand one morning, and Mr. Coles had shortchanged him, cussing him out and pulling his gun on him and refusing to give him back his change. The EMT was glad when he found out that someone had taken advantage of him. It helped him to remain professional.

When the ambulance arrived at the hospital, Ricky was there waiting for Mr. Coles. While he was unattended, Ricky approached him. "Well, did you get all the pleasure you was looking for?"

Mr. Coles began yelling, and Ricky slapped him with as much force as he could and disappeared.

The doctors ran to Mr. Coles's aid but couldn't understand what had upset him so much to make his heart race so fast. And Mr. Coles was too afraid to tell. He just held his face and wept. He was interviewed by the police, but he would not tell them anything. Although they assured him that they knew many similar attacks had happened in his area, just like all the rest, Mr. Coles wouldn't talk. He knew he had been a victim or involved in those attacks and would only be implicating himself and making things worse. He kept quiet and pretended not to heal very well during his hospital stay.

Too afraid to go home right away, he stayed an extra two weeks in the hospital so that he could find another place to live. Then he moved out of the neighborhood altogether, knowing he'd never be safe there again.

Ricky searched the island for Carlette but came up with nothing. He thought she would never go back to her aunt's house, and didn't attempt to look for her there, afraid that her aunt would have him jailed for allowing Carlette to live with him and marrying her before she was of legal age. This was another rumor that had gotten back to Carlette while she was sifting through the small island of gossips.

CHAPTER 20

As the plane landed, Carlette closed her journal and watched as the runway got closer and closer.

Outside of the Atlanta airport, she hailed a cab. The driver smiled politely, said something in a language she didn't understand, and began putting her bags in his trunk. She got into the cab and opened her journal.

As the cab drove up to Cora's house, Carlette closed her journal and gazed out of the window, widemouthed.

Before the driver could help her inside, Carlette hopped out of the car, grabbed her bags, and headed up the wide brick steps. Cora held the door open for her with a welcoming smile and summoned her with an open hand.

Waddling as fast as she could, Carlette forged ahead with excitement. Standing in the doorway of what she considered a pristine palace, she stared in amazement as she looked around, admiring the beautiful art and finishes. Carlette had never seen such a magnificent place before. The interior looked as magnificent as the outside, and compared to her aunt's small cottage, it was a castle.

The other ten girls occupying Cora's house stood looking at Carlette, smiles on their faces, as Cora introduced her to them. "And this is Jaha, Seeta, Carrie, Olara, Jasmine, Clover, Tovia, Mary, Lola, and Puhshell. It would probably be useless for me to give you their last names, since most of them will be gone before you really settle in. And depending on how I feel, I might not keep the house open. Carlette? Carlette?"

Carlette looked at Cora.

"Carlette, how was your trip over here?" asked Cora.

Carlette was still dumbfounded.

The girls giggled.

Cora knit her brows. "Carlette?"

Carlette blinked. "Huh?"

"The trip over here, was it okay? How was your trip?" Cora quizzed.

"The trip? Over here?" Carlette snapped out of her daze. "Oh! It was nice, very nice. They feed you well, and the seats are very comfortable."

Cora smiled. "That's good, Carlette. We want to make things as comfortable as possible for you here, too. Come on, I'll show you to your room."

Carlette picked up her bags again.

"No, Carlette. We'll have someone else bring your bags up. We don't want you lifting too much, okay?"

"They're not that heavy. I carried them in here. I can carry them to my room."

"Nonsense. Someone will take them for you."

Carlette didn't argue. She smiled politely and thanked Cora.

One of the girls took the bags, and the others followed her up the stairs, giggling cheerfully. Carlette watched them. Their blissful attitudes made her feel good to be there. She was also at ease with Cora. The house was impeccable. It seemed to have a million rooms, although there were only twenty, not counting the baths, the library, and the recreation room.

Cora took Carlette's hand and headed upstairs. "So, are you okay being here?"

"Yes, Cora—"

"Call me *Auntie* Cora. All the others do."

"Auntie Cora, I'm very happy that I came. At first I didn't want to, but now I'm okay with it."

"Well, that's good. We're going to make sure that you get nothing but the best while you're here. All young ladies should want the best."

"Oh yeah . . . I'm sorry about being pregnant."

"No, no, no. I'm not referring to that." Cora sat down on the bed, patted a spot for Carlette to sit next to her, and took her hand. "This will be your room." She proceeded to explain her statement. "I'd never hurt or embarrass you that way, Carlette. Everyone makes mistakes, and things that we have no control over happen to us all the time. What I'm saying is, you still have a future. Have you thought about anything you'd like to do after you've finished school?"

"Yes, Auntie Cora. I'd love to be an accomplished

flutist or flautist, or however you're supposed to say it."

They both laughed.

"It doesn't matter how you pronounce it . . . as long as you live out your dream," Cora told her.

"Thanks, Auntie Cora."

"My Lord, you *are* well mannered, just like Genevee said."

"Aunt Genevee said that about me?"

"Yes. She thinks the world of you. She also thinks you're the most beautiful child in the world."

Carlette's somber expression turned into a proud smile. She was almost light-headed with pride.

Cora released Carlette's hand. "I'd agree with that if I didn't have so many daughters and grand-children myself who I feel the same way about." Cora looked around the room and smiled. "The reasons why we bought this big house. Have you ever thought of modeling?"

Carlette folded her hands in her lap and shyly looked down at them. "No, but Aunt Genevee said the same thing, and I only noticed myself right before this happened to me." Carlette patted her protruding stomach.

"Were you raped, Carlette? Many of the girls who come here were raped."

"No. Well, yes. No, not really. I just love my child's father so much, I wanted to get the feeling I'd heard so much talk about." Carlette hunched her shoulders. "I just loved him, Auntie Cora. I still love him."

"Do you want to tell me what happened?"

Carlette began talking almost without taking a breath. She broke down in tears again as she described to Cora what had happened between her and Ricky. She explained everything, from the night she overslept at his house and was too scared to go home to her aunt, to the night that Ricky took her virginity. By the time she was finished, she was shaking and crying uncontrollably.

"Don't worry, Carlette. When we find him, we'll have him arrested for that."

"No! No! It's okay now. It's okay. We're married. I love him now. Please, Auntie Cora, don't hurt him. He asked me before he had sex with me. I agreed."

Cora looked confused. "I don't understand."

"Well, he told me why he did it. I mean, he never touched me again after that, until I allowed it, and we were married by then. Please, Auntie Cora, don't send my husband to jail." Carlette lowered her head. "And, to be quite honest, I liked it and loved him more but pretended to be angry and tried to hate him so that I wouldn't like something so unheard of." Tears dropped from Carlette's eyes between her thumbs.

Cora patted her hands. "Okay, Carlette, okay. Let's just forget it and move on." She sat on Carlette's bed in silence for a while. She took her hand again. "Carlette, are you at all wondering why I take girls like yourself in?"

"Yes, but I figured that was something you just liked doing."

"I do like helping all of you, but there's a story behind it. A story about me."

"You have a story, too, Auntie Cora?"

"Yes. And it's not half as pleasant as yours."

"What happened? I mean—"

"It was similar to what happened to you, except . . ." Cora hesitated. "Except . . ." She hesitated again. "When I was seventeen, I was molested by the town handyman, who everybody trusted. I looked about twelve, but I was seventeen, naive, immature, very small for my age, and a loner. Anyway, he told me my cousin Bobbie Pearl was waiting for me near an abandoned building and he would walk me there. My parents had warned me to never go near those buildings, because they were unsafe, in more ways than one. But because I was with him, I thought it was okay.

"We waited and waited there. It got dark, and I asked him if we should go home, because we had very little daylight and only the streetlights that shone through the windows as a guide. He told me perhaps Bobbie Pearl had got lost inside the building and we should look for her before heading home. He took me by the hand as we walked through a dusty, narrow door. We both kept yelling out for Bobbie Pearl as he led me through the structure. He started running up and down the hallways, and I was struggling to keep up. My palms were sweaty, and my hand slipped out of his grip. I didn't know where he went, and I couldn't see anything. To make matters worse, I didn't know my way back out. I started calling out to him as I walked aimlessly throughout the building. That's when he came out of nowhere, grabbed me by my waist with one arm, lifted me up, and turned me around. I panicked and started screaming. He put me down and said, 'Shh! Shh! It's only me, Cora.' I started getting scared and told him I wanted to go home. I could feel that something was wrong, very wrong, and it was.

"He got harsh and loud. 'Now you quiet down, Cora! You had no business coming to this building with me! It don't look good! You know that, don't you?' I began pulling on my thumbnail and nodded yes. My mother had told me to never go anywhere without her or my father's knowledge, or without telling them who I was going with, and he knew that. He also knew that I wasn't allowed in the abandoned buildings. He knew everything about us.

"He touched the belt on my jeans. I grabbed his hand to stop him. He said, 'Let go, Cora, or I'll tell your momma. She'll be very disappointed in you, and so will your daddy, and all the people I tell that you were here with me.' That made me panic. All I could think was, Oh, no! All the people? All what people? Is he going to tell everyone? They'll think that I asked him to come in this building with me. Oh, no! Tears started rolling down my face. He knew he had me then and continued his bullying. 'Are you going to be quiet until we're through here, Cora?' When he said that to me, I nodded in agreement."

Carlette could see that Cora was clenching her fists tighter and tighter. She laid her right hand on Cora's.

"He undid my belt, unbuttoned and unzipped

my jeans. He told me to take one leg out of my jeans and panties, saying it would be quicker that way. That's when I started begging him to just let me go. I told him I'd never come back to the vacant building again or disobey my parents again if he'd just let me go that one time. You see, Carlette, my perception back then was that, whenever I was disobedient, any adult was entitled to punish me however they chose. So I stepped out of my clothes, like he'd ordered. As soon as I did, he pulled me by my skinny little arm until I was close enough to him, then got down on his knees and assaulted me. And, like you, I squealed with disgust, and he made me tremble and get weak-kneed from his attack."

Cora wiped a tear before it fell. "Carlette, my whole butt fit into that monster's hand. Can you imagine that? A full-grown man, probably a lot older than your husband, whose one hand alone is the size of your butt, taking advantage of you at a young age? I wasn't only weak and wobbly legged when he was done. I was totally humiliated. Did I mention that he was a white man? And that in those days it wasn't only shameful for a girl to be molested, but black girls were considered whores if they even looked cross-eyed at a white man? He even told me to get used to what he was doing to me, because I was going to grow up to be nothing but a whore, anyway, because that's what all black women are. Whores. I believed him, Carlette. Yeah, I believed him. At the time, there were no programs, groups, or talk shows, no one to talk to, turn to, or tell it to. Absolutely, no one to tell, and he kept making me meet him there, until we moved away."

"So he got away with it?"

"No. I held on to my sanity for a good year and a half before having nightmares about him. My mom took me to the doctor, and I told him. I had to describe a lot to the doctor in front of my mother. She almost passed out in his office. That wasn't a common thing in our neighborhood at the time, Carlette, and it was even less common to get help from an outsider."

"Did he get you pregnant, Auntie Cora?"

"No. He told me he wasn't going to do something like that to some little nigger girl, and on top of that, he told me I was black and ugly. That's the way he felt about our entire neighborhood. He was taking our money, taking advantage of me and possibly many others, and pretending to be our friend. For a long time after his abuse and negative comments, I really believed I was ugly and not good enough, but mostly because he was white. Back then, lots of blacks thought that white had to be right. Some of us are still ignorant enough to think like that."

"But you're very pretty and educated, Auntie Cora, and what he was doing to you was nasty, wasn't it?"

"Yeah, and the way he did it made it worse. He would tell me what to do, was overly descriptive about what he was doing to me and my body parts, and he'd groan and make sounds like a dog while he abused me. After going to college and getting my degree in communications, counseling, and psychology, I learned that his insulting me was to cover up the way he really felt about himself and his indecent behavior. His insults were to make me not realize how vulgar he was. He even let me know that he would never do something so disgusting to his wife, which made me the outlet for his repulsive little fantasy."

"They arrested him for what he did to you?"

"No, but they tried to build a case, or so they said. But before they could, he was caught doing it to another girl. I don't know who she was or what he'd done to her, but I remember the police coming to our door and telling my mom that they'd picked him up on similar charges, and questioning me. I believe that girl was white and he'd been having sex with her, too. I hope that she didn't get pregnant by that man. I just hope to God she didn't. Makes me always wish that I'd said something sooner."

"Did they ask you those embarrassing questions again, Auntie Cora?"

"Just a few. All they really wanted was for me to identify him and for me and my mother to confirm the report we'd originally made."

"My Ricky had many girls before me, Auntie Cora. I've never been with anyone else. That man must have done that before you. Did he have a police record for doing that or something?"

"Yeah, but they didn't find that out until later. They didn't have the technology back then that's available today, so it was months before they even found out that he had been a janitor in a school in Indiana and had abused some girls there, too, black and white."

"At least he didn't get you pregnant. I'm glad that didn't happen to you."

"Yeah, me too. But I was messed up for a long time. Helping you girls is what helps me stay sane. But we're both lucky, Carlette, you and I. Latest statistics show that every six minutes a rape is committed by two or more attackers. By the time your baby's a teen, it'll be worse. That's why I believe that we need to talk openly about sex and what has happened to us. We don't need to use vulgar language, but we need to be descriptive. Children these days are smarter and sexually active sooner. They need to see the big picture before they get a true idea of what can happen. All the big words and false language only confuse the parent and the child. I have always believed that sex is a straight-talk subject and should be dealt with while children are young."

Cora shook her head. "Maybe I've said too much, but the fact is, you're in a home for girls who have faced many outrageous attacks, and I have to discuss with them whatever will make them keep their sanity. When my husband was alive, he was the one who made me forget everything that happened to me. He gave me straight talk, and from then on, I knew that my parents should have given me the talk he ended up giving me. Boy, did I love that man." *I sure do miss you, Samuel Knight.*

"You were married, Auntie Cora?"

"Yes. I wouldn't lie to you. And that's how I got my girls."

Carlette smiled. Even for a rhetorical question, she realized it was silly.

"My husband's pension and the insurance money he left me are how I afford some of this big, old, beautiful house. There's no way I'd be able to have someone keep all this wood clean for me without it."

Carlette felt much better after Cora told her story and explained some things to her, and she couldn't help but offer Cora a little comforting. "Auntie Cora, you need a hug." Carlette leaned over and hugged her.

"I knew we'd hit it off, Carlette, but I never thought you'd be one of my favorites. Get yourself together. I'm taking you to a movie, then dinner, tonight. You deserve it. You've had a long trip, and you've been through far too much at your young age. You need to relax."

"Auntie Cora, I have to be honest. I wanted Ricky to have me. I was wishing he would do it so that I could get as close as we did. I wanted him so bad, but I pretended to be upset when it happened. I still love him and want him. Sorry for lying." Carlette looked away.

"That's okay, baby. We have emotions. Those of us who don't are dead."

Both laughed like little girls.

Cora touched her thighs as she stood. "I just want each girl that comes through here to understand that sexual abuse is not their fault. There is something wrong with an individual who believes in using their body to punish another. Our bodies are important—sacred. Using your body to punish people in any sexual way degrades it. You never get rid of former contacts, and some of them surely don't deserve your body, man or woman, whether you know them or not. I just want to make sure that each person I am responsible for knows this. Some of the abused go out and try to get revenge by doing the same thing that brought them here."

Carlette squinted with disbelief.

"Before you leave this world, baby, you will learn and see lots of things that are stranger than fiction. Now get ready for our girls' night out." Cora left the room.

Carlette prepared for the fun. She would write in her journal when she returned from their time on the town.

Chapter 21

Approximately two months later, Carlette's baby arrived at 3:00 a.m. in the middle of the week, and everyone was sound asleep. Luckily, Carlette was with Cora, who knew exactly what to do. She timed Carlette's contractions, called the house doctor, and took her to the hospital.

Carlette kicked, screamed, gagged, and cursed Ricky. She called for her mother, daddy, aunt, God, and Cora, and vowed to never have sex again. By the time the doctor knocked her out for the C-section, she was exhausted.

After the arrival of baby Ricky, she slept for almost three days. She ate very little during her stay, and when Cora came to pick her up from the hospital, she was still weak. That frightened Cora. Most of the girls were ready to wear tight jeans and partied during their hospital stay.

Cora's reasoning for Carlette's poor condition was her age and low blood count, and she was right. She had always been able to figure out a person's ailment, what caused it, and how to treat it. That was one of her gifts. In fact, she'd wanted to be a doctor until she found the girls.

For weeks, Cora fed Carlette foods high in fiber and iron, plenty of milk, orange juice, and lots of green vegetables, especially collards, turnips, and mustard greens. Carlette had to remain in bed most of that time and wasn't allowed to do more than hold her baby a couple times a day. Breast-feeding was definitely out of the question. She barely had enough energy or nutrients in her frail body for herself, so there was no way the baby would get enough nourishment to survive. And there was a possibility that Carlette herself wouldn't survive breast-feeding.

Carlette felt guilty about not being able to breast-feed her baby, and about having Cora and the other girls wait on her hand and foot. That was something she wasn't used to, but she didn't have a choice. Although she loved her aunt Genevee, and they were closer than ever, Carlette even tried to resist her attention during her visits, but Aunt Genevee was definitely not having that. She was far worse than Cora. She worried about Carlette's health, and just like Cora, she pampered and spoiled Carlette as much as possible while she was in town. She would even sit on the side of her bed, hold her in her arms, and kiss her forehead.

Carlette could only take in a deep breath, sigh, and roll her eyes. To her, the attention was embarrassing, but Cora and Genevee would never know. She didn't want to hurt their feelings or appear ungrateful. They were her foundation, the ones giving her the chance to do all the good things that lay ahead for her.

Until she recovered, she stayed in bed, wrote in her journal, read good books, watched television, and tinkered with the laptop Cora and Genevee had bought her for Christmas. She really hated the way they fussed over her and, wanting to keep the attention down to a minimum, asked for as little as possible.

CHAPTER 22

The special education Cora provided for Carlette, which she received at home, helped her to advance quickly. After recovering from childbirth, she went straight to junior college and finished in a year and a half. Then she went on to get degrees in business and the arts, which she obtained in four and a half years.

A four-year grant check had been issued to Cora for Carlette. The termination of the funding was coming upon her fast. She wanted to give her friend's niece every opportunity to get her career in order. Unlike most of the residents at Cora's house, who were able to get extensions on their grants through age twenty-five if needed, Carlette wasn't eligible for an extension, because her school record from the island indicated that she was gifted. She was considered a high achiever and hadn't started from ground zero, like many of the girls in the house.

Positions at different high-profile companies were offered to Carlette after college. She would take one position and, after a short while, apply for another that would pay her more. She had a child to support.

After almost five years she grew tired of her work schedule, and she had little interest in her work. Carlette wanted to be more than a meager nine-to-fiver, and her potential made her crave a fulfilling career in music or theater. However, she knew she had to provide for herself and her son. She could not keep relying on Auntie Cora's help at the house.

Thinking about her dilemma made her stomach do flip-flops. In her youth she had constantly wished to be independent and out on her own. Now that the time had come, she couldn't figure out which way to go, only because she now loved dancing, acting, and the flute, which she'd thought she hated. She was afraid that Cora and her aunt would disapprove of her making any of those a priority before trying her hand at working for a big business first, so she had done that. With Ricky Jr. soon to be ten years old, if she was to seek a career in music or theater, she would definitely have to leave him behind.

CHAPTER 23

"No, Carlette, I don't see a problem with you using your other talents, but you might want to confer with your aunt before you make that type of move. She always tells me how concerned she is about you ending up in some mediocre position, like she did. You need to call her. She's the reason for you coming here and getting such a great start in life."

"I did call her, Aunt Cora. She said it would be okay with her if you thought it was a good idea."

"It's a wonderful opportunity for you, Carlette, but what about Ricky?"

"Aunt Cora, I know I've received a lot of support from you. You're the best thing that's ever happened in my life. I mean, other than baby Rick and Aunt Genevee, but will you take care of him just for a little while . . . until I'm settled?"

Cora smiled at Carlette. "Of course, I will." Cora loved Ricky. There was nothing else for her to do now, and she was hoping that Carlette would leave him behind. Although Carlette and her son were semipermanent guests, Carlette was the last girl to be accepted into her home. Now retired, Cora had too much free time on her hands and couldn't think of a better way to spend it than taking care of Carlette's son while Carlette chased her dream.

"Are you sure you don't mind, Auntie Cora?"

"Ricky's like one of my grandchildren. He won't be a problem."

Carlette jumped up and gave Cora a big hug. "Thank you, Auntie Cora! Thank you!"

Cora giggled and pried Carlette's arms from around her neck. "Carlette, you're welcome. Go ahead now. Make your plans. You've seen how fast time can go by. You're not getting any younger for the theater business. You'll need to make rapid plans if you want to become famous before you're an old, worn-out thirty."

Carlette giggled. "Thanks again, Auntie Cora! Thank you!"

CHAPTER 24

Journal entries had to be set on the back burner. With only a little over a year's savings, Carlette had to search vigorously for auditions. Luckily, she signed a twelve-month contract with the first modeling agency she went to. The job, which included commercials, paid her enough to support herself and commute back and forth to see Ricky and Cora. Carlette continued to go to auditions but signed a new modeling contract when the old one ended.

She had been away for almost six years and was close to giving up, until she was welcomed into a play titled *Born Struck!*, about an African American female who chased her acting career and found it. The part Carlette auditioned for was that of a black dancer like herself who was destined for fame.

David Portugal, the producer, the director, the everything of the show, had taken a liking to her and had hired her right on the spot. At thirty-eight he looked twenty-five, with his dark skin, wavy hair, and muscular physique.

His show had been running in many different places for almost a year before he asked Carlette to dinner. He told her he needed to go over some important changes concerning her character.

"I have big changes for you, Carlette, really big changes. Changes that will not only make you a lead, but a star."

"Do you really think that I'm that good, Mr. Portugal?"

"Carlette, don't you?"

"Well, no, I don't know."

"You must realize by now that the audience is really applauding you. The others are just there. You're carrying everyone."

"Really, Mr. Portugal?"

"Call me Dave. We've been formal for too long."

"But I can't—"

"Nonsense! I won't have it any other way. Call me Dave."

Carlette put both hands around her water glass and looked down at it. "Okay, I'll call you Dave."

"Good. Now tell me. How would you like to be a star? A big star?"

"That's why I'm here, Dave. I've wanted to make it big in acting for a long time."

"Then come with me to my apartment tonight."

Carlette looked puzzled.

"Don't look so confused. We don't want everyone knowing our plans, now do we?"

"I guess not."

"Carlette, to be a star, you need to be more

sure of what you want than that. Are you sure you want to be a star?"

"Yes, Dave. I'm positive."

"Then come with me. There's lots to go over."

Dave paid the check and led Carlette by the hand to the door. When the valet brought Dave's car to him, Dave told Carlette to drive. He had seen the way her eyes lit up when he had picked her up earlier that evening. She wouldn't decline the offer to drive the pretty little red sports car with the black convertible top, and she didn't.

Grinning stupidly, she jumped into the driver's seat. Dave had her drive around for a while so she could get a feel of the good life. Before heading to his apartment, he released the convertible top to allow Carlette's long ringlets to blow in the wind.

"How would you like a car like this one, Carlette?"

"I'd never be able to afford anything like this."

"I thought we were going to have confidence? Be positive."

"Oh, Dave, I'm sorry."

"If you're going to make it, your attitude will have to change drastically, my dear, or you'll go nowhere fast."

Carlette looked sad.

Dave quickly cheered her up by telling her that they would work on her attitude together.

They rode around for a while without speaking. Carlette looked over at David. "It's gotten so late, and I'm very tired. There's a certain amount of sleep—"

"Nonsense, Carlette! As good as you are, you can do whatever you want with only a minute's rest. Come on, we're going to my place. I'll show you how to get there. I want to show you how good you'll be living soon."

Dave's apartment was beautiful. Skylights, marble floors, large sliding-glass doors that looked out over the city, and marble steps that led up to his living room and other rooms welcomed her.

"Oh, my God! Dave, this is beautiful!"

"See what you were going to miss?"

"Yeah! I have to admit, this would be worth losing sleep over."

Dave went over to the bar and poured wine, while Carlette relaxed on the sofa. He walked over to her with a glass of wine in each hand. "Here, Carlette. Have a drink."

Dave extended the glass of wine he had laced with Three Hour, a subtle knockout drug that had to be timed. It allowed victims approximately three hours of wake time after they'd consumed it before blacking out for three hours. Then they'd wake up in somewhat of a hallucinogenic state.

"I don't drink, Dave." Carlette pushed the glass away.

"It's only wine, my dear. It won't hurt you. Just sip on it. You'll see."

Dave set the drink on the table near Carlette and took a seat on the sofa, next to her. He watched her with a smile and slanted eyes while he continued talking about himself. Just to be accommodating, Carlette picked the wine up and sipped it until it was all gone.

Dave stared at her deviously.

Carlette yawned. "Dave, I have to go home now. I'm getting very sleepy."

"No, you don't. You can sleep here."

"No."

"Carlette, don't be silly. There's plenty of room right here. I'm not asking you to sleep with me or anything like that. It's late, you're sleepy, and we both have to be in the studio by nine thirty in the morning. We can ride in together. Besides, you don't want to be responsible for me having to drive around the city after drinking, and at this hour, do you?"

"No, Dave. No, I don't."

"Then you won't argue with me anymore. You'll take one of the bedrooms up here next to my living room, and I'll sleep downstairs in one of the others."

Dave got up abruptly. He needed to work fast before Carlette fell asleep where she sat. He quickly went downstairs to get her a towel, a washcloth, and some of his sleepwear.

"Here, Carlette. There's a bathroom right next to your bedroom. Help yourself to it. I'm going to shower and go to bed myself. I'm also tired and sleepy." Dave pointed the way to her bedroom.

Dave showered and went into his bedroom, and Carlette did the same.

As soon as Carlette crawled into bed, she seemed to black out.

Later, she woke up groggy and naked in a dark room, her face buried in the pillow. She felt a lump under her, as if her legs were entangled. She reached down to straighten out the twisted comforter, but her hand grabbed a head of hair. Carlette screamed and tried to roll away but couldn't move. *I must be dreaming.* She tried to sit up, but her slender body was jerked so hard, she fell facedown into the pillow again.

Carlette shrieked, "My back! You've hurt my back!" The room seemed to be spinning, and she was weak. She could only lie still, hallucinate, and listen to the vulgar things she thought were being whispered into her ear, until she blacked out again.

When she woke up again, she was in her own apartment, in her own bed, and fully dressed. She immediately called Dave to question him.

"I never touched you, Carlette. Don't you remember what happened? You began screaming frantically and complaining about wanting to go home in the middle of the night, so that's what I did. I don't know what happened to you from there."

"I'm not a fool, Dave! I remember what you did to me! You had your mouth all over me. Did you have sex with me, Dave? Did you, huh? Did you?"

"Carlette, I'd never violate you in any sexual way without your permission. I have too much respect for you to do that. Listen, Carlette. I'm trying to tell you what happened. We drank some wine together. After that, you went into one of the guest rooms, and I brought some fresh soap, a towel, and a washcloth for you to bathe with, and something to sleep in. The next thing I know, you wake up screaming, telling me that you want to go home, and that's all I did. I swear to you, Carlette, that's all I did. Maybe you're allergic to the wine, because as soon as I put you in your own bed, you blacked out. And unless you got up and removed everything, you were fully clothed then."

Carlette was confused. How could she have felt someone so vividly but end up fully dressed and in her own bed? She distinctly remembered her experience with Ricky and Mr. Coles but was too ashamed to tell Dave that. "B-b-but why are my back and breasts so sore?"

"Probably because each time I tried dressing you, you'd fall back down on the bed, and you kept crossing your arms across your chest, saying you didn't want me to see you naked. Now, I'll admit, Carlette, your body is beautiful—all of you is—and what man wouldn't want to be with you in any way that he could? But I never ever touched you like that, and I never would without your consent. I swear to God, I wouldn't."

Carlette began to think. *Did he swear to God? He must be serious.*

"Carlette? Carlette? Are you still there?"

"Yes, Dave. I'm here."

"Why are you so quiet?"

"I'm ashamed, Dave. I shouldn't have called you like this. I practically accused you of raping me."

"It's okay, Carlette. I'll understand if you don't want to see me again."

"What about the things we talked about?"

"What things?"

"You helping me to become a star, Dave. You said you'd help me with that."

"Oh, Carlette, sure. I thought you were talking about something different. Of course, I'll help you with that. Nothing has changed my mind about your stardom. I thought that maybe after our conversation you wouldn't want to come back to my apartment ever again. But I can still make you famous, if that's what you want. Is that what you want?"

"Yes, I still want you to help me."

"Would you like to come to my house tonight? We could start early. I don't want you to get the wrong idea about me. We could go there right after rehearsal if you want to, that's unless you're afraid of me."

"No, Dave, I'm not afraid of you. We can go to your apartment after rehearsal, but no more wine for me, okay?"

"Okay. But you will have some champagne, won't you?"

"No! That'll make the same thing happen to me again, won't it?"

"No, Carlette, not at all. The only thing I buy is the expensive stuff. Besides, champagne tastes more like soda pop and isn't nearly as strong as most wines. Please, have just one drink with me. Please, Carlette, please."

"Okay, Dave. I'll have one."

"Now you're being a good sport. That's what stardom is all about. We'll meet up after rehearsal and go to my apartment so we can work on making you famous."

"Okay, Dave. And please forgive me for almost accusing you of something so vile."

"It's all forgotten, Carlette. Besides, how can anyone be angry with someone as beautiful as you? See you later?"

"Yes, Dave, you will."

Carlette hung up the telephone and blew out a nervous breath. She had almost blown the chance to work with someone who knew what she needed to do to get where she wanted to go. Professionals like Dave were hard to find, let alone get close to. Tonight she would be more proficient and would definitely act more polished.

CHAPTER 25

At his apartment Dave and Carlette went over several scripts. He tutored her in walking, talking, and various acting techniques before he popped the cork on the champagne. Dave told her to go over some of the scripts again while he went into the kitchen to get glasses.

He poured Carlette's drink in front of her, then poured one for himself. They both sipped the golden liquid.

"This is better, Dave."

Dave smiled. He took another sip and began filling Carlette's head with "star" talk. "Now let's see your walk, Carlette."

As Carlette strutted across the room, Dave dropped the drug into her drink. He pretended to be topping off her glass when she came toward him. Carlette sat down, finished her drink, and began to chatter.

Dave slurred his speech. "Come on, Carlette. I'd better get you home before I get too drunk."

"Maybe I should stay here tonight. We've both been drinking."

"Are you sure? You were so upset last time."

"I know, but it's okay now. I don't want either of us getting into trouble by trying to drive with alcohol in our systems."

"Okay. I'll get you what you need so that you can get ready for bed."

Again, after Carlette showered, she collapsed on the bed and woke up in the dark, facedown on the pillow. She thought she was dreaming again and relaxed. She didn't want Dave to think she was some sort of lunatic or sheltered fool who wouldn't be able to handle the stardom he'd promised her.

Carlette blacked out again.

Dave turned on the light in Carlette's room and began shaking her. He told her he'd heard her having a nightmare. "Carlette! Carlette! Are you okay?"

Carlette was too groggy to really understand what he was talking about.

Dave shook her again. "Are you okay?"

Carlette became a little more coherent. She'd had the dream again. Not wanting Dave to get the wrong idea, think she acted too psychotic, and decide not to help her, she answered as rationally as she could. "I just had a bad dream. I'm okay, I'm okay." Then she passed out again.

Later, as Dave drove Carlette home, she remained quiet. He became worried and began a conversation with her. "Do you want to talk about it, Carlette?"

"About what?"

"You seem to have something on your mind. Are you okay?"

"Yes, I'm all right."

"Carlette, I'm worried about you having bad dreams. I can help you. I can take you to my doctor."

"No, no, no. I'm okay. I'm fine. Really, Dave, I'm fine. I've had nightmares since I was a child." Carlette was lying. She'd always slept like a rock, even when her aunt Genevee had been at her worst.

"Okay. I guess I won't bring it up again."

"Dave, really, there's no need for you to. I'm okay. I'm fine." She hopped out of Dave's car and ran up to her apartment.

Dave yelled out to her, "Standing commitment every day after rehearsal!"

Carlette continued moving without looking back.

Dave drove away, whistling. He knew that he was the root of Carlette's bad dreams. From their conversations, it was apparent to him that she hadn't been with anyone for a while. Back at his place he had thought about taking advantage of her some more, but he had lost track of time and after almost three hours, he knew that the pill would wear off at any time. She would have really known what was going on and would never come back to him.

He had wanted her from the beginning and didn't think she would give in to him so willingly, but he wasn't prepared to do the work, take the time, or use the energy to make her physically want him. He had his sights on too many others and wasn't going to make that type of investment.

And he surely wasn't going to mess up his arrangement with her.

CHAPTER 26

"Thanks, Renee," Carlette said softly to her co-worker.

"You're welcome, Carlette. Are you sure this is where you want to go?"

"Sure, it is."

"Okay. Be careful."

Squinting, Carlette said, "Of what?"

"Nothing. Just something we girls like to tell each other." The cold response made Renee think twice about giving any other motherly advice. Besides, all of what she'd heard around the set could be rumors.

Carlette jumped out of Renee's car, a slight chip on her shoulder, and headed into the apartment building without giving her a second glance.

Mr. Shimer, the doorman, smiled, nodded, and allowed her entry without a hassle. He thought she was stunning. When he'd seen her come into the building two nights ago, being escorted by someone he deemed the nicest man in the complex, he'd made that comment. It was obvious to him that the two had immediately become an item. What man in his right mind wouldn't latch on to this young beauty as quickly as possible? Mr. Shimer took off his hat and scratched his balding head as he continued to smile and thought that he might have missed ogling Carlette if he hadn't come in early to relieve Donovan Kirktale, the day doorman.

Carlette almost hummed as she stepped onto the elevator and pushed the button for the floor she wanted. When the elevator stopped, she arrogantly strolled off and headed for her destination.

More excitement rushed through her body as she approached the apartment. As she stood in front of David Portugal's door, she could hear blaring opera music. Dave was expecting her. She hadn't seen him after rehearsal, but they had a standing commitment. He had just been too busy with one of the other actors to give her a ride.

Carlette knocked, but no one answered. She turned the doorknob, and the door opened. She heard moaning coming from upstairs. Worried, she followed the sound. The door to the bedroom where she had slept was slightly open, and she could see Theresa Stock, one of the seventeen-year-olds who portrayed one of the children in the play, in the bed with someone.

Carlette's face wrinkled. She pushed the door open some more. Dave was with Theresa and was doing to her what he'd told Carlette was just a bad dream. He put an arm around Theresa's small waist and pulled her closer. She held on to the antique bedposts and swung on Dave's arm like a gymnast as he explored her, then filled her with his manhood.

Theresa wasn't struggling or refusing the attention. She turned her head to relax and rationalize the situation—what she was allowing for fame. Her eyes became tear filled as she looked toward the door and spotted Carlette.

Carlette's heart felt as though it would jump through her throat. She became so confused and fearful from disbelief, she backed up and almost fell over the railing, sheltering her screams with her hands.

Suddenly Theresa felt guilty about what was happening, about Dave's exploring and fully invading her. Her parents would hate her and be disgusted. She was already lying to them and calling them sporadically. She squirmed with shame to free herself.

Dave hadn't noticed Carlette, and he wasn't concerned with Theresa's discomfort. Feeling her tension, he used his toned arms, legs, and chiseled body to hover over her and quickly locked her in.

Theresa completely collapsed with defeat as she felt his strong body against hers. There was nothing she could do to reverse the situation. Another cast member had discovered her dirty affair with Dave. And the way she was allowing him to use her made it more humiliating.

Trying to force him away from her might make her regret the action. He could be a monster at times. She had tried interrupting his pleasure in the past, and he had shown her that side of him. She would have to accept the situation, look into Carlette's face, and probably deal with the other cast members' whispers when she went back to work. If Carlette was like the others, she would blab the entire ugly scene to anyone who would listen. She, too, must have been there to please Dave. The jealousy would make her talk, even if she wasn't a gossip.

Theresa tried blocking out their sinful sounds.

As Carlette ran to flee the ugly situation, she covered her ears, believing she could still hear the last words Dave had said to Theresa echoing in her head. Not wanting to face anyone, she took the stairs down all twelve flights and held on to the railing as she staggered down the steps.

Mr. Shimer saw her as she headed for the revolving door and tried to engage her in conversation, but she passed by him like a bolt of lightning.

Once outside, she jumped on the first bus she could get, headed straight to her apartment, packed her things, and left town. The embarrassment and shame she felt were too much to deal with. She had to get as far away from David Portugal as possible.

CHAPTER 27

As Carlette entered Cora's house, she could hear moaning sounds. Thinking Cora was sick, she almost broke her neck running up the stairs. When she got to the room where the sounds were coming from, she was shocked at what she saw. Some little white girl was with her baby, her son, her only child, and had his private parts in her mouth.

Carlette went berserk. "Boy! What the hell is wrong with you!"

Ricky had never heard his mother raise her voice or use a curse word before. "Momma!"

"That's right, Ricky! Momma! You! Little girl!" Carlette was pointing. "You! Go home to your mother! Right now!"

The girl instantly sprang to her feet and ran, pushing past Carlette and almost knocking her over. Carlette had to grab on to the door frame to keep from falling.

"But Momma—"

"Boy! Are you crazy? Have you lost your damn mind?"

Ricky sat quietly and stared at his mother in confusion. He had never seen her so furious. And she was using slang, not real words, like she had been educated to do and which she always tried to get him to use. She wasn't the poised and proper person that he had known all his life, but an irate, cussing, slang-using, fire-breathing Carlette, who spat her words with an island accent.

"Momma . . ."

"Boy! Don't even speak to me! Just don't say nothin'! You got a girl in Cora's house, doin' this? That girl's going to turn you over to the cops!"

"No, she won't, Momma. She's my girl. That's Cashette. Her name almost like yours."

"Boy, I don't give a damn if her name *Cashew!* She white and a womon! I caught you two together! Now she's going to make up a story 'bout you! Just look to be in court, Ricky! Just look to be in court!"

"It ain't like dat, Momma. It ain't like dat."

"What do you mean, it ain't like dat?"

"She's my girl, Momma. Just one of my girls."

That made Carlette even angrier. "Boy! How many girls you datin'?"

"I ain't datin' none of 'em, Momma. They just my girls, my bitches, my hos. They give me whatever I need when I need it. That girl was just doin' her job when you walked in."

Carlette's face turned red from anger and shame. She could only stare at her sixteen-year-old boy, who was sitting on the bed, his pants still around his ankles. She couldn't believe this was her son, and she didn't want to believe it. This display of indecency was not what she had taught him.

She thought back to the day on the plane, when she had touched her stomach while thinking about her cousins, Keith and Kellen. Maybe she had marked the boy without realizing it. Maybe it was a new era, but she wasn't accepting the new-era behavior from her son.

Taking a deep breath, she began to count to herself. *One, two, three, four, five, six, seven, eight, nine, ten.* "Ricky!" she shouted. Then she lowered her voice. "Ricky, that's no way to treat a woman, baby, and you don't call them names like that."

"This the twenty-first century, Ma. It ain't like when you was young in the old days. They like it, so why not?"

"Because, Ricky, baby, you love yourself more than that. Pull your pants up." Carlette sat down on the bed.

Ricky stood up and tugged on the oversize jeans until they were secure enough to be fastened.

"Come on, baby, sit down next to me. Me and Cora have done all we can to make sure you get the best education and moral training we can give you, and that money can buy. How can you believe that it's okay to treat any woman like a machine?"

"All my boys do it, Momma. And them girls, they be beggin' you. It's like a man is a god or somethin' to 'em. They just gotta have somebody to make 'em whole, to make 'em feel good about theyself. If they wanna pay me to do that, I don't see nothin' wrong with it."

"Well, I do, Ricky. Suppose, just suppose, I told you that men have treated me and Cora that way."

"I'd kill 'em, Ma!"

Carlette crossed her arms and smiled smugly.

Ricky smiled stupidly. "Oh . . . I see what you doin'. You tryin' to make me mad. You usin' psychology."

"Am I, Ricky? Am I using psychology, or have I been abused? I got pregnant with you when I was just seventeen. Now tell me, Ricky, which is it?"

Ricky lowered his head to hide his hurt, but Carlette could see the tears form in his eyes.

"You might think these girls' actions make them weak, but they believe they're showing you love, and that love is all about giving. One day you will see how they feel."

Ricky kept his head lowered. "Nah, ain't no female but you can get a whole lot from me, Ma."

Carlette patted Ricky's thigh as she stood up. "There's always that one, Ricky. There's always that special one who can make your heart and knees weak. And, believe it or not, fifteen, sixteen, seventeen, or twenty years wasn't that long ago."

Carlette left Ricky's room and went to hers. She sat on her bed, reached in her nightstand drawer, took out her journal, and opened it. She thought, *I have neglected you for too long, best friend. It's definitely time for me to catch up.*

CHAPTER 28

Carlette decided that military school was best for Ricky and shipped him off that fall, but the incident with her son remained on replay. *Maybe touching my stomach while thinking of my cousins did mark him, but his father's ways are definitely embedded in his genes. Oh, well, at least Cora wasn't home and I was the one to catch him.* But the thought didn't make Carlette feel any less guilty.

As she sat thinking, the phone rang. She took a deep breath and let it out through her nose as she spoke. "Hello, Cora's house. This is Carlette speaking."

"Carlette Roxen?"

"Yes, this is Carlette Roxen."

It was Dave Portugal on the other end. He had missed Carlette's body and was also fearful that he might have gotten her pregnant. It wasn't routine for him to use any protection, but he'd used the old condoms he kept in his nightstand, because he'd planned on having Carlette a few times before trying to convince her to be in a consensual relationship with him. She was special to him in a sexual way, but he didn't want that baby momma drama that using old condoms could cause. He also knew that Carlette wasn't the kind who'd be easily talked into an abortion, like most of the others he'd conned and lied to once they realized what he'd really done. His usual sob story—of them being so beautiful and he being so shy deep down inside that he didn't know of any other way to approach them—had always worked. They'd break down. Then he would explain that they both had careers, and the next and last step was abortion. He would then be in the clear, and he would not be bothered with them again, even if they begged him.

Dave spoke softly. "Carlette, it's Dave."

Carlette screamed and dropped the phone.

Dave knew something was wrong, but he was determined to talk her out of the truth. He wanted to be with her one last time. "Carlette! Carlette! Carlette, are you there?"

Carlette slowly bent over and picked up the phone. "What do you want?"

"Carlette, you sound irritated. You're not pregnant, are you?"

"No, I'm not. Why would you ask me a question like that?"

Dave was relieved but tried to play it off with artificial concern. "You left six months ago without a word. I thought we were working on making you a star. Are you coming back? Are you okay?"

"I'm fine. I'm not coming back."

"Why not, Carlette?"

"You're a liar!" Carlette could no longer control

her fury, and the shouting, which was rarely heard coming from her, kept coming. "You told me everything that happened to me in your house was just bad dreams from drinking, but I saw you, Dave! I saw what you did with Theresa!"

"Carlette, please let me explain. She's young, but she loves performing oral sex on men. She chased me around the studio until I gave in, and I let her."

"What? Are you kidding me, Dave? You had her do that, too?"

"Wait a minute, wait a minute, Carlette. Now I'm confused. Tell me what you thought you saw."

"I didn't *think* I saw anything, Dave! I *know* what I saw!"

Dave was shaken. "Then calm down and tell me what you saw. Come on, tell me. It's very unfair of you to scream in my ear and accuse me without me being able to tell my side. I should be able to defend myself."

"I saw the way you pulled little Theresa to you and had her wrapped in your arms so tight. She was almost swinging before you wrapped your arms around her and pulled her so close to you, she could barely move."

"Aw, Carlette, that's no big deal. As much as she had done for me, I owed her something. A good time!"

"Did you owe her the luxury of taking her virginity?" Carlette was just pulling at straws. She wanted to know just how evil David Portugal could be, knowing he would never get another opportunity to touch her.

Dave breathed nervously.

"Just answer me, Dave! Did you owe her that?"
There was an uncomfortable silence.

"Dave, she saw me standing in the doorway. Her eyes told me how embarrassed she was with me seeing you and her together. They seemed to beg me to keep quiet. How could you, Dave? How could you take advantage of a child that way?"

"Well, that child is following me around now, Carlette, and begs me for all the stuff I made her do, did willingly, did to her, or forced her to do, or whatever you might think."

"You're pathetic!"

"If you thought she was so innocent, why didn't you help her? Why didn't you help her get away from pathetic me? Were you jealous? Huh? Did that bother you? Did it make you so angry to see me enter another woman in ways I hadn't allowed you to experience?"

"You're filthy."

Dave became tired of Carlette's high-and-mighty routine. "And you feel good inside, Carlette, real good. No matter how a man takes you, you feel good inside. You're lucky that I wanted you bad enough to drug you to take what I wanted. That's the only thing that saved you. If you had stayed longer, I would have taken you the same way I did Theresa. I would have made you a star, all right, my star, the same way I did her. And you would've been following me around, crawling for me, and begging me to be with you, just like she does now."

"Shut up, Dave!"

"Don't hang up, Carlette. Don't you dare hang up that phone until I've finished talking, or you'll be sorry. Very sorry. Everyone will know about us, including that kid of yours. Are you listening, Carlette? Are you listening to me?"

"Y-y-yes."

"Theresa might be a whole lot younger than you are, but she's a lot smarter. Carlette, you're just plain stupid. Educated, but stupid. You can't even put two plus two together and come up with four. You're an idiot. Why would a woman who thought she was having dreams of a man raping her and who was experiencing soreness continue coming to his apartment? Didn't that add up for you?"

When Dave realized Carlette was really frightened and listening to his entire nonsense speech, he got excited and became bolder and nastier. "You remember me squeezing, touching, biting you, my face buried in your vagina, and my penis there, too? And by the way, boy, are you good from behind." Dave laughed hysterically.

"You bastard!" Carlette slammed the phone in its cradle. She didn't care what he told people about her. Carlette wanted to tell Cora, but with the type of house Cora governed, she knew Cora would disapprove if she learned that Carlette had witnessed a rape incident and hadn't done anything to stop it. There was no telling what Cora would do. She might even make her and Ricky leave.

Dave leaned back in his chair and laughed even harder. "I can't believe she held the phone so long. She's an idiot. An idiot. A pretty, educated, airheaded idiot . . . with good stuff! This shit's too funny, too funny for words." Dave was in tears from laughter. "If she hadn't caught me with Theresa, I really would've had her following me around, too. And what nerve, asking me, Dave Portugal, how I can do a young girl like that. Oh yeah! Give me a break! She can watch me do what I did, but I can't have consensual sex with her? My woman? Why'd she watch me do it? Why didn't she help her? She saw what was going on and didn't do a thing, did not even get that poor child some help. Women and their double standards. What a bunch of hypocrites."

Dave was arrogant enough to believe that Carlette would keep her mouth shut about the incident. She was too shy and introverted to blab about something so extreme.

CHAPTER 29

Cora remained retired, but because there were so many calls flooding her line from displaced mothers and rape victims, she opened the doors again, and Carlette took over.

Late one Sunday night the doorbell rang, and Ricky, out of military school and now a sophomore in college, answered the door. There stood the most beautiful pregnant girl Ricky had ever seen. She was holding two pieces of luggage and crying. Ricky let her in and called Carlette to aid her.

Cora, hands folded in front of her, followed Carlette, and they entered the living room with smiles to greet the new guest.

Carlette was about to extend her hand but froze when she recognized Theresa Stock. A pregnant Theresa Stock. She reminded Carlette of herself when she had first arrived at Cora's. She and Theresa stood in the entrance and stared at each other.

Cora was still smiling. "Do you two know each other?"

Although Theresa was still crying and sniffling,

she spoke up. "No. At least, I don't think we do. A lot of people think they know me when they first see me." She blew her nose. "I'm Theresa. Theresa Stock. I have one of those faces that people find familiar."

"You do look familiar." Carlette spoke up to divert suspicion. There might be a problem if Cora found out that she had failed to help Theresa in her hour of need.

Theresa hid her clenched teeth behind her tightly closed, quivering lips as she cut her eyes at Carlette.

"Come on in, Theresa." Cora took Theresa's hand and led her up the stairs to the room she would be occupying. She had Ricky bring up Theresa's bags and told Carlette to go get her something to eat.

While Theresa unpacked, she cried silently.

Cora talked to her, trying to calm her down. She sat Theresa down on the bed, sat next to her, and hugged her tightly, rocking her back and forth.

Theresa let go of her pain, and the crying got louder.

"He-he-he-he-he treated me like dirt. He promised to help make me a star, but he ruined me."

Carlette was on her way to Theresa's room by then but was too ashamed to go in. She stood by the door and listened.

"He had me doing everything. Everything!" cried Theresa.

"Come on now, Theresa. You don't have to explain anything to me or anyone else."

"But I have to. It hurts so bad. I just wanna die!"

"No, Theresa, no. We hurt, we make mistakes

and have regrets, and even secrets, but we never, ever, want to or try to die. We never let another person win by allowing them to make us feel that way, or worthless. Every man is priceless, Theresa."

"But you just don't understand, Cora."

"Call me *Auntie* Cora. Why do you think I'm here, if I don't, Theresa?"

"I dunno."

"Theresa, most of the females who've been through here were much younger than you are when someone took advantage of them, including me. Some of the ladies were carrying babies by men who'd raped them."

"I'm sorry. I guess I'm just being silly."

"No, you're not. You've been through quite an ordeal, or you wouldn't be here. I'm not trying to downplay your situation or make you feel silly because of it. I'm just letting you know that you're not alone."

Theresa began rummaging through her purse. "Here. These are my papers. They said that I needed to show them to you. You'd understand me better if I did."

Cora looked them over. Theresa had been in psychiatric care two months prior to coming to her and had still been going to counseling up until she was released to Cora.

"Okay, I see." Cora didn't back down from the challenge. "Is there anything you need to add to these comments, Theresa?"

"Only that David Portugal is the reason for them."

"David Portugal?"

Carlette was still outside the room, listening.

She swallowed hard. She couldn't remember if she had mentioned his name to Cora or not, and remained as still as possible to hear the entire conversation.

"Yes, Auntie Cora, David Portugal. I'm carrying his baby."

Carlette almost dropped the food tray.

Cora's response was quick. "Those are the ones who seem to stress most women, Theresa, the ones who get them pregnant and then leave. Do you need me to contact anyone? Maybe your parents?"

"No, don't call my parents. They know I'm pregnant, but they don't know everything I've been through. I tell them only good things. They raised me right. I don't ever want them to know about any of this."

"Come on, Theresa, talk to me."

Theresa swallowed. "He fooled me. He told me he could make me a star. He kept giving me money and letting me drive one of his cars, the pretty red sports car with the black convertible top. Because he had a few, he'd let me keep it as long as I wanted. My parents asked me about it, and I lied to them. I told them that Mr. Portugal let me borrow it because we had so far to go for rehearsal and he didn't want to have to drive so far out of his way to pick me up.

"I really thought he was nice. Other than my parents, no one had ever taken so much time with or interest in me the way he did. He was taking me to restaurants, sneaking me into nightclubs, which I wasn't allowed in, because I was too young, and he was letting me drink wine and champagne and giving me marijuana while we were out and at his apartment. At first, he was like my best friend, a big brother I could talk to, tell anything to, and have fun with. The fun ended the night he took me with him to the strip bar where they have live sex shows."

"You two hadn't had sex before then?"

Theresa looked away. "No. And I didn't want to go to that bar. It made me feel uncomfortable. Dave was already high, and I stayed because I thought we were friends and that he might need me to drive him home 'cause he was so high."

Cora knew lying when she heard it and guilt when she saw it. She continued to listen intently.

Theresa took a trembling breath. "We sat at a table close to the front. The show got him excited, and he put his hand on my leg. I was like, 'Okay, he's high. I won't say anything. Besides, I have the car keys, if he gets stupid.' Then he put his hand under my skirt. I screamed and jumped up from the table, but he grabbed my arm, slammed me back down in the chair, and kept touching me. Nobody paid us any attention. In fact, they all seemed to be okay with whatever went on in that bar. Other people were doing freaky things, too, but it made me feel sleazy. I had to fight back the tears of fear and humiliation, but I stayed seated, kept quiet, and pretended that nothing was going on. I was too embarrassed to do anything else.

"I thought he'd just take me home after that for not cooperating. That's what the boys I'd been with before him always did, but he didn't stop touching me until he got a reaction from me. When that happened, I said his name like I was just yelling at him. He laughed like it was all a big joke to him, but it wasn't funny to me at all. I was totally humiliated, and furious. Auntie Cora, I didn't want anyone to know what he was doing to me in that bar."

Theresa sniffled. "We sat there for a while, and after he watched some more of that disgusting act, he said, 'Come on.' I got up and straightened out my clothes. He slapped me on my butt and said, 'Did you like that, TT?' God, Auntie Cora, I just wanted to turn around and start scratching up his stupid face, but I controlled myself because I thought we were leaving after that. But we didn't.

"He took me to a booth in the back of the club, where it all got worse. Before I could refuse, he pushed me in first and made me hurt my leg on the table. He was feeling all over me and stuff. I was trying to push him away and fight him off, but he was so strong that nothing I did fazed him. He even pulled up my shirt and unfastened my bra, and nobody, not a soul, ever looked our way. Then he told me to take off my underwear. I pretended not to hear him and wouldn't do it. While I was trying to fasten my bra and pull my shirt back down, he went under the table and did it himself. Auntie Cora, that did it. I couldn't get him off me. He had me pinned in that booth, and I was too scrunched up to do anything.

"In the entire seventeen years I'd lived, I'd never felt so much like nothing. That took most of my pride from me. He explained to me later that he had been drunk and wouldn't have disrespected me under normal conditions. I believed him and kept hanging out with him. I still believed he was my friend and was going to help me to progress as an actor, and I let him fool me into going to his apartment. He got me there by letting me drive that car until late, and offering me wine and smoke. I accepted his hospitality, and he did it again. He got me drunk and high on hashish, then conned me into going up to one of his bedrooms. All I can remember from that night was him asking me, 'Do you like it, TT? Do you like it?' as if we were both in agreement with what was going on in that bedroom."

Theresa had heard the rattling of the tray and knew Carlette was listening outside the door. She wanted Carlette to relive what she'd seen Dave do to her.

Cora stared at Theresa with the most convincing straight face possible, her expression holding no indication that she hadn't heard Theresa say anything about resisting David Portugal up until now. As she listened to Theresa's story, she tilted her head in an effort not to frown.

"That was the worst feeling ever, Auntie Cora. It was even worse than what he'd done to me at the bar. I felt like the life was being drawn out of me, but I couldn't stop him. After he was done, he got up, and I thought he was finished with me, but he continued to have more sex with me. I asked him what he was doing, but he wouldn't tell me. He just whispered in my ear, telling me he was going to get what he'd paid for. He was saying that I couldn't wear tight-fitting clothing, super-short dresses, and skirts with splits in them, drive around in his car, take his money, have him satisfying me in clubs, like he had just done, without him getting anything out of it. He said that he knew I wasn't that naive or stupid, and he finished destroying my body.

"I didn't want to just suddenly stop coming to rehearsals. I thought it would look suspicious. I was afraid of the gossip if others put me and him together. I was just going to go to a few more rehearsals, then make up an excuse to my parents for why I didn't want to be in the play anymore. But he called me before our next rehearsal and told me that I needed to be in the studio by seven thirty the following morning to go over some of the parts that were changed for the child stars.

"When I got there, the doors were open, but there was no one else in the studio. As soon as I removed my jacket, that's when it hit me. I was being set up again. I tried to make a beeline for the door, but he grabbed the back of my sweater and pulled me inside. He's very muscular." Theresa was breathing heavily as she stared at nothing. "Very muscular. So not many men can fight with him and win. I was like tissue paper to him. He picked me up like I was a baby and kissed me right on the mouth." She closed her eyes and swallowed hard. "I tried to turn my head. I'd never really kissed a boy up to that point, and he hadn't kissed me, either, but I knew he was going to stick that nasty tongue of his in my mouth. I just knew it."

Cora wanted to shake Theresa. She clenched her teeth to control her facial expression and emotions and allowed Theresa to continue her lie.

"I didn't want him to, especially after what he'd done to me before he'd picked me up. And I almost puked. He proceeded to take me behind the curtain, and that's when I lost all control and started kicking, screaming, and clawing up his face, but it did no good, Auntie Cora. It did no good. He raped me, and I got pregnant." Theresa began to cry full force again.

Cora sat quietly beside Theresa and waited until she was somewhat composed before speaking to her again. "Where's the baby, Theresa?"

"There's no baby. After he raped me that morning, he told me that I'd better be quiet about what had happened, because I'd gotten off easy. He said he wanted to take care of me for scratching his face up like he did at his apartment, but he let me go home out of the goodness of his heart. But he knew that I was too hysterical to be at rehearsal. They might have all found out what he was doing to me if I broke down. He had to call it off because of me, and his face."

"You two had never kissed?"

Theresa swallowed hard. "Uh, no, no, never. And I was glad I scratched his stupid face up. He was always talking about other girls and women."

Cora thought the statement was strange but wouldn't say a word against Theresa's testimony.

"Anyway, he called me later that evening and threatened to tell my parents and everyone he knew all sorts of lies about me if I didn't keep quiet about what had happened, and urged me to continue coming to rehearsals and the plays as if nothing had happened. I'd been driving his car, taking his money, and other things. Auntie Cora, can't you see? It would have looked like I was a cheap little gold digger and whore, so I had no choice but to continue going.

"He'd send me through hell, though, Auntie Cora. He'd send me through hell. While they weren't watching, he'd rub up against me or feel me up. I was in the bathroom one day, and he came into the stall and put his mouth on my breasts and performed oral sex on me again, and none of it felt good. He was getting ready to have anal sex with me again, but someone started calling for him." Theresa's eyes fluttered as she tried hard not to close them and reminisce about Dave. "He told me to stay in the bathroom for a while after he left, and I did. He finished rehearsal as if nothing had ever happened. He came by my parents' house one day while I was house-sitting for them."

A quick, sneaky smile interrupted the serious look on Theresa's face, but she promptly changed her expression. Cora noticed.

"I opened the door but left the security lock on it, and he exposed himself to me," Theresa added.

"You should have slammed the door on his private parts!"

"And purposely cause a clamor? My parents live in one of those very upscale apartment buildings. Someone would have surely come out to see what was going on. Besides, he'd already stuck his foot in the door. He was high, and when I tried to close the door, he threatened to start yelling."

"And you believed him, Theresa?"

"Well, yeah. He's sick or something."

"He's sick, all right. Did you let him in?"

"No."

"He just came there to flash you and leave?"

"No, Auntie Cora. He made me do things to him."

Cora was getting tired of Theresa's lies. She wondered what was taking Carlette so long with her food, so she could leave the room, but continued to humor Theresa. If Theresa was on the edge, she just might finish sliding downhill. She crossed her arms. "He made you perform oral sex on him while he stood on the other side of that door?"

"No, no, no, not exactly. Just other things. He told me that he was teaching me how to pay him back for that, though."

"But most buildings like those have guards or security cameras, don't they?"

"My parents' does, but he was good at making scenes. And I didn't want him to start shouting and acting like a fool around the apartment complex, so I buzzed him into the lobby out of fear, although I had no intentions of letting him inside the apartment when he came upstairs. And the way he was standing in the doorway when he flashed me, it looked as if he was only talking to me through the door."

"Why didn't he just force you to let him come inside?"

"He was angry about me trying to slam the door on him after he'd exposed himself to me and wanted to make me as miserable as possible. At least, that's what he said. But I think what he did was intentional. He wanted things that way. It excited him to be standing on the other side of the door that way. I think he needs a doctor for the things he likes and does. I think he's perverted. I think he needs psychiatric care."

"Theresa, take it from someone who's dealt with these types of matters for a long time. He does." Cora wanted to say they both did, because she knew Theresa had enjoyed most of what had happened to her and what she had done to her supposed tormentor that day.

"I believe you because when the morning sickness came and the news that I was pregnant followed and I told him, hoping that would stop him from bothering me and hurting me so bad, he got worse. He wouldn't be seen with me in public anymore and wouldn't let me do the shows or come to them, but he was still messing with me. You see, nobody knew I was pregnant but me and him. I'd put on a little weight, but my parents thought that it was because I wasn't as active and ate more.

"He kept telling me how fat and disgusting I looked, but he was still forcing me to have sex with him. He was rougher with everything, like he was purposely trying to make me lose my baby, and I did at three months. The second one, at six weeks. Luckily for me, both times I got sick at his house, and he took me to the hospital. He'd tell me to call my parents and tell them that I was on the road with him and that I'd be okay. Then he'd take the phone to confirm it.

"He came to see me every day. The staff thought he was my guardian. Each time I lost a baby, he acted as if he didn't care, but as soon as I was released, he'd come get me and apologize. He'd even cry, like he really cared about the babies, and promise to marry me. I'd soften up, and he'd start messing around with me again. And things kept getting worse and worse. He'd mess with me in every way, no matter what was going on with my body, or what condition I was in. So, you see, Auntie Cora, he is sick. He needs help."

"Hold on a second, Theresa. Are you saying that he wasn't concerned about the changes your body went through, and he'd mess around with you, anyway?"

Theresa held her hands together tightly. "Yeah. But we sort of went back to the way we were. He'd be with me more openly in public because he wanted his friends to see him with a young girl, but he was still trying to hide the relationship and his vulgar attitude at rehearsal and in certain public places. His personal friends were just like him—strange. He said that lots of them did things like that, too, so he didn't care what they thought."

"Things have really changed since I was young, Theresa. I mean, I was sexually abused, but until recently, I'd never heard of men being that intimate with a woman without being concerned with her body changes. It is a bit sickening."

Theresa, tears streaming down her cheeks, tilted her head and gave Cora a stern look. She almost shrieked, "I know that, but there wasn't much that I could do, Auntie Cora! He had me too afraid of him." She calmed down and relaxed a bit. "By then, I'd started liking him, feeling close to him, and I let him do almost anything he wanted. So, most of the time, if he did things to me when my body wasn't right, I'd just keep quiet and throw up after if it made me too nauseous. It would make me just that sick, Auntie Cora. Thinking of it still makes me sick at times. I'm surprised that I was able to distinguish the sickening feeling that his freakiness gave me from morning sickness."

Cora wanted to shake her head because of all the lies Theresa was telling, but she continued to play along. "Why didn't you use some sort of birth control?"

"You act as if I'm the one who's to blame."

"No, Theresa, no. I've had several girls come through here accusing men of irrational behavior, only to find out that they were willing. After the men got tired of the relationship, the girls became pregnant to try and keep them, or wanted to have them arrested for their own mistakes, just to get even. Some of them had more than ample chance to get away and move on with their lives, but they were all trying to turn rejection into love. I really don't know you, Theresa. Maybe you did that, too. I just don't know until I ask . . . until we talk and I get to know you. What type of counselor or person would I be if I were to allow an innocent person to be prosecuted for no reason?"

"I guess, not a very good one, Auntie Cora."

"Well, I know I wouldn't be a very good one if I didn't try to get the entire story. Did you get birth control pills?"

Theresa thought Cora was getting suspicious, and had to think fast. "No, Auntie Cora, but I thought he was finished with me after the first time. I wasn't ever going to have sex again after he raped me, but as soon as he'd let me back in the show, it would all start again. You know what? I even stopped going to the bathroom at the theater, but that didn't stop him. He still got a hold of me. This is my third pregnancy by him.

This one happened willingly, Auntie Cora. I stopped just liking him and feeling close to him and fell in love with him after a while. I guess, part of me thought no one else would want me after what he'd done to me. And the things he'd do to me and taught me did the rest. It's true, Auntie Cora. I fell in love with him. It felt good being able to please a man so much older than me in so many ways, and to know all the sexual things he taught me, but I also felt trapped."

Carlette dropped the tray. She could relate.

"Carlette, is that you, baby?" called Cora.

"Yes, Auntie Cora. I tripped, and this darned tray of food fell out of my hands. I'll go get another one." Carlette had also become a frequent liar.

"Hurry up, Carlette! Theresa's starving!"

When Cora turned her head to address Carlette, Theresa smiled deviously. *Bingo! She heard me.*

Carlette cleaned up the mess and hurried back downstairs, the similarity of her situation and Theresa's story on her mind. She had gotten pregnant by someone older. She loved Ricky's dad but had also felt trapped by her circumstances. "If I had said something, we could have done something about David together. Theresa had to endure almost four years of his abuse because of me."

Carlette took the other tray upstairs, but by the time she got to the top of the steps, there were new revelations about David.

"He let me stay with him this last time I got pregnant because my parents found out. They wanted to know who the father was, and I let him know that. He begged me not to tell and promised he'd take care of me and this baby. He claimed to want a family and wanted to marry me. He said that he really would marry me this time." Theresa started crying again. "But when I came back from the doctor's office, I caught him in bed with a *guy!* They were both naked. Dave had just finished giving him oral sex and was getting ready to have anal sex with him. That's what sent me to the institution and then here. They said that I had a knife after them and was chasing them both around the apartment while they were both still naked, but I don't remember that part, Auntie Cora. I can't remember anything past their intimacy."

Aha! The other man is why she left David! Cora almost snapped her fingers. "Then why are you still crying?"

"I dunno, Auntie Cora. Maybe because of this baby, or the last thing I saw going on between Dave and that guy. I dunno."

Theresa's tray rattled in Carlette's shaking hands.

"Carlette, is that you?" Cora called.

"Yes, Auntie Cora. Here's Theresa's food," replied Carlette as she walked in the room.

"What's the matter, baby? You seem to be awful shaky tonight," said Cora.

"You know how clumsy I can be at times." Carlette still refused to acknowledge Theresa and wouldn't even look her way when she set the tray down. She quickly averted her attention to Cora. "Auntie Cora, I haven't been able to spend much time with Ricky. He wants me to play the video games with him. Is it okay for me to leave you alone with Theresa?"

"Sure. She and I are getting along just fine. I think she's calming down some," replied Cora.

"Yeah, you go ahead. I'll be fine. I always am," Theresa added.

The comment gave Carlette a sheepish feeling and sent a chill through her. She almost lowered her head but walked out the door as if the comment hadn't affected her.

Carlette sat down next to Ricky, who was already playing the games.

"Hey, Momma. You playin'?"

"Yeah. Gimme that control!"

The two played game after game, and Ricky won them all. But Carlette refused to give up. She had to stay away from Theresa.

"Hey, Momma, do you know that lady? You know her, don't you?"

Carlette knew something would put her on edge as soon as she got comfortable, but she couldn't lie to her son. "Yes, I know her."

"I knew it. I knew it. You can fool Aunt Cora, 'cause she sweet. I mean, you sweet, too, but Aunt Cora naive like you and don't think you'll tell a lie."

A lie? A lie? Is that what my son just said? Carlette was more than disappointed in herself; she was disgusted. Her son knew she was a liar. Did he think she was low and cowardly, too? Had he put everything together?

"Where do you know her from, Momma?"

Carlette cut off the questioning by telling Ricky that she couldn't concentrate on playing the game with him talking to her, and Ricky agreed to be quiet.

She casually turned to him. "And don't you ever call me a liar again. Do you understand me?"

Ricky didn't argue. He nodded and continued playing. He didn't want his mother to make another scene like the one he'd witnessed the day he had one of his so-called girls "treating him right." He covered his laugh with a fake cough.

Carlette wanted to leave the room after the first question, but she played a little longer with Ricky, to not show her guilt and to appear as if she was in control.

As soon as Ricky went to bed, she went to check on Theresa to see if she was asleep. Before she could close Theresa's bedroom door, she heard the lamp click on.

"He raped you, too, didn't he?" said Theresa.

Carlette thought she was hearing things.

"He raped you, too," Theresa repeated.

"Theresa?"

It was time for Theresa to twist the knife. "Carlette, I know he did it. We used to laugh and talk a lot about the things he'd do to people."

"If he told you that he raped me, then he's a liar!"

"He didn't tell me that."

"Then why are you saying these things?"

"He told me that he'd never allow a woman to come to his little showplace without giving up something one way or another, and I knew he meant that."

"Then why were you there?"

"I thought I was an exception."

"Had he told you that?"

"No. I assumed it because I thought we were such close friends."

"Well, he never touched me. He never touched me."

"I thought it was you because he told me about this woman who left the play suddenly, who thought she was too good for him, who he'd drugged with Three Hour, and how he literally tried to suck the life out of her and made her believe that it was all a bad dream. He said that after he'd convinced her that it was a bad dream, he was clever enough to get her to come back. He gave her some more Three Hour and almost broke the bed down having sex with her while she moaned and could only allow him to throw her body around like she was some sort of rag doll. She thought she was having violent dreams, because the Three Hour can make you hallucinate like that, so it was easy for him to convince her that she might be allergic to wine, and she just went with the flow. He assumed that she didn't want him to think that she was loony or something, that she didn't want to seem unstable to 'the big producer,' because she wanted to become a star so bad."

Carlette was embarrassed to the point of being irrational. "I-i-it couldn't have been me, Theresa."

Theresa was angry and jealous, and snot flew out of her nose as she spoke. "He bragged about the way he put his hand under your stomach to balance you while he assaulted you, and how he held your long, shiny hair back in a ponytail while he did it, Carlette. He described everything about you to a T. It was as if he was obsessed with you."

"You need to keep your voice down. My son and Auntie Cora are sleeping."

"You do have beautiful hair, pretty brown skin, and a perfect figure, just like he described. You're older than me, but I can see what made my man so obsessed with you."

Carlette turned her back to walk out the door, but Theresa wasn't going to let her get away that easily.

"It's funny how a man can look so clean and be so dirty, isn't it? At least, you got away before he really did suck all the life out of you. Good night, Carlette." Feeling pleased with her lies about Dave raping her, too, and the low, filthy words she'd spat out at Carlette, Theresa clicked the lamp off and smiled smugly in the dark.

Carlette felt sick. How could Theresa say such filthy things to her? How could such dirty things come out of her mouth? Was she jealous of her because of the way Dave had felt and talked about her? Did she still want him back after all he'd done to her and after what Carlette had witnessed him doing to her? Carlette didn't know what to think, how to handle Theresa or her comments, and immediately went to Cora's room to wake her up for a talk.

CHAPTER 30

Theresa lay in the dark and reminisced about her childhood. How sweet her father and mother had always been to her, how supportive and trusting they were, and how they'd always gone on trips as a family. As hard as she thought, she couldn't understand how any man could act the way Dave did. After all she had done for him, he had chosen not to make her exclusive. She had been the one to force the relationship and had loved all the dirt they did. She had always gotten what she wanted, so there was no way she was going to allow David Portugal to deny her. He would love her if she could just produce one of his children. Then she could turn him into her father, a respectful man, a gentleman, a real man, who she thought at times had gone overboard with his sweetness, as had her mother.

She had seen her mother get jealous because of her father's extreme politeness, but that was something she had to live with, because that was the way "General Stock" was. And whenever it became a discussion, he'd tease her mother by telling her, "There's enough of my politeness to go around, Sheltae Montaneese Stock. You never know whose life you might be saving by showing a little extra attention." Then he'd kiss her mother on the lips, hand, or forehead. Her mother couldn't help but take her father's hand, because the statement made sense to her.

Although Theresa's mother could have put most models and actresses to shame, Theresa knew why her mother became jealous from time to time. The general was gorgeous. Theresa was his daughter and could see it, so other women had to be salivating.

One last tear escaped Theresa's eye and slid down the side of her face. She felt it seep into the tight, crisp sheet. Then she drifted off to sleep with pleasant thoughts of her father.

CHAPTER 31

Cora was lying on her back and snoring lightly. She was still wearing her glasses, and her novel was on her chest.

"Auntie Cora! Auntie Cora!" Carlette shook her awake.

"What, Carlette? What? Is the house on fire?"

"No. I need to talk to you."

"And what's wrong with daylight? Are you afraid of it?"

"No, no. This is urgent."

"What's wrong?"

"It's Theresa. I know her. I lied."

"Is that why you woke me up?" Cora sat up in bed, caught her novel before it hit the floor, and removed her glasses. "I figured that out before you almost dropped that tray while listening outside her room the second time."

Carlette wrinkled her eyebrows in confusion as she stared at Cora. "And you're not mad at me?"

"No. I'd seen that name Dave Portugal on some of your papers, and I knew you didn't come running back home for nothing. When Theresa mentioned him, I figured he must have been your reason for being here, too. But why did you and Theresa deny knowing each other?"

"I caught her and Dave, you know . . . She looked willing but embarrassed, and she's so young. Then I heard her scream like a wildcat, and I ran and didn't stop running until I got here."

Cora almost grinned at the way Carlette expressed herself. Cora remained quiet and kept her composure. She doubted Theresa's screams were of anguish. She bit her bottom lip so that she wouldn't expose Theresa's little act too soon. "Oh, Carlette, baby."

"Auntie Cora, I know I was wrong, but he'd just drugged me to do some of those things to me, also. I was afraid he'd hurt me, too."

Cora became genuinely serious. Was Carlette also lying about this David Portugal? "Then why'd you go back there?"

"I didn't realize what was really going on until I saw what he was doing to Theresa. He'd made me believe I was hallucinating and having bad dreams."

Cora clenched her teeth. "How'd he do that?"

"He gave me this stuff called Three Hour—at least that's what Theresa said it was—and it can do that to you. I heard about the stuff on campus, but I never worried about it because I never went out with anyone."

"How'd Theresa know he'd given you the drug?"

"She said that he was talking and laughing about it with her. She said he gave her my description but not my name. I guess she put the rest together and came up with me when she saw me the day he was raping her."

"*Raping* her?"

"You don't think he was raping her, Auntie Cora? It looked like it to me. She's so young."

Cora took a deep breath. "I've known nasty men like him, Carlette. They usually get what's coming to them sooner or later."

"What about me, Auntie Cora? I ran off and left Theresa."

"Theresa's no angel in all this, either, Carlette. She laughed with Dave about him taking advantage of people. She put it all together and came up with you. Why didn't she at least tell you that he was drugging you?"

"I don't know. I just don't know anything anymore." Carlette hung her head and began to cry.

"Come on now, Carlette." Cora put her hand under Carlette's chin and lifted her head. "Let Auntie Cora see a smile, or she's going to get real mad . . . have to take you over her lap, spank you, and make her old knees hurt."

That made Carlette smile. She had seen Cora's persistence and firmness, but she had never seen her get mad at much of anything.

Cora wasn't even mad at the man who'd taken advantage of her. She always thought that she and the other people in her neighborhood were mostly to blame for that. They shouldn't have put so much emphasis on skin color and appearances. She felt as though that was what got her into trouble, the weak-mindedness of her community. She had even told Carlette later on in her stay that she had seen the same man come out of one of the abandoned buildings, wiping his forehead with a white handkerchief, before he attacked her. A few minutes later her friend Bethany came out crying, trembling, and walking the opposite way real fast. Cora never said anything to her friend, but Bethany definitely acted differently after that day, so she was guilty of the stupid don't-tell mentality also.

Cora sat up on the edge of the bed. "Honey, listen to me. I'm not saying that you or Theresa were right in your actions, okay? What I am going to say is that for every action, there's a reaction. She didn't bother warning you about Dave and got mixed up in his savage, exhibitionist behavior. You had to face her again, and now you have to live with what happened, and so does she."

"Well, I know she can be as cruel as he is. The way she talked to me tonight proved that. She has a very nasty mouth and spirit."

"She is very direct, but right now she needs to be if she ever wants to get through this thing."

"But she sounded so much like him, Auntie Cora. He said that she is more mature than I am."

"When did he tell you that, Carlette? Before or after he'd taken advantage of you?"

"It was after. He called here. When I told him that he was wrong for tearing Theresa apart the way he did, he took offense. He said the same things you did, and he was right. I didn't help Theresa. But he also began saying personal things about what he'd done to me, how he'd done them, and how stupid I'd been for coming back there, even if I did think that I was hallucinating. I was ashamed, so I tried defending myself, but he was so harsh. I was no match for him. All I could do was yell, 'Shut up!' I was going to slam the phone down in his ear, but he threatened to tell Ricky and everyone else what he'd done to me, so I listened to his rude, vulgar talk until I just couldn't take any more, then hung up. I haven't heard from him since."

"That's because he was bluffing you. He doesn't want everyone to know who he really is, Carlette. If the word got out to the wrong people, he'd be ruined."

"Especially if that gay part got out, Auntie Cora. I heard Theresa telling you about that. I bet it was this actor named Julian Montgomery. He is real good-looking, but gay, and he is also younger than David. David was always trying to find ways to make conversation with him. Hey, you know what? I saw Julian drive that red convertible, too. That car must be his date catcher. Did Theresa say that Julian was drugged or forced to do anything against his will?"

"No. What you heard was probably all that was said. But Julian was probably more of what Dave wanted. Dave's the type of man who'll use women to satisfy his perversion until the right man shows up, and he doesn't want the fact that he prefers men to get out. He catches those women by looking and acting macho."

"You mean he's really gay?"

"Well, Carlette, it appears to me that Dave does things to different women to gain sexual satisfaction and to cover up some of his sexual desires and insecurities, but it ends in abuse, because they can't really please him. He might find himself

feeling even more inadequate after intimacy
with a woman. He might be a good lover, act like
a Casanova, or demand to be in control the way
he thinks a man should be, but it's a facade. The
reality is, he can't separate his femininity from his
masculinity, and most of the time he sees himself
as pliable and dainty, like many women do. He
really hates women, which is why it is so easy for
him to mistreat them."

"But Theresa said that he was infatuated with
me, that he talked about me all the time."

"Gay men can become infatuated with women,
too. Not many lose their true desire for them,
Carlette. They're still men, and they still fantasize
about women at times. There's always a chance
that a woman will come along that will interest
them in some way, with her pretty legs, hair, face,
nice breasts, maybe the entire package. Gay men
have complimented me on many of my attrib-
utes. Some have wanted me, but I knew it was a
temporary desire. But it seems to me that Dave
was so infatuated with your looks and figure that
he probably wanted to be with you, and the only
way to get you was to drug you. That could also
be the reason why he took advantage of you the
way he did. He was jealous of you and wanted to
hurt you. When he told Theresa about you, it was
like two girls talking, and the envy was raging
inside of him—inside of both of them—for you."

"If she was like a friend to him, then why'd he
take advantage of her? And why didn't he drug
her, too, to do it?"

"At some point Theresa had shown personal
interest in Dave, so she wasn't a threat to him,

Carlette. He'd gained her confidence. There was no need for drugs. He uses drugs on those whom he believes won't be willing to be with him whenever he wants them to. Once he'd gotten Theresa to lie—and I'm sure she'd told him personal things that she didn't want anyone else to know about herself—there was no longer a risk of him getting involved with her, no matter what her age. When they became intimate, she became you or any other woman who he thought was using him, and no woman was going to do that and get away with it, not even a friend. And he was going to get back what she or any other woman owed him through her, and he didn't have to cover that up. He knew that after all the lies she'd told her parents about his car and other things that he'd done for her and she'd willingly done with him, she'd be too afraid and ashamed to tell anyone anything about what he did to her. My real opinion . . . Theresa was having sex way before she met Dave, but he taught her to be a good liar. Dave wants to destroy whatever he feels threatened by, and everything, including your attitude, threatened him."

"But he hired me, Auntie Cora."

"To get you close to him, Carlette. There was no way he was going to let someone so beautiful and proud looking walk out on him and not put them in their place. He's a sick man, and it's a good thing that you and Theresa got away from him. He was only pushing Theresa further to the edge."

"Theresa still loves him."

"She gave me that impression, too, but why do you think that?"

"She called him her 'man.' She said that I have

beautiful hair, pretty brown skin, and a perfect figure. 'You're older than me, but I can see what made my man so obsessed with you.' Those were her exact words."

"Well, we could be right. I'll have another talk with her. I also need to let her know that you're in charge."

"Auntie Cora, I need to talk to you about that, too. I need to leave for a while."

"Why, Carlette?"

"I'm not ready to have a confrontation with someone I'm supposed to be helping. Can I go see Aunt Genevee for a while? Can you handle things if I do?"

"Girl, you've made me come out of retirement twice now. Okay, go ahead. When do you want to leave?"

"In the morning would be perfect."

"You really are afraid of confrontation, aren't you?"

"I hate it."

"Well, if you plan on running my house or having any job at all, you're going to have to learn that confrontation comes with the territory."

"I know, Auntie Cora, but I don't want that lesson to be now."

"Okay, get packed, but don't take Ricky. I need his company. He's very helpful with these ladies."

"He has to go back to school in a few days, anyway, and I'm sure that I'll need to be away longer than that."

"Carlette?"

"Yes, Auntie Cora?"

"I know that I've spoiled you and Ricky, but

from now on you're going to have to face your problems. You can't run away from everything that makes you uncomfortable."

"I know that."

"Then you'd better get prepared for stability, because running this house is no easy task."

CHAPTER 32

Theresa woke up extra early. She wanted to irritate Carlette, be vicious to her behind Auntie Cora's back. She went into the kitchen and glanced around. Then she walked into the living room, pretending to need to stretch, so that she could look for Carlette, but she was nowhere in sight. She went back into the kitchen, where Auntie Cora was standing over the stove, making breakfast.

"Where's Carlette, Auntie Cora? You said she's usually up before you are. I thought she'd be up by now."

"Oh, she's gone. She left early this morning."

"Did she take her son with her?"

"No. He's headed back to school in a few days."

"Oh." Theresa was disappointed with both answers.

"Was there something important you wanted with her?"

"No, no. I just didn't see her, that's all."

"Theresa, don't tell me that you'd rather have Carlette looking after you. That would hurt my feelings."

Theresa giggled and got comfortable. "No. I just thought she'd be here. I like you, Auntie Cora."

"Is there something about Carlette you don't like?"

"Oh no!"

"Good. Because she's usually the one who runs the house, and if you didn't like her, we'd have a problem, a big problem. We'd have to find you another place. I'm really retired. Carlette was the one who begged me to reopen after the high level of calls we received when I retired. If it wasn't for Carlette, not even the few girls who are here now would have anywhere to go."

Theresa dropped her head and began to cry. "I don't know why you think that I don't like Carlette. I like her!"

"That's not what she tells me."

Theresa sniffled. "Why? What did she say?"

"She said that you spoke very cruelly to her."

"I didn't mean anything by what I said to her."

"Calm down, Theresa."

"I've been through so much, and now this."

"Everyone who comes here has been through a lot. That's why they're here. That's the purpose of the house."

"I guess you're just going to take Carlette's side and not hear what I have to say."

"You have that opportunity, Theresa. You've had it since the first day you walked through my door. You pretended not to know her. Now there's a problem. Do you want to talk about it?"

"She watched him rape me! I thought I could just let it go, but when I saw her again, I got mad."

Instead of addressing Theresa's lies about being raped, Cora stayed on the path of the conversation. "And you said things to her that weren't pleasant."

"Yes, but she could have helped me. I spent over three years being abused by Dave."

"How many years did you allow to pass before you said something about the things he was doing to her, and possibly to other females, that she didn't know about?"

Theresa looked surprised. "What things?"

"Dave never told you about or described someone that he was giving drugs to so that he could take advantage of them? Did you two laugh about it together?"

"Carlette told you that?"

"Yes, she told me. Did you say that?"

"Yeah, but that was different."

"Why was that different?"

"I didn't know who she was."

"So it's okay for someone to be taken advantage of or hurt as long as you don't know them?"

"Yes. I mean, no. I mean, if I'd known it was her—"

"Theresa, it doesn't matter."

"But the things he did to her weren't that bad. He did worse things to me."

"What he did to her was just as bad. He touched her sexually without her consent."

"But he had anal sex with me and made me lose two babies, Auntie Cora! Oral sex ain't that bad!"

"Theresa, don't tell me it's not that bad! It was

my first introduction to sex, an unwanted introduction." Cora almost slammed down the spoon
she was using to stir the food in the pot. "I was
groped, kneaded, and spoken to vulgarly for hours
while someone like David Portugal took my life
from me." Cora wiped her eyes with the back of
her hand. "Because once he'd done that to me, I
felt dead. And he kept that up for almost two years.
To have someone's saliva touch your body in
places that intimate without consent is just as insulting. Didn't it insult and humiliate you when
Dave did it to you at the bar and then again at his
house against your will?"

"Yes, but the other things were a lot worse."

"Anything other than willing sex is the worst
thing, Theresa."

"But he still thinks she's better than me. If he
didn't, he wouldn't have thought he needed to
drug her."

"Theresa, you're not being rational. You're a
beautiful girl, just as pretty as Carlette."

"But her hair's longer."

"Theresa, listen to me. You're a pretty girl. Hair
doesn't make you beautiful. If you had stayed
away from Dave, and Carlette had gotten friend-
lier with him on his terms, she'd be you and you'd
be her. Dave is jealous of what he can't have and
will go to any length to destroy it if he can get
close enough."

"But I wasn't willing."

"Maybe not at first, and I'm not too sure about
that. But he knew that he had the toys to impress
you enough to keep you coming back so that he
could do whatever he wanted and get away with

it. The apologies, gifts, fake niceties, and the pregnancies are what made you fall in love. It was a forced attachment that made you feel as if you were in love."

"But I *do* love him!"

There was a short silence between the two.

"You still love him, Theresa?"

"I can't help it, Auntie Cora!" Theresa started crying in earnest. "It's as if I can't breathe without him. And he's in love with *your* Carlette! I can't help but hate her! I'll just stay out of your way until you put me out!" She ran upstairs without eating the breakfast that Auntie Cora had put in front of her while they were talking.

Cora removed her plate from the table. *That girl has some real problems. I'd better go up and talk to her. The man is a sleaze, but why she insists on lying about him, knowing that she wants him back, is beyond me. As a matter of fact, I can't figure out why Carlette won't press charges, even though she's shy. Oh, well, I can't do what they won't.*

Cora finished fixing the breakfast plates for the other girls, who would be down shortly.

CHAPTER 33

"Girl, look at you. You more beautiful than when you left."

Carlette blushed at the compliment her aunt Genevee greeted her with when she got off the plane. "Thanks, Aunt Genevee, you look very pretty, too. Who been doin' your hair? It's beautiful."

"Girl, you remember Lo-Lo Veeda's?"

"Yeah, I remember 'er. She be doin' your hair now?"

"Yeah, girl, and I don't have not one complaint, neither."

"I can see why not. She good."

"Come on, let's go to the house and have some tea and something to eat. We can catch up on things there."

Genevee took one of Carlette's bags, and Carlette carried the other. They traveled in Genevee's new red car back to her house. The car reminded Carlette of that dirty David Portugal. She quickly refocused on Genevee's hair.

"Auntie, your hair looks really good, but what's with them shiny hairdos now, you know, the ones with all them colors, and the ones that look like they be plastered to a woman's head with grease and lacquer? And the extra supertight jeans these girls be wearing now?"

"I don't understand that style, either, Carlette, and it seems to me they wouldn't wear such a look if they trying to attract a decent man, the way they claim they do. It look tacky to me, like it would run any respectful man away, or attract a man who only fake, but I'm an older woman, so I can't say."

"I ain't that old, Auntie! It look tacky to me, too. A lot of the girls who come to Auntie Cora's come in with that style—and broken hearts. It looks too trashy, and so do the low jeans on boys. You know those boys are showin' their drawers now."

"No, Carlette, you kiddin' me."

"No, I'm not, Auntie. And I don't know which is worse, the drugs they sell or the prison clothes they wear and think they're designer gear. But those boys are wearing them saggy pants, showing their drawers, like they're thongs now. Wasn't it bad enough when they were showing their cracks like a plumber? My goodness! All of it is just ugly, in more ways than one. A girl has to be crazy to want a man who shows all his behind to the world. And those girls, they'll always be complaining about any man who is attracted to such a plastic look. Shoot! Their hairdo look more like candle wax than weave. The more fake you look, the more phony your crowd. And, Auntie, some of those men aren't half as good as the girls. But they always try not to be seen with them day or night, like they have some great something they need to protect by being seen in the company of the wrong female. And the men with those pants showing their drawers act like they look attractive. I don't know, Auntie. Maybe it's okay to some women, but I don't want to be looking at no man's drawers. I barely wanted to look at Ricky Jr.'s when I had to buy them. I just don't know what's going on with all these kids now and their parents, but I stopped Ricky from wearing them pants. And the tattoos— I told him I could write on his skin with an ink pen or marker and make him look just as dirty as something he had to pay for. The tattoos are a definite no-no. It's nice to have him around, but that boy is going to be a real man even if he never sees his father or another man ever again."

Genevee giggled but kept her eyes on the road. "Well, if the young people today were like your parents were, especially your mom, they would be more selective. Lord knows, she was similar to a cat when it came to men. If anyone invaded her territory, she considered it tainted and would never go back there. The only reason she forgave me and remained in love with your father was because he was a good, honest man, and I was her sister."

"So my dad wasn't her first?"

"I didn't say that. He wasn't the first man she dated, but I do believe he was the only one she ever lay with. And she didn't do that until after your father married her." Genevee sighed. "He was a good man, an upstanding man."

Feeling a little sad, Carlette didn't comment. Instead she took in the scenery. She couldn't help but notice all the changes. She turned in her seat.

"It's really getting modern around here. When did they build all these new houses and stores, Auntie?"

"Almost as soon as you left."

"Oh, I see. They were waiting for Carlette to leave."

Genevee and Carlette both laughed. They talked about crazy things and laughed some more. They went into the newer shops and bought some things before continuing their journey.

When they arrived at the house, Carlette couldn't believe her eyes. Aunt Genevee had added on to it so much, Carlette almost didn't recognize it. It looked like a small mansion with a pool. It was no longer that fire-engine red, but a mild yellow with white trim, and hedges grew around it now.

"Wow! Aunt Genevee, this is so pretty! How many rooms do you have now?"

"Eight. I added a family room and bedroom downstairs, and one bedroom and bath upstairs."

They went inside. There was all new furniture.

"Aunt Genevee, did you hit the lottery or something?"

"No. Come into the kitchen with me. We need to talk."

Carlette followed her aunt into the kitchen, her main counseling area. Carlette held her breath when she entered the kitchen, which looked brand-new with everything built in, including the stove. The eating area was now an island. She stared at everything and smiled.

"Go ahead, Carlette. Have a seat."

Carlette noticed that her aunt was looking very serious. "What's wrong, Auntie?"

"For the past year your husband has been coming by."

"Ricky's been here?"

"Yes. He's big in construction now, and he's all legitimate and everything. Oh, he has plenty of money. I've told him many times that I'm not angry with him because of you and that I don't want any of his money, but he gives it to me, anyway. If I don't take it, I find things in my house or something new being added on to it. That's how my house has gotten so huge. He always says that he has to do something to make up for not taking care of you and his baby all these years. Carlette, you're going to have to take him back, or I won't be able to find my way around here after a while, girl. The only room that he hasn't gotten to is your old bedroom."

"I never rejected Ricky. I still love him. Do you know where he is?"

"Yes."

"Why didn't you tell me before now, Aunt Genevee? We've called each other, and you've visited me many times."

"But you never ask about him. I thought you didn't care or want to see him. He asks about you and Ricky Jr. all the time, but I didn't want to make any problems for you, so I didn't say anything."

"That's okay, Auntie. You did the right thing. But do you know where he lives, or do you have a phone number?"

"No, but he usually stops by or calls me to see

how I'm doing. Actually, he should be coming around today, about noon."

"What? That's in about an hour. I gotta go get cleaned up. I don't want him to see me looking any way but good."

Carlette dashed into her old bedroom, the only room that Ricky hadn't altered. She threw one of her bags on the bed, flipped it open, and looked for an outfit she knew he would love. *A satin fitted blouse, a pair of jeans, heels? No, no.* She rummaged through her closet. *Here they are, my satin bridal slippers.* She put her feet in them. They still fit, and they looked new. She removed the slippers, stood at the mirror, and wrapped her hair before getting into the shower. It all had to be perfect for Ricky.

Smiling as she stepped out of the shower, Carlette thought about why Ricky hadn't touched her room. It was the memory of their first encounter. A memory of her. Of them. It made her feel good, and she owed it all to her aunt Genevee for bringing them back together.

Carlette looked in her bedroom mirror and removed the wrap. She combed and brushed her hair until it wrapped around her neck and both sides met, then fluffed up her short bangs. She stood back and looked at herself. She loved the way her hair cascaded to the front and covered her bosom, and the way it touched the floor when she bent forward and went back into place when she stood up straight, as if guided by a magnet. Her jeans and blouse showed her comely figure, and like most of her clothes, they fit her like a glove. Not many women in her town had a beautiful figure like hers and Genevee's, but Genevee was buxom and hippy, "draggin' lots of wagon."

Carlette finished her preparation by applying a small amount of dark fuchsia lipstick and her clean-scented perfume, which people always complimented. When the doorbell rang, she ran out of the bedroom and sat on the sofa, pretending she was reading a magazine.

"Genevee, how are you today? I just came by to check on you."

It was Ricky. Carlette would know that sexy voice anywhere.

"I'm fine, Ricky. Come on in."

Ricky entered the house somewhat reluctantly. Genevee had never seemed so hospitable, no matter what he'd done for her, how many times he'd been there, or what he'd said to her. The openness made him a little curious. "Genevee, you okay?" He stepped inside. "Oh my god! Carlette!"

Carlette, trembling with excitement, rose from the sofa.

Ricky's eyes welled with tears, and as soon as he hugged Carlette, they both began to cry.

Genevee was so filled with joy over the re-union, she also cried.

Carlette began to feel emotions that she hadn't experienced since Ricky left. She wanted him to make love to her but didn't want her actions to be suggestive.

"Let me look at you, Carlette," said Ricky.

Carlette was tingling from his touch but coolly stood back while Ricky held both her hands to get the whole picture. His eyes slowly roamed her body. She could barely stand to stare at Ricky for long. He always seemed to have that special something that stimulated everything inside of her. His eyes seemed more mesmerizing and mystical than she remembered. His hair had a touch of gray at the temples, which made him more handsome than ever. That set her on fire with temptation.

Ricky smiled. "You look so good, Carlette, and smell so nice. You're more beautiful than I remember. Did you marry again?"

Carlette thought that was an odd question and looked at Genevee, who hunched her shoulders. "No, Ricky. How could I? We're still married, aren't we?"

"Yes, yes, yes. That's if you have waited for me all this time and didn't divorce me."

"No, Ricky, I didn't divorce you."

"Then we're still married. Do you want to remain my wife?"

"Yes, Ricky. I still love you."

"I love you, too, Carlette. I want us to be together, all of us. Where's our son?"

"I left him in the States, with Auntie Cora. He's still in Georgia, but he's going back to school in a few days."

"When will I be able to see him?"

"Any weekend that we choose, as long as he knows we're coming. He is very active and won't sit around expecting company."

"I bet he's gotten tall."

"Ricky, that boy's more than tall. He's somewhat muscular, too. He's built just like you, and he looks like you, too. He's incredibly handsome." As soon as Carlette made the statement, she wanted to recant it. She became embarrassed by Ricky's immobile stare, pretty smile, and twinkling eyes.

"Am I handsome, Carlette?"

Carlette blushed.

Ricky couldn't help but melt from her innocence. Just looking at her in that state took him back to the first time he'd touched her sexually, and the way she'd made him feel. Now Ricky was blushing. He had to clear his throat to speak again. "You don't have to answer me, Carlette. It's okay."

Genevee laughed at them both.

Ricky and Carlette decided to take a walk. As soon as they left, Genevee's doorbell rang again. Genevee smiled broadly and hoped Carlette and Ricky hadn't seen her visitor.

CHAPTER 34

Ricky had been on the phone all day, calling his friends. He had one more day at home, so he wanted to meet up with everyone that day and have a good time. That way he could sleep in the day before returning to school and be well rested.

When he walked through the door after his farewell partying, he saw Theresa sitting in the living room. She was still up and playing his video game.

"Theresa?"

"Come on, Ricky. Come play with me."

"Nah, I'm tired. You go ahead and play. I'm going to bed."

"I guess nobody around here likes me."

"You okay, Theresa. I'm just sleepy, though."

"Okay. I understand." Theresa went back to the game.

Ricky watched Theresa play alone and could see the sadness in her eyes. "Scoot over, Theresa."

Theresa moved over.

Ricky picked up the other control to challenge

her, but Theresa was so good, by the time it was his turn, he'd fallen asleep.

Theresa got down on her knees, unzipped Ricky's pants, and began to honor him with what David Portugal had taught her.

Ricky woke up to the manipulation and tried pushing Theresa away from him. "Don't, Theresa! Don't!"

Theresa ignored Ricky, until she had made the breath come out of him. "Ricky, I love you. I've always loved you. I'm leaving. Will you come with me?"

Ricky was angry enough to be belligerent with Theresa but managed to maintain his self-control. "Theresa, I can't believe you did that."

"But I love you, Ricky."

"What about your baby? Do you love your baby?"

"Yeah, I love my baby."

"Naw, Theresa. Naw, you don't. You don't love that baby. If you loved that baby, nothing in this world would've made you do something like that to me with your child inside you. You don't even know me."

Theresa began to cry.

"Theresa, them tears might fool Momma and Aunt Cora, but they don't fool me. I'm more from the streets than them, and I done had women just like you before, girl. You don't care about nothin' but yourself and that old, no-good man who done got you pregnant."

Theresa dropped her head.

"Do you know what you just did to your unborn child, Theresa?"

Ricky was waiting for an answer, but Theresa, too ashamed to answer, kept her head hung.

"I asked you, Theresa, do you know what you just did to your baby?"

"Nothin', Ricky, nothin'."

"Girl, shut up! You just fed the wastes of a man you don't even know to your baby. You don't know me, Theresa. You don't know me. You just put yourself and your baby in jeopardy. You don't know who I might've been with before I came in that door, or what kinda diseases I might have."

"You don't have no diseases."

That stupid comment made Ricky furious. He wanted to call Theresa a stupid female dog, but the conversation he'd had with his mother when he was sixteen prevented that. Her words had touched him deeply, and he refrained. "Just get up, Theresa! Just get up!"

Theresa stood up. "Are you going to tell your mother and aunt?"

"Why would I tell them something so stupid and disgusting?"

"Because that's what I deserve for doing something so obscene to you."

"You didn't do nothin' to me, girl. You did it to yourself and that baby you carryin'."

"Please, Ricky, please. Don't be mad. Tell on me, but don't be mad."

"You want me to tell, don't you, Theresa? You hate my mother, and you want her to know what you've done to me. You're trying to hurt my mom. That's why you wanted me to run away with you. You thought I was just that stupid."

"No, Ricky."

"Yes, you did. But let me tell you somethin'. I ain't goin' nowhere with you, and I ain't tellin' her nothin'. Nada! You won't get what you're lookin' for. You wasted all that perfection for nothin'!"

Theresa looked at Ricky. She couldn't squeeze out any more tears.

"Where are the tears, Theresa? They evaporate?"

Theresa didn't know how to respond and, as usual, said the first stupid thing that came to mind. "I thought you'd like me back."

"I did like you. You know what, Theresa? That man got you crazy, girl. He gotchu crazy."

"No, he don't. He loves me."

"Theresa, you only a couple years older than me. I know good and well you didn't always do what you did to me. A man have to get hold of a girl early to teach her what you know. And for you to do somethin' like that to a man you don't hardly know, with a baby inside of you, he was tryin' to turn you into his prostitute."

"No, he wasn't. He was gonna marry me."

"Let's not go there, Theresa."

"He was gonna marry me."

"When, Theresa? When?"

Theresa didn't know what to say.

"Come on, Theresa. If he was gonna marry you, tell me when."

"He didn't give me a date."

"That's because he didn't have one, wasn't gonna make one, and didn't want one. I know men like him. I used to hang out with 'em. They start them girls out real young by doin' things to 'em to get 'em attached. Then, if the girls don't want to do it back, they threaten to leave 'em or beat 'em.

When they do it, the guys start gettin' more and more distant, anyway. The girls want to be with 'em, tell 'em how much they love 'em, and be beggin' to be with 'em. That's when they start askin' the girls to do more and more stuff for 'em to prove their love, and even if they do it, they still don't pay 'em much attention. They end up gettin' pregnant by 'em, thinkin' that's gonna hold 'em, but it don't.

"Some of the guys just call it a business. Some of 'em be real freaky. They watch they girls havin' sex with other people even while they pregnant, 'cause they don't give a damn about that baby or the mother. They don't have no love for either one. I've known men who've pimped they woman, and shared they woman with another man while they all slept in the same bed together. I've even known men who had sex with they women in certain ways to make 'em miscarry, 'cause they don't want the kid, or the girl hangin' around."

Theresa put her hand over her mouth and ran to the bathroom, and Ricky followed her, afraid he'd gone too far. She was over the toilet on all fours and vomiting when he reached her.

"Theresa? You gonna be okay?"

Theresa could only gag and puke.

"Theresa? You gonna be okay? You want me to go get Auntie Cora?"

"No! No! I'll be okay in a minute!"

Ricky stood at the door until Theresa was through. Then he went to the medicine cabinet and gave her something to control her nausea.

"Why are you helping me, Ricky? You said I'm disgusting."

"I want your baby to be okay. He don't have

nothin' to do with your choices. He didn't ask to be made."

"You're so righteous. You know what? That's what I'll start calling you. *Righteous* Ricky. So what kind of pimp were you, Righteous Ricky? The kind that performed oral sex on real young girls to get 'em? And don't be callin' my baby a him, 'cause you don't know what I'm having, Mr. Righteous Ricky."

"Ain't none of what you sayin' hurtin' my feelings. You know why? 'Cause I could've been a pimp, but my mother stepped in before that happened, and I'm glad she did. She stopped me before I got too stupid. She let me know that anybody can claim to be a male, but certain things, like honor, loyalty, and responsibility, make you a man." Ricky waved his hand in exasperation. "Do yourself a favor, Theresa. Let go of that man . . . the hate, and the envy. Especially the envy and hate you have for my mom. You'll never be able to get back at her for something that probably wasn't her fault."

"You don't even know what happened."

"I know that man did you wrong, 'cause you here, and that my mother's real pretty, and you gotta be jealous of that somehow. You went out of your way with me tonight. You didn't do it because you love me, and you surely didn't do it for nothin'. People don't take action for nothin'."

"I'm sorry, Ricky, okay?"

"That's cool. But you'll never get better if you don't start taking your life seriously like I did." Ricky walked away to go to his room. He glanced down at his watch. It was almost 3:00 a.m., an indication that he would be sleeping late the next day.

CHAPTER 35

Ricky slept until almost 4:00 p.m. He was sitting on his bed, wearing only his jeans, listening to music, when he was interrupted by Theresa's voice on the other side of his bedroom door.

"Ricky? Can I come in?"

"Sure, Theresa."

"Ricky." Theresa couldn't help but stop and stare at Ricky and feel some desire to have someone like him. He was handsome, the complexion of his toned body was beautiful, just like his mother's, and he was filled with wisdom. Although he'd said some things she didn't like, Theresa liked the idea of a man caring enough to say them to her, and there was a coolness about him that was indescribable, desirable, and irresistible.

"Theresa, you were going to say something?" Ricky couldn't fool himself, either. He knew that Theresa was just as pretty as his mother, and had imagined what she would look like without the baby in her stomach. Even naked.

"Ricky. I'm sorry. I mean, I apologize. That's

the word they tell us to use. People who say I'm sorry usually are, I guess. But I mean it from my heart, Ricky. I apologize. Will you forgive me?"

"I forgave you last night. It ain't a thing."

"It is to me, Ricky. I violated you, and I shouldn't have."

"Forget it, Theresa. It really ain't all your fault. I've fantasized about you many times."

"Really?" Theresa wished she could have controlled her enthusiasm more.

Ricky laughed at her response. "Yeah, really. You good-lookin'. I can look at you and tell you came from a really good family. You even speak well. I don't know how that loser ever got you in this situation."

"He conned me, Ricky. I told your aunt he raped me in every way, because after I had done all he wanted, it felt like, like he even raped my mind."

"So why you so mad at my mother?"

"Because I was ashamed. Your mother saw Dave with me and ran away, frightened, and he'd talk all nice about her, like she should be put on a pedestal or something, and then treat me like dirt."

"And that made you jealous? Why, Theresa? He's dirty."

"He thought your mother was too special to take naturally, so he drugged her. Me, he just took and took, and he took me when I was pregnant and used me without compassion. I believe that's how I lost two children. That's what made me throw up last night. You reminded me of that."

Theresa had become humble, but Ricky didn't

have time to notice that. He was more concerned about his mother.

"He took advantage of my mother?"

"Yeah, that's why she came back home so soon."

"And that's why you two acted as if you didn't know each other?"

"Yes."

"You saw him taking advantage of her?"

"No, but he talked about it."

"Then how'd you know it was true?"

"He described her from that play we were all in, and I know how he is. He gives and offers, and then he takes what he thinks he deserves. He's just like the men you were describing to me last night."

"Wow! Aw, man!"

"Don't tell your mother I told you. I'm serious this time. Please don't tell her. She's embarrassed by it. I only told you because you made me think. Maybe I needed a man all along to tell me what a fool I was being."

"He really made you lose your babies?"

"Yeah, I believe so, just like you said last night."

"He's a sorry somethin'."

"Tell me about it."

"Do you still love him?"

"Yeah, I guess I'm too stupid not to."

"You're not stupid, Theresa. People can't help who they love."

"I could love someone like you, Ricky."

"Don't start that again, Theresa."

"I mean it, Ricky. I mean it. Maybe it's a crush. I don't know. I've never had a real boyfriend before, but I have feelings for you."

"I'm flattered."

"I'm not trying to flatter you, Ricky. I'm too frank for that. I've been with boys before, but Dave's the only man I've been with my whole life since them, and I haven't been with him since I conceived this baby. I've been checked out and everything. I'm okay. Will you make love to me? I've never experienced that feeling, Ricky," she said, stammering. "I'd like to experience that with someone like you, a good person with dignity, respect, who's warm. I won't try to force you into a commitment or anything. I'd just like to see what it feels like to be that close to someone that I respect. And maybe you respect me, too. I don't know. But I need someone who makes me feel like a lady, like a warm blanket is wrapped around me."

"Theresa, you're pregnant."

Theresa still didn't know what to say. "I have protection, Ricky, don't you?"

"Well, yeah, but . . ."

Ricky saw the desperation in Theresa's eyes and couldn't refuse. He had wanted her since the first time he'd seen her in Auntie Cora's doorway. He got up from the bed, locked the door, and led Theresa by the hand back to his bed and gave her a speech, to mask his feelings.

"Theresa, I shouldn't be doing this, but someone needs to show you how the father of your child should be acting toward you."

Theresa threw her arms around Ricky's neck, and he wrapped his arms around her pregnant waist, and they hugged for what seemed like hours. To Theresa, that alone was better than anything Dave Portugal had ever done for her.

CHAPTER 36

It was 8:00 p.m., and Ricky had dozed off with Theresa lying in his arms, her back to him, still crying from the passion.

When he woke up, he pulled her close to him and massaged her stomach. "You okay, Theresa?"

Ricky's breath felt like a heavenly breeze touching Theresa's ear. "Yes, Ricky, I'm okay." She closed her eyes, drew in a breath, and slowly let it out.

"Good. Now don't you go forgetting me when you get married, you hear?" Ricky was hoping that Theresa would say that she wasn't going to marry, because she wasn't really in love with Dave Portugal. He lay very still as he waited for her response.

"Ricky, I could never forget you, or this night." Theresa was still crying. "I think I'm in love with you, Ricky, and I think that I have been since I first saw you. I wish I'd had better judgment. Maybe we'd be in college together, we'd get married, and this would be your child I'm carrying."

Theresa continued crying until she fell asleep.

* * *

The following morning Ricky leaned up on one elbow and stroked her hair. He wondered what it would have been like if he had met her under different circumstances. He'd had his share of disappointments, too. The females he'd dated just weren't as honest as he wanted them to be. He could relate to Theresa's situation and couldn't help but kiss her cheek and whisper in her ear. "Nothing is ever the way it appears, sweet Theresa. No one has it all." Ricky had realized that just because Theresa had been exposed to sex didn't mean that she was no longer innocent.

After Theresa left his room, Ricky lay on his bed, wide awake, waiting for her to leave for her appointment. He had become infatuated with her. He needed to know and wanted to know more about the bruised angel he'd spent the night with. She was more than a unique soul; she was special to him.

The sound of multiple footsteps prancing down the long hallway told him she was on her way out. He waited until he heard her dainty feet run downstairs, then opened his door. He walked out and stood on the top step. When he heard the front door shut, he rushed downstairs.

From the living-room window, he spied on the van that transported the residents of the house who had appointments, wanted to shop, or desired general entertainment. As soon as the van was out of sight, he just as swiftly headed back up to Theresa's room. He would go through the belongings of his mysterious beauty, the only girl to come to the house who had piqued his interest. He needed to know more about her wanting to hurt his mother. Maybe he could find something in her room that would somehow satisfy his curiosity. Most of all, he wanted to know more about her. She did something to him inwardly that he couldn't explain. Something he had never felt with any other female, no matter what the circumstances or what they did for him. So what if she was carrying a child and had been less than perfect? He just couldn't allow her to get back with that man.

Ricky opened the first piece of luggage, a duffel bag, and saw a little red book trimmed in gold with a lock on it. *This must have some really deep stuff in it. She got it all locked up. But I gotta get into it. This girl definitely got my heart, and she holding back too much. I'll just keep quiet if she asks who opened her book.* He smiled when he went to snatch the lock off and it opened on its own.

He proceeded to recline on Theresa's bed, then got up quickly and went to the bedroom door to search the hallway. When he saw the coast was clear, he headed back to his room. He turned on his music, sat down on his bed, and opened the diary.

Up until Theresa was sixteen, her life had been like a fairy tale. Even the photos of her parents that fell out of the little book were fairy tale like. Her penmanship was beautiful, until she began to talk about her life as a child actor and about David Portugal.

Ricky touched the pages with his finger as he read.

I had done things with boys before, starting at age twelve. I had vowed to keep our hugging, petting, kissing, and nude touching encounters a secret even from you, Diary. But once David Portugal took my virginity, I had to let you know all about him. I love him. I love him. I love him. He is like no one else I have known. I pretended to want to be just friends with him, hoping that he would take me to the places he had talked about when he'd told me about his female conquests. When he finally took me in ways that he had made me dream about for almost two years, I felt like I was floating. Oh, God, how I want him each time I see him, and in any way he wants me and with anyone he wants me to be with. Or even if he just wants to watch. He has taught me so much, and I giggle each time he calls me his "passion whore." He thinks it's a title that turns only him on, but I, too, am turned on by it. At least I used to be.

I was even okay with him when he taught me how to sell myself, have threesomes for money, and to please women. He had my head filled with the fantasy of us becoming rich if I continued to please all the prospects he brought home for me to cater to, especially his most important client, Julian. He, I, and Julian, the three of us, meet often. Julian is always rough with me. I think he hates me for what I do to please David. He even choked me one night after watching me and David being intimate. When it was his turn, he never wanted to look at me and held my face against the mattress as he unnaturally pleased himself, almost choking me to death in the process. David pulled him off me, but the two still used me until they were tired. Then David gave me bus fare and sent me home. He and Julian were drinking champagne when I left.

Diary, I never thought any of this was suspicious. Why? Because I was doing all that I could to please David. I didn't want him to think that I was crowding him, like I hear so many men say women do—except my dad. But, anyway, I just wanted to please him in every way. And if that meant I had to give him and Julian their time, that was what I felt I had to do. But when I came over for the very first time uninvited and caught them—that filthy David, the man who should have loved me for all I had done, and that freaky, low-down Julian—and David was treating him better than he ever treated me, I went crazy. He was taking so much time with Julian, making him moan out his name while Julian held on to his big-ass head!

Ricky laughed. He continued reading.

And he had the nerve to get ready to mount that man after that, and I lost it! As I chased both of them around David's apartment with that knife, all I could think about was how intimate I had been with both of them, what they were probably doing to each other, and what might be inside of me after seeing what those two were really up to. I wanted them both dead. And, as God is my witness, that was where I would have been if the neighbors hadn't called the cops. Thank you, God, for rescuing me. David would have won twice. And thank you for finding Cora and this nice family. They are good people, truly encouraging people, and I think that I am really in love this time. But maybe he doesn't think that I am good enough for him, and he's probably right, although my parents raised me better than I allowed myself to be. I have begun to write some poetry. The tributes are from my soul. The rest really describe that old deceitful imp, David Portugal.

THE DEVIL'S HORNS

He was the most beautiful man I'd ever seen in my young life. We'd been seeing each other for almost a year. He'd been nothing short of a gentleman. I'd fallen in love with him, and there was no turning back. Although he had me all wrapped up in emotion, I knew there was something frightfully different about him.

It wasn't until that night, that horrible, regretful night that I accepted his unholy invitation to share my bed and allowed him to take my pure virgin body out of wedlock, that I saw what he really was. The night that he would plant the seed he needed to bring him a strong, furious, ungodly child.

The moment I said yes, the room grew cold, and the lights dimmed. And even before he touched me, I knew that was all he'd been waiting for, a formal invitation to enter my home and innocence.

His body changed almost instantly. First, his facial expression darkened; then he grew horns, a tail, hooves, a beard, and grotesque wings. He expanded so much, his body literally ripped his suit, shirt, and shoes off, and he appeared to be exceptionally broad winged and muscular. Even his shadow accentuated itself on my walls as he transformed himself.

I saw his hand go up. It had long claws. He brought it down swiftly and without compassion.

He tore his nails across my face and body. Instantly there was a pain and burning from the scars he'd clawed into my face, breasts, stomach, and thighs. He'd marked me. Yes, he'd marked me. I belonged to him.

My clothing, including my underwear, hung open. They looked like they'd been through a shredder. My mouth flew agape in astonishment, and my eyes widened in disbelief. He gave me a look that made me fall into a deep trance. I knew what I was doing and what he was doing to me, but I couldn't resist him.

He pulled me to him with his spearlike tail, palmed the top of my head with one of his clawed hands, and forced me to do things to him I'd never done before. I was a virgin in every way.

As I was following his command, he threw out his tongue, which was a replica of his tail, and howled like a wild dog.

He immediately reversed the roles once his needs were met. He used that wicked-looking tail and tongue of his to feed his lust and my concealed desires by placing them in the lower openings of my body, making me scream. There was no sensuality, no feeling of love, no warmth whatsoever, just this awful pain that made me want to pass out, but I couldn't. He was controlling me. All I could do was scream. While I did, he howled in delight, drowning out my agony.

Finally, he released me. It was as if I fell to the floor in slow motion and passed out. When I regained consciousness, it was morning. He was gone, but the signs of his passionate lust remained. My bedroom had definitely been disturbed.

Immediately, I ran into the bathroom to gaze into the mirror, hoping it was all a dream, but it wasn't. He'd been there, and he'd marked me all right. The scars from the night before were very distinctive. It wasn't a dream at all. He'd had me, and there was no denying my new prophetic senses. He'd definitely planted his demon seed inside of me. It grew rapidly, and I aborted it. He returned to me, angry and violent. He made me more aware this time, aware of everything that happened. It was my punishment for not wanting his child, for murdering his unborn, and for killing his plan. I'd been his chosen virgin for the new order, but now I was no good to him. He'd taken my virginity. I was tainted. Yes. Tainted, disobedient, and uncontrollable. He'd been humiliated, and my punishment had to come.

The first time he'd been with me, I hadn't seen his male organ, although he'd forced me to please him unnaturally. He exposed himself on the second visit. He wanted me to see his organ. He wanted me, this ex-virgin, to see exactly what she'd been forced to sinfully please. It was horrifying and unsightly. There was nothing at all human about its form. It was more hideous and uninviting than his wicked-looking tongue and tail.

He forced me to satisfy him again. He would not let me rise like before. With a tight grip on my head and neck, he pressed my face hard into the pillow.

I could barely breath, and I passed out. When I woke, I was lying in a hospital bed. They told me that I'd hemorrhaged and lost a lot of blood. They said that a woman dressed like a nun had come to my room, prayed for me, and I'd suddenly begun to recover. They said that my landlady had found me, and that was how I got to the hospital. There is no landlady. I live in and own my condo. It's even paid for.

After the attacks, I noticed another change in me. I'd have these weird dreams of girls I'd never seen before, young girls, virgin girls, who were being stripped of their pureness and having all sorts of sex with all sorts of men and women. I'd become a stripped virgin, who'd been forcefully given the knowledge of a bordello queen with a spiritual sixth sense. I'd often awaken sweating, shaking, gasping for air, and crying. Was God trying to tell me something? Was He showing me what happens each time a woman's virginity is taken from her out of wedlock? Is she not only giving in to an unknown lust, but also romancing and sleeping with the devil? At the time, I wasn't sure, but I knew that my mother had warned me about invitations to evil. Once a virgin has invited the evils of the devil to her body, there is no limit to how far Satan will go to finish destroying her soul. To him, it's just another conquest.

Yep, Diary, you guessed it. This is my distorted rendition of the real David, and there are probably a lot more like him. But this is also me. I have my freedom from the demon. I have taken my life back and away from him.

THE LAST HO STROLL

*6:37 a.m. It was almost light and freezing cold. I
was still at Carter's Den, the main ho stroll. A selective spot to earn the "subvert dividend." I was
the last ho left on the stroll, when I heard this click,
click, clicking sound on the sidewalk that made me
spin. I stopped, turned, and looked all around,
trying to find the clicking sound, which was
coming from the cold ground. I abruptly stopped,
and the clicking ceased. I then began to pick up my
pace. Again, I heard that click, click, clicking
sound, so I continued walking at a faster rate,
clutching my thin coat and trying to keep the cold
wind out of my face. As the clicking got closer, it
was obvious to me that it was indeed following me.*

*In a fright, and with a racing heart, I picked up
my pace some more and then broke into a run.
Faster! Run faster! My dizzy mind and scattered
thoughts caused me to panic, but there was no
escape from this frightening clatter. As I picked up
speed, the sound came again, that horrible, click,
click, clicking on that cold, cold cement. Just a few
more blocks to the busy section . . . I'll get away!
Somebody will be there, anybody. Then I'll be free!*

*As I reached my destination, the click continued. I
looked around and saw nothing, but I was sure I'd
heard the clicking just before I'd turned around. I
began walking with my back to the wind, and that
was when the clicking began again. While coming
down from my pain-free high, I realized it was my
shoes, my stilettos, that were making that sound.
My stilettos, my companions, part of my entice-*

ment, made me frightened as they echoed on the cold, cold cement.

I'd come off a high that had kept me pain free, a high that had made me forget all about me. A high that had me running from me, and so blind, I couldn't see. As I became more conscious and feeling as if the fear was over, sudden flashbacks rendered me sober. That was when I began to remember what made me disrespect my gender. Wait a minute. That pimp didn't love me. Neither did the johns. The wife-in-laws pretended we were all one, while the world passed by and spat on me and my con.

In my apartment I began to really think. Why am I doing this? What's wrong with me? Oh yeah. Now I remember. It's all clear. I was raped. Now I feel worthless. That's why I'm here! Almost instantly, I remembered the first big money I'd made, and the man who told me he'd protect me and we'd both be rich if I stayed. "Just obey and endure, girl. We'll both get paid. With me to protect you, why are you afraid?" His love was in my heart, mine in his hands. I said to myself, "Girl, you can take a chance. You love that man."

Now that I am alone and free, I'm able to think. Think for me. So I'm thinking. He's not out there freezing every night, feet hurtin 'n' burnin, trying to keep things right. That's right. He's not out there, nor the man who took me against my will. And what about the one who gave me my first big bill? He's somewhere else, laid up, getting his thrill.

I don't need this life. It ain't doin' me right. It don't make me feel cuddled, nurtured, or bright.

*My body is special, but it's been used and abused.
Guess what? So have the persons I've serviced and
tutored.*

*Who's to blame for my treatment and my tricks' in-
discretion?*

*This lady told me some years ago to always pray, no
matter what people say, what you do, or where you
go. She told me there's a God who watches over me.
There's nothing done that He doesn't see. I don't
think she was lyin', and each night I be prayin',
cryin'. Sometimes I feel like dyin', 'cause that stroll's
gettin' harder and more tryin'. God's going to move
me far from this stroll. He's promised me a life better
than gold.*

*God has already spoken to me. He told me He sent
that lady to help me. He said, "Sweet, sweet baby,
don't continue following the wicked streets. There's
a better way. It's all been planned for you. The
lady that I sent can show you the door. She under-
stands you, sweet baby. Let her help you through.
You'll completely see the strife you're living now
and welcome the escape from this cruel, cruel life."*

*All the books of Christ never touched me as deep as
the voice I heard in my moment of grief. I knew
that the voice was of God no man could be so mer-
ciful, so tender, so sweet. I instantly began to cry
and just as quickly rose to my feet. "Dear Lord," I
said, "send that woman to me again. I know,
dear Lord, that I must try to become more aware
that there are many like me who are in pain and
need my care."*

I thank You, Lord, every day. You showed me love. You didn't throw me away. I'll always be indebted to You. With my heart and mind, I will dedicate myself to helping others through.

I thank You, Father, again and again for that early morning that was the end of my ho stroll and even more for my new beginning and walk with You. A walk that I will always dedicate to You.

This is how I feel now, and I have made a vow to find decency and restore the values taught to me by my loving parents. Other girls, boys, females, males, women, men—everyone needs to know that they deserve to live their lives without being mistreated, that they don't have to be ashamed, and they must be willing to prove to themselves, their families, and the world that they are what they were born to be. A true productive citizen that doesn't need anyone pimping them and filling their head with dirt that will make them feel weaker than ever.

Ricky says he loves me. I hope that he will still say that after I tell him the truth. Up until last night I thought that I would never want to be truthful again, but after seeing another side— a decent side of someone so beautiful as he is— it doesn't matter what I have been through. All that matters is that I do not deceive him in any way, no matter what happens later. He is as good as David Portugal is evil. God, I really love Ricky. This is truly a feeling that I have never experienced, and I don't believe I will ever discover it with anyone else again.

It is almost morning, but I must add these last thoughts, God. They are dedicated to all the underdogs in society.

WHY

Why do some insist on being slaves? They blame it on others until they reach their graves.

If you take them out of Egypt, they find ways to return. If you pull them out of a blazing fire, they'll find other ways to burn.

Upon mountains they'll climb, never reaching the other side, never going around them, that route is for the non-blind.

How long will they let themselves be foolishly controlled by those less aggressive, less bold?

When will they realize that they have no life? 'Cause life ain't all struggle and strife.

WHAT IF

What If Black People Really Cared and Respected Each Other?

What If They Wouldn't Backstab Each Other, Then Blame Another Race for Self-Destruction?

What If They Would Stand by Each Other, Whether Sister or Brother?

What If They Would Build Their Neighborhoods into Flourishing Communities?

What If They Established Reputable Businesses and Supported Each Other?

What If They Used Their Strength and Power To Stand Up for What Is Right? Their Boldness to Fight What Is Wrong?

There Would Be No Need to Hide Behind Organizations or Other People in Fear of Self-Identity.

There Would Be No Need to Shout Black Power and Really Mean "My Power."

There Would Be No Need For Someone Else to Tell You How Special You Are.

There Would Be More Fathers and Mothers Who Love Each Other.

There Would Be Fewer Fatherless Children in Need of Both Parents and There'd Be No Need for Welfare, no Warfare Against Your Own (No Drugs, No Thugs, No Guns, No Violent Gangs. More Neighbors and Less Hoods in Our Neighborhoods).

There Would Be More Greeting Each Other, Happy Faces, and Acknowledgment of Your Brother.

If Black People Really Cared and Respected Each Other, There Would Be No Need to Continually Bring up Inventions of Past Minorities to Feel Authority.

The Same Talents Are in the Present with More Potential. Is This a Fact or Coincidental?

Good night, God. See you in the morning. Maybe in my dreams.

Ricky chuckled again. He realized how much he and Theresa had in common, and tears slid down his cheeks with a will of their own. *Theresa is so beautiful. How could any man treat any woman so horribly? She was somewhat at fault, and I have done some bad things to women, but I had the decency to apologize to all of them. I even bought them stuff and looked like a punk in front of my friends. Now I see why my mom wants me to respect our people no matter where they come from and doesn't want me doing certain things to females. If Theresa tells me she loves me, I mean, if Theresa wants to be with me or whatever, I'm going to make that happen, no matter what it takes.*

Ricky wiped his eyes and held the diary to his chest. He lay back on the bed, his eyes closed. He would never tell Theresa that he knew the truth or that he had read her secrets.

After a short time, he jumped up. *Man, you're acting like a little love-struck girl!* He quickly returned the book to its rightful place and went back to his room. He wanted and needed Theresa more than ever.

CHAPTER 37

Carlette and Ricky Sr. had gone out on the town. Almost every man they saw had tried talking to Carlette. Ricky had felt proud and had even teased her about having to beat them off with a stick. They had had a wonderful time and were both anxious to go back to Ricky's house.

Ricky's residence had also changed. He had built a new home with all the conveniences, including an ultralarge pool and a separate pond with tropical fish. The entire yard was lit and made the clear water glisten, accentuating each ripple the fish made.

Carlette was impressed. She wished she didn't have to leave. She wanted to call her son and tell him to meet her there, and she wished they'd both stay with his father forever, but she knew that was impossible. She still had the responsibility of the girls back at Cora's house.

Ricky Sr. turned the key and led Carlette inside the house.

Carlette gasped. "Magnificent! I didn't think the

inside could look better than the outside. Ricky, this is beautiful. Your home is absolutely fabulous."

"This is *our* home, Carlette. I owe you this and so much more. Come on over to the sofa and sit down so that we can talk. I'm going to get us something to drink. Here's the remote. Direct it at the wall in front of you, and press this button. You can watch whatever you'd like on TV. I have satellite."

Carlette took the remote. She didn't see the television that Ricky referred to, but pressed the button anyway. She could hardly believe her eyes. Two doors on the wall opened up, revealing an eighty-inch screen built into the wall that was attached to a surround-sound system identical to a cinema's.

Ricky walked back into the room. He laughed when he saw the look on Carlette's face. "What's wrong, Carlette?"

"Ricky, this television is like a movie screen. It's enormous."

"I know. I thought it would be stupid to buy a regular wide-screen TV with these fifteen-foot ceilings. I have the same one downstairs, in my game room and bedroom."

"This house must have cost you a fortune."

"No, it didn't. Except for the screens, I built everything myself. All these things are paid for. I even made a contracting deal with someone to get those screens put in. It's my luxury SUV that costs. I couldn't build myself a vehicle, so I went ahead and bought it, but my work truck and antique cars are also paid for. I had to do a lot of traveling and building to afford all these goodies."

Carlette, her eyes slightly teared up, laughed

at the comment. She had known that Ricky Sr. would be the success he had promised to be, and their son would soon follow in his footsteps.

Ricky handed Carlette a glass of wine and set his on the table so that he could get comfortable next to her on the sofa.

Carlette remembered what had happened to her with Dave and was reluctant to take it.

"Carlette, is something wrong?"

"No, no. It's just that you're so mature. I still feel like a kid around you at times, that's all."

Ricky sat down next to her, put his hand around her waist, and pulled her close to him. His hand almost fit around Carlette's petite waistline. "You don't need to feel that way, Carlette. I'd never hurt you the way I did that time. While we were apart, I thought I'd die if I never saw you again. That's why, no matter what I changed in your aunt's house, I never touched your room. I needed that memory. It was all that I had to remind me of you. I swear to you, Carlette, I'd harm myself before I'd hurt you again. Now that I've matured, I know that I shouldn't have taken you at such a young age."

That made Carlette feel guilty, but his expression "taken you" also aroused her. She spoke quickly so that Ricky wouldn't notice. "Oh, Ricky. I know that."

Ricky sat up and lifted his wineglass off the table.

Carlette rubbed Ricky's head while he sipped his wine. He put his free hand around her waist and kissed her.

He's doing that tongue thing again that I like. Carlette felt light. She could smell and taste the wine on Ricky's tongue and inhale the cologne on his body. The essence of the two mixed together, and the way he was kissing her made her face feel like it was on fire. God, how she loved everything about him.

Ricky took Carlette's glass from her and set it on the table along with his. He removed her fitted top and bra. His lips made Carlette tremble and cry silently. She had missed him so much, she could no longer deny her feelings.

Ricky lifted Carlette from the sofa and carried her into the bedroom, where he repeated his actions from the first night he'd lain with her. Only, this time she had no complaints.

CHAPTER 38

It was time for Ricky to head back to school. Theresa had slept with him his last night at home. They'd set the alarm to wake up extra early so that they could make love again before sneaking out of his room and so that they could say their good-byes.

As they stood at the front door, Theresa began to cry. "Good-bye, Ricky."

Ricky rubbed her stomach and kissed it. Then he kissed her lips. "Good-bye, Theresa. You'll write or call me, won't you?"

"Almost every day, Ricky."

Theresa had fallen in love. The natural feeling had erased the hate she thought she had for Carlette or anyone else. All she wanted was to have her baby and be with Ricky forever.

Ricky gently kissed her forehead, nose, and lips. He rubbed her stomach again and talked to the baby. He didn't want to leave Theresa. Out of all the women he'd dated or been with, Theresa seemed to know him best and love him the most. He had also fallen in love with her. He gave her one last hug before running out to the waiting taxi.

CHAPTER 39

Ricky daydreamed about Theresa as he sat in classes. She hadn't called or written, as promised.

Theresa had become quiet and less militant. Cora thought she might be going back into her depression, but the reality was that Theresa missed Ricky. She hadn't written him, because she thought his nice gestures were out of guilt for their intimacy, and assumed all she had were memories of their nights together.

Days had gone by, and Ricky hadn't called Theresa. He would call to talk with Cora, hoping she would mention Theresa, but would never ask about her. He wanted her to call him because he thought there might be friction between her, Auntie Cora, and his mother if Auntie Cora and his mother found out about their affair and disapproved. Afraid of giving his secret away before he could make up his mind about where his feelings for Theresa were really going, he wouldn't even ask about his mother or call her.

He began dating again, but after being with Theresa, all the girls seemed so shallow and silly.

He waited until it was late one night before calling. He wanted to make sure that Auntie Cora was asleep. The phone rang until the answering machine picked up the call, and he left a message for Auntie Cora to call him. Worried about Theresa, he was determined to tell her about them.

Cora returned the call and informed him that Theresa was in the hospital. She had delivered a stillborn baby girl.

Ricky's heart began to race like an overactive engine. He almost hung up the phone before Auntie Cora could say good-bye. He packed a few things, left school, and went straight to the hospital from the airport without telling anyone he was leaving.

CHAPTER 40

"Theresa Stock's room, please."

The nurse looked up in a blasé manner. She could see tears in the eyes of the young man standing over her. She had seen grieving parents before and knew how hard it was for them to lose a baby. She spoke as gently as possible. "Are you the baby's father, sir?"

Ricky, near to breaking down, said what he thought he needed to say to get to Theresa. "Yes, yes."

"Right this way, sir."

He followed the nurse along the green line, then the yellow, which led to Theresa's room. He felt confused and dizzy. More than anything else in the world, he wanted Theresa's baby to be healthy, but she didn't make it. He felt let down and vulnerable.

As he entered her room, he could see Theresa lying in bed, with an IV, and staring blankly out the window. To him, she looked more beautiful than ever. Although he walked swiftly toward her bed, she seemed miles away from the door.

"Theresa."

At first, Theresa didn't see Ricky approaching her bed. She turned slowly. When she saw him, she burst into tears.

Ricky quickly stepped over to the bed, took her hand, stroked her hair, and assured her that everything was going to be all right. "Theresa, why didn't you call me?"

"Because . . . I thought you were just trying to be nice to me."

"Would I be here now if all I wanted was to be nice?"

"I don't know. Maybe you feel guilty because I lost my baby, but it's not your fault, Ricky. It's not your fault. The stress David sent me through is what killed her. Her own father killed her, not you."

"Theresa—"

"It's true. David murdered all my children, and I've accepted that. There's no need for you to be here or feel sorry for me anymore. I've accepted my mistakes."

The more Theresa talked, the more Ricky fell in love with her. He was wishing that they'd never had harsh words and that none of the other negative things in her life had happened. It all made him feel stupid now that he'd fallen in love with her.

He leaned over her bed and tried to sound as sincere as possible, trying not to release the tears he'd been holding back since receiving the phone call from Auntie Cora. "Theresa, I love you. I mean it, Theresa. I love you. I want you to be my wife. Will you marry me?"

"And have your mother and Auntie Cora disappointed in you for the rest of your life? No, Ricky, no, I won't do that. I love you too much to put you in that situation."

"Do you believe that I've always been the person who's here with you today? I sold drugs, pimped women, sold illegal things, and stole stuff. The only difference between me and you is that you were forced into getting pregnant and doing what you did by that whatever he is, and I *was* him at one time. I told you, Theresa, if my mom hadn't come between me and those streets, I'd be in a lot of trouble right now, serious trouble."

"David really didn't force me. My emotions did. I actually flirted with him first. And did you forget about what I did the night we were playing the video game? You told me how horrible I was, and you were right. I'm no good, and that's probably what contributed to my baby's death."

"No, Theresa, no. I know I said some cold things to you. Some of it was out of anger, but the rest was to hide my feelings for you. The night you touched me had me too crazy to think. I didn't want you to know that, so I lashed out at you and used the idea of you wanting my mother to know what happened as fuel. But I love you, Theresa, and I'm going to prove it."

With those words, Ricky fell to his knees, gently laid his head on Theresa's leg, held her hand even tighter, and released the tears he'd been struggling to hold back for so long.

Now Theresa was stroking Ricky's hair and comforting him.

Ricky had already known the real story about Theresa and David Portugal, so her admitting it hadn't change the direction of his heart. He wondered how he had gotten so weak for Theresa, then remembered the comment his mother had made to him when he was just a teenager. *There's always that one, Ricky. There's always that special one who can make your heart and knees weak.* Ricky knew Theresa was that one.

CHAPTER 41

Cora was curious about Ricky leaving school suddenly. He'd told her that he felt stressed and needed a longer break and could help her with some things for a while, but she insisted that he call his mother before making that decision, since she didn't want to be held responsible.

Ricky talked to Carlette, who supported his decision. She never told him about his father, because Ricky Sr. wanted to surprise him, to which she'd agreed. Not even Cora knew. They were saving that for when they all met face-to-face.

Ricky visited Theresa every day at different times so Cora wouldn't get suspicious, and tried not to act any different than he would during his regular visits home. He even went out with the same friends, who definitely noticed a change in his concentration level and interests. Whenever they asked him if he was okay, he'd just tell him he had a lot going on at home.

But Ricky couldn't fool one of his best friends,

Bykerk Mannara. After so many downbeat get-togethers, Bykerk finally pushed Ricky's head, smiled, and said, "If you love her, you better do whatcha gotta do, boy!"

Ricky knew he was right. As a matter of fact, he was way ahead of Bykerk.

Theresa was released from the hospital in the middle of the following week. Ricky told Cora to rest, that he would bring Theresa home.

As they drove, Theresa noticed that Ricky was going a different way. Instead of questioning him, she sat quietly, assuming he was going to stop by the store for something. When they pulled up to city hall, she looked at him, wondering if he was serious. Ricky got out of his SUV, walked around to the other side of it, opened the door for her, and lifted her out of the passenger seat. He kissed her, and she hugged his neck tight.

While filling out the marriage application, they both realized that there were small details they didn't know about each other. Theresa never knew that Ricky's parents were from the islands; Ricky didn't know that she was originally from California. But there was one thing they were both certain about—the way they felt about each other.

Ricky took Theresa back to Cora's as quickly as possible so that they wouldn't be missed. Curiosity might get in the way of his plan to marry Theresa on Friday.

CHAPTER 42

Ricky stayed at a friend's house all night Thursday. It was hard for him to stay away from Theresa and not call her, but it was even harder for her. When the phone eventually rang, Theresa snatched the receiver up to her ear and identified herself immediately.

The voice on the other end of the phone was familiar but cold. "Theresa, you okay?"

Theresa remained quiet. She wanted to hang up.

The voice became more stern and controlling. "Do you hear me talking to you? Are you okay?"

"Look, Dave. I don't want any trouble."

"Did I ask you what you wanted, Theresa, or did I ask you if you're okay?"

"Dave, I'm fine."

"Good. Then you can come home on the next plane out of there."

"I'm not coming back."

"What do you mean, you're not coming back?"

"I'm not coming back there, Dave."

"You don't miss me?"

Theresa noticed that he hadn't asked about the baby at all and wouldn't answer him.

"Theresa, did you hear me? Did you hear the question?"

"Yeah, I heard it."

"Well, do you miss me, baby?"

He'd never called her that before, and she couldn't think straight. "Dave, after what I saw you doing—"

"All you saw was a man who needs different types of pleasure from time to time. That doesn't mean I don't love you."

Did he say love? Now Theresa was totally confused. "You love me?"

"What did I just say, Theresa?"

"And you want me and the baby back home?" Theresa wanted to know where he was really coming from.

"You had the baby? It lived?"

"Dave, I asked you a question. Do you want us both back?"

"Sure, baby, sure."

Theresa knew he wasn't sincere. From his response, she knew that he'd done precisely what Ricky had told her those pimps did to women to make them miscarry.

"I'm not coming back!"

"Theresa, please, come on now."

"No, Dave."

"How can you throw away all the years we got together? All that I went through to get you for myself? Remember the money, the dinners, the car, the night I wanted you so bad that I made a scene at the bar to show you how much I cared."

"You told me that would have never happened if you hadn't been so drunk."

"No, Theresa, no. I lied. I wanted you, baby. I wanted you real bad. I thought you were going to like it. I thought it would make you care for me."

"It did after a while. Even though you were making me do other things, after a while, it did. You know what, Dave? I'm going to be real honest with you. Although you made me do stuff that I'd never dreamed real people did, what you did to me that night in the bar is what got me hooked on you real bad."

"That one night, Theresa? That one night got you hooked on me? Then you should come on home and take care of me."

"No, Dave, not that one night. All the nights you'd abuse me, then make up to me that way, to make everything right. No one had ever touched me that way, Dave. No one had even kissed me for real before you. You kept doing things to me, showing me stuff, and I started getting used to it and liking it. But you killed three of my children with the things you did to me, with your fake love. I don't ever want to see you again."

"You said the last baby is alive, Theresa."

"No. I asked you if you wanted me and the baby to come back to you. I never said she lived. How could she live through the trauma you put us through?"

"It was a girl?"

"Dave, you're not onstage now. You can stop acting."

"Look, Theresa, I don't care about anything else you have to say. If you don't get back here so that you can take care of my needs, I'll tell everybody about the way you came back to my house after you got out of the institution, begging me to love you like you thought I loved Carlette, and crawling around my house on your knees, crying and begging me to let you—"

"Dave! You just go ahead, 'cause you've probably done that, anyway. I know how you are. You love to brag! Besides, I got me another man. He's made love to me, Dave. Real love! I don't have to beg him for nothin', and he don't have to beg me. And I sure as hell don't have to crawl around on my knees for him. He's not a freak and user like you. He doesn't care if I do those things or not. He loves me for me."

"You've done that to another man, Theresa?" Dave thundered.

Theresa frowned and held the phone away from her ear, trying to prevent Dave's shouting from making her go deaf.

"You've done that to another man? I know you're in the same house with Carlette. Did she put you up to this? Are you two plotting against me? You just remember, Theresa, I'm the one who treated you right in the bar that night! I'm the one who bought you all those nice things and let you drive his car! I'm the one who taught you all those things you pretended to hate when we were together! And you had the nerve to mess with another man like that, now that I've fallen in love and decided to be with just you? And I've stopped talking about Carlette, like you asked. Girl, I'll kill you!"

"To do that, Dave, you'd have to come and

get me. And guess what? My new husband wouldn't approve."

"You're not marrying anyone, Theresa! You're not marrying anyone, unless it's me!"

Theresa pretended to be interested. "Oh, Dave, you were really going to marry me?"

"Yeah."

"Well, too bad! I'm already married!" Theresa slammed the phone down and went to her room.

Cora came running to see what was wrong with her. "Theresa? Theresa? Can I come in?"

"Sure, Auntie Cora. The door's open."

"Theresa, what's wrong, honey? I heard you shouting, then running upstairs."

"Nothing's wrong. That was Dave."

"How'd he know you were here, Theresa?"

"I told him that I was being sent here after I left therapy. It was stupid, I know."

"You still love him, Theresa?"

"No. I just think about the sex a lot, but now I know I don't love him. I'm not going back to him."

"He asked you back?"

"Yeah. Can you imagine that, Auntie Cora? He kills three of my kids and wants me back so that I can get pregnant with more of them he can kill."

"Do you think he really wanted you, or did he want the sex, too?"

"I don't know. He said he had gotten rid of everyone else and had decided to be true to me, said that I should get there and take care of him, and that he was going to marry me." Theresa rolled her eyes upward. "I told him I was already married and didn't want him anymore."

"Why'd you lie about being married?" Cora

thought that there might be some truth to what Theresa was saying.

"I wanted to hurt his feelings, Auntie Cora. I wanted him to feel a little of what he made me feel all those years."

"I know, Theresa, but lying—"

"Auntie Cora, look, I know you're trying to help me, and I appreciate that, but I have a lot of hate built up inside of me for him. He's put me through so much."

Cora nodded with understanding.

"Auntie Cora, I'm sorry about being harsh with you, but it's going to take some time before I get over what David Portugal did to me. But you know what the saddest thing about all this is? Now that the light's come on, it's almost too late for me to see the road. I've got a lot of work to do to make up for all that trashy talk that he did about other people and I listened to. I've gotta somehow make up for all that, and what he did to me. I've lost a lot of my life to that lowlife . . . up to the night I came here. I was stupid enough to go over there the night before I came here. I thought he'd let me stay with him and I wouldn't have to come here. He told me I could stay with him, but he'd definitely had enough of me. He wouldn't touch me, and he'd be with others, no matter what I did to try and stop him. He said that I was too pregnant to be desirable to him in any way, except for one, and he'd see what he could do for me after I dropped the load, but he was definitely going to see whoever he wanted in his house, whether I was there or not. That's why I was crying when I got here."

Theresa began to cry again. Cora hadn't seen her cry since their discussion about Carlette. Theresa had seemed happier than ever lately, and Cora had been happy about that. She'd seen no need to pry and ask her why. She hugged Theresa and let her cry. Maybe she had been too hard on her. After all, Theresa had always been well mannered and respectful around her, and had never given her any real trouble.

CHAPTER 43

It was finally Friday! Theresa gave Cora the excuse of wanting to get out of the house and go shopping, but Cora disapproved.

"Auntie Cora, please. I'll be fine. I've either been cooped up here or making visits to the hospital for checkups since I've been home. I need some air, Auntie Cora. Some real air and exercise. I gotta get outta here, or I'm going to be insane again."

"Okay, but I'll have to come with you."

"Please, Auntie Cora. I need to be alone. I need some time to myself. Please try to understand how I feel just this once."

Cora felt guilty. "Okay, baby, okay. But please, Theresa, don't stay away too long, okay? You know how I worry about you."

"Okay, Auntie Cora. Can I have about five hours? All I need is five."

"Theresa, it's eleven a.m. Be back by seven, okay?"

Theresa snatched up her purse and almost

sprinted out the door. Ricky was waiting for her not too far away, just like he'd promised. He and Theresa drove through two counties to be pronounced husband and wife.

"Ricky, I have to be back by seven."

"What? It's our wedding day, Theresa!"

"I promised Auntie Cora. You know how she is."

Ricky did know how she was, so at the end of the day he took Theresa home and stayed out until after midnight before joining his wife at Cora's, to avert suspicion.

CHAPTER 44

A week had gone by, and all Ricky and Theresa could do was look at each other longingly while Auntie Cora was awake, but they slept in the same bed every night, either in his room or Theresa's. Ricky and his mother kept in touch and spoke with each other every other day but neither wanted to divulge their secrets over the phone.

The night before Carlette was to arrive at Cora's, Theresa was stable enough for intimacy. As usual, she and Ricky waited for Cora to go to her room and gave her enough time to fall asleep before one went into the other's bedroom.

They had been touching, caressing, and kissing for over an hour before Ricky slid away from Theresa's lips, placing his lips first on her breasts, then on her stomach and torso, and finally resting on her sex.

Theresa jumped. "I thought you didn't know how, Ricky."

"I never said that." Ricky continued.

"Don't, Ricky. You don't have to."

Ricky continued as if he hadn't heard her.

She slowly exhaled from Ricky's touch. As soon as she touched his curly head, the door flew open.

Ricky instantly remembered that he hadn't locked it.

Auntie Cora was standing in his doorway. She had gotten up to get a glass of water. She'd seen Theresa's door open and noticed she wasn't in her room. "Ricky, have you seen, Theresa? I'm worried about her. Boy! Theresa!"

Ricky, naked and dangling, had reeled up on his knees. Theresa grabbed the covers and tried covering herself, pulling them from under Ricky and almost knocking him to the floor. He regained his balance and managed to get the top sheet away from Theresa to cover himself.

"Auntie Cora! Auntie Cora! Auntie Cora! I can explain!" Ricky cried.

Cora wasn't having it. "Ricky, there's no way you can explain this type of behavior to me in my house! We've raised you better than this, me and your mother."

"We're married, Auntie Cora. We're married." Ricky's tone was flat.

Cora's eyes were big in disbelief. "What? What did you say?"

"We're married. Theresa's my wife."

"Does your mother know about this?"

"No, Auntie Cora. No, she doesn't," Ricky replied.

Cora shook her head. "When were you planning on telling her? After you and Theresa had your first child?"

"We wanted to tell her face-to-face. We were

going to tell her as soon as she came in tomorrow," explained Ricky.

Cora looked disappointed. "Ricky!"

Ricky was sure of what he wanted and felt. He wasn't going to back away from or out of his responsibility or love for his Theresa. As far as he was concerned, they'd all have to deal with the situation. "Auntie Cora, I'm sorry to sneak around behind your back this way, but me and Theresa love each other so much. We really do. She's the only woman that I've known, other than you, Momma, and Aunt Genevee, who's mature and caring. We couldn't let you or my mother disapprove of us loving each other."

Cora looked sad. She had lost her baby.

"Auntie Cora, I love you and Mom, too, but I'm so in love with Theresa—and I have been for a long time—I don't know what to do. Maybe you don't understand how I feel. But it's a feeling I can't get rid of, and I don't want to. I knew she was the one when I first met her. I know this looks disrespectful to you. We shouldn't have been in your house this way. We both respect you too much for that. We have money. We can go to a hotel, but please don't tell my mom about this before I can, please, Auntie Cora."

Ricky's words had pierced Cora's heart. She looked up at him only to see a look of desperation on his face, which weakened her heart even more. She grabbed Ricky as if he were still a little boy and hugged him, then let him go before he lost the sheet he'd thrown around himself for cover. Still puzzled, she looked from one to the other. "Theresa, is this what you were talking

about on the phone that day I walked in on you?
Were you and Ricky married then?"

"No, Auntie Cora. I didn't lie about that,"
Theresa asserted.

Cora gave Theresa a partial smile. Her honesty
was somewhat cute, like a little child's.

Ricky didn't flinch. He knew the conversation
Auntie Cora was talking about. He had called David
Portugal himself and cussed him out with everything he had, even after Theresa had begged him
not to. He was waiting for Auntie Cora to tell him
that she'd overheard that conversation, too. He was
going to tell her flat out that he'd basically threatened to kill David Portugal if he even as much as
looked in Theresa's direction again. But Cora knew
nothing of that conversation. She was concerned
only about Ricky's and Theresa's future.

Cora giggled softly and shook her head, look-
ing at Ricky and Theresa. "Ricky, baby, you and
Theresa stay here. When your mother comes in,
I'll help you explain everything to her."

"Really, Auntie Cora? Really?" said Ricky.

"Yes, baby, really." Cora really wanted to laugh
out loud at her self-adopted grandson's awkward-
ness as he stood in the middle of his room, looking at her. Instead, she remained in control. "And
you two can stay in either her room or yours. I was
on my way out, anyway. I need some things. I
won't be back for a while."

Ricky and Theresa looked at each other, wondering what Cora could be picking up at that hour
of the morning, but kept quiet. They were just
happy that she had agreed to help them explain
the situation to Carlette, and to let them stay at her

house, instead of sending them to find a hotel at that hour.

The only thing Cora was going to pick up was her telephone, to call Perry Williams, the man she'd reluctantly begun to date almost four years after her husband died. He lived across the street from her, a few houses down. She could drive her car down there, and the kids would never know. She would stay awhile with him just to get out of their way.

She called Mr. Williams, explained her situation, and left for his house. She thought to herself, *At least they had enough grace to get married. Perry's asked me to marry him more than five times, and I haven't done it. My mother didn't teach me to live this way, and I know God doesn't approve. There's no way I can frown on what they've done. If they love each other and want to touch each other in private ways, they should be married. I'm really proud of Ricky and Theresa for doing the right thing. Oh, well, I'll just have to do my best to help them make Carlette understand.*

CHAPTER 45

Carlette and Ricky Sr. arrived at Cora's house early Saturday morning. Ricky Sr. paid the cabdriver and took all the luggage out of the trunk himself. When they entered the house, they could smell the breakfast Cora was preparing.

"Put the luggage down, honey. They're all in the kitchen." Carlette took his hand and led the way. When they entered the kitchen, Ricky Jr., Theresa, and Cora were all seated, heads bowed in prayer.

Cora was the first to look up. "Carlette! Baby! We've missed you! You have to tell us all about your trip!"

Ricky Sr. stood smiling while Cora and Carlette chattered and giggled, forgetting that anyone else was in the room. Theresa felt too uncomfortable to look up, and Ricky Jr. stared in confusion.

Ricky asked his mother, "Who's he?"

Theresa looked up and gaped. The man had to be his father; they looked like twins. She'd never met the man, but why couldn't Ricky see that? For him, it had to be like looking in a mirror. Hadn't

Carlette ever talked about his father with him? Hadn't she ever shown him pictures? That had Theresa thinking that Carlette was even weirder than she'd originally believed, and she couldn't help but stare in disbelief.

After a moment of silence, Carlette spoke up. "Ricky, this is your father."

"What father?" Ricky said, angry and embarrassed. He looked at Theresa, who quickly put a smile on her face.

Carlette gave Ricky Jr. a terse answer, while holding on to her smile, trying to save face. "He's your father, Ricky."

"Ma, why is he here now? I'm almost twenty-three. What do I need with him around here?"

Carlette stared at her son. "Ricky."

"No, Ma, I don't want to hear it! He ain't had nothin' to do with us! Now that I'm grown and you doin' good, we don't need him!"

"Ricky, baby, it wasn't like that," said Carlette.

"Then how come you never talked about him before? Why is it you never told me anything about him, other than you loved him and he was from the islands?" Ricky quizzed.

Carlette now began to realize that this wasn't the best way to introduce Ricky to his father. The matter was more private than she had realized. "Ricky, can we go in the other room and talk?" She started walking toward the living room.

"Sure, we can, but without him!" Ricky Jr. forced his chair out from under the table with his legs and followed her.

Carlette waited until they were both seated and comfortable. "Ricky, the reason why I never talked about your dad, other than to let you know that you had one and where he was, is that I thought we'd never see him again."

"Why'd you think that? Because he left you?"

"No, Ricky. Because we got separated some-how . . . well, by a deceitful person."

"Why didn't you tell me that, Ma? Why didn't you tell me?"

"Because I really didn't know how, and your father just confirmed the deceit and how it all happened. It's not a very pleasant story, no matter how you look at it."

"But, Ma, all that time I was hangin' with those boys in the streets, I thought my father was just like theirs, uncaring, negligent, and disrespectful. If I had known that he had no other choice but to be away from us, it would have saved you the heartache of seeing me almost become that way. Momma, I wish you had told me about him."

"Ricky, you know I told you how old I was—"

"Yeah. And I also remember you telling me about that girl I had in the house, and you asked me how I would feel if I thought you and Auntie Cora had been treated that way. Did he rape you, Ma? Did he? Did he rape you?"

Ricky knew what Theresa had told him about Dave and his mother, but he wanted to know what had made his mother get pregnant and marry so young. "Did he, Ma? Did he rape you?"

"No, not really."

"What?"

"I was in love with him. I wanted him, he wanted me, and it happened. I was disappointed at first, but he really loved me and married me.

He took good care of me, Ricky. Aunt Genevee had just treated me so cold that it was a blessing to have your dad there for me and to be carrying. You were an even bigger blessing."

"Then how'd you two get separated?"

"This man who owned the house that your father lived in lied to me. He said that the rent wasn't paid and wanted me to sleep with him for it whenever it was due, and I left. I went back to Aunt Genevee's, but that was the last place your dad looked for me. She told him that I'd left the island, and not to bother me, that I was trying to get over some things and get my life together. He never had a way to call or write me, and I didn't know he was even looking for us until now. I'm sorry, baby. I didn't intentionally mean to hurt you."

Carlette put her face in her hands, and Ricky took them in his.

"That's all right, Ma. That's all right. I've also been keeping something from you."

"What, Ricky?"

"Ma, I'm married."

"Married? Did you get one of those girls at your school pregnant?"

"No, Ma. I married Theresa."

"Ahem, ahem, Rick. Ahem!" Carlette choked, almost strangling on her own saliva.

"Ma, I'll get you a glass of water."

"No, Ricky, no, I'm okay. What made you marry her?" Carlette's nose was wrinkled in disapproval.

"Love, Ma, love."

"Are you sure that's what it is, Ricky?"

"Ma, I know about her past, and I know that

you and her didn't like each other too much, but she wants to apologize so that we can be a family."

"Yeah, right, and I'll believe that when hell freezes over."

"Momma, Theresa's just like you. She's been through some hard times, real hard times."

"Is that why you married her, Ricky? Because she's had hard times and you felt sorry for her?"

"No. I married her because I fell in love with her the first night I saw her. When we got to know each other better, I knew she was the one. She don't hide things from me and lie. She tells me what she wants me to know, and she stands by me. I love taking care of Theresa, but she don't want it that way. She believe in helpin' herself and her man if he need it. I like that, too. It makes me comfortable to know that she would have my back or could survive if somethin' happens to me."

Carlette's sarcastic face turned soft. Maybe her baby *was* in love. It sure sounded like it. Maybe she had misjudged Theresa because they had gotten off on the wrong foot. Regardless of what she felt, she had to say something quickly, not wanting to run her son out of her life. "Ricky, if you love her, then I'll have to try and love her, too."

"It won't be hard."

Ricky and Carlette rose from the sofa simultaneously and went back into the kitchen, where Cora, Theresa, and Ricky Sr. were sitting at the table, engaged in lively conversation. Ricky Sr. was promising everyone tours of the island, and Cora jokingly promised to fatten him up in exchange, because he was too thin and pretty. Theresa was laughing so hard, she had tears in her eyes.

When they saw Carlette and Ricky return, the room became silent. Ricky Sr. stood up from the table. His son rushed over to him and threw his arms around his waist. Ricky Sr. hugged him back and brushed his hair, and of course, the female tears began streaming. Ricky and Ricky looked at each other, and they were both tearing.

Then the laughter started, and the hugging continued. Theresa hugged Carlette and apologized to her, and the tears streamed again and kept flowing, until everyone had hugged and apologized for one thing or another that they thought had hindered their relationships.

CHAPTER 46

Carlette and Ricky Sr. decided to go back to the island. Although Cora never wanted Carlette to leave her permanently, both she and Ricky Jr. supported her decision, but Cora kept Ricky Jr. and Theresa as ransom. That was her guarantee that Carlette and Ricky Sr. would come back to visit soon. She also needed the company and help from Ricky Jr. and Theresa with the remaining clients.

After Ricky Sr. and Carlette left, Ricky Jr. and Theresa flew out to meet her parents. They wanted to give them the news of their nuptials together. Theresa's family was thrilled with Ricky. Her father loved him so much, he monopolized his time while they visited. Theresa teasingly accused her father of trying to steal Ricky from her after he bragged to her that he thought Ricky would have been the perfect son. He even allowed Ricky to call him Clifford, his real name, which was reserved for only special people.

Even her mother called her father General,

but Theresa had figured out not too long ago that he wanted it that way for a reason. The smiles on their faces had given that big secret away one morning, when she caught them kissing and cooing after leaving their bedroom. Embarrassed, Theresa had immediately stopped teasingly calling him General, or G, and just called him plain old Dad or Daddy. General or G made him sound like her mother's stud.

Theresa and Ricky Jr. both wrote and called the island often. They had to keep Genevee, Carlette, and Ricky Sr. up to date on what was happening with them and when they planned to visit.

Genevee was anxious to meet her great nephew's wife after hearing all about how pretty, strong, and intelligent she was.

Cora wasn't one for writing, but she called everyone frequently and sent boxes of what she called *stuff.* Her stuff boxes consisted mostly of canned fruit, vegetables, smoked meats, or the bread she would make, which did not perish easily, and also included clothing, figurines, anything she thought would be interesting.

Cora had just stuffed one of her boxes when the doorbell rang. When she looked out the peephole, she could see that it was a young white girl with brownish blond hair in a ponytail, who looked to be no more than fourteen years old. Cora opened the door and called loudly for Theresa. She knew that she and Ricky would be in his room, listening to music.

Theresa knew the familiar tone and immediately came running downstairs, jumping off the last step. "Cora? Cora, do we have a visitor?"

"Yes, Theresa."

Cora invited the young girl to step inside.

Theresa extended her hand. "Hi. My name's Theresa Roxen. What's yours?"

"Ginger. Ginger Moore."

"Come on in, Ginger. I'll show you to your room. Ricky will get your bags." Theresa led Ginger up the stairs and through the long hallway until they reached the bedroom almost at the end.

Cora tiptoed up later to critique Theresa's counseling skills. She listened outside Ginger's door just in case Theresa wasn't able to handle her.

"You can hang your things in there, Ginger. Are you hungry?"

"A little."

"Then after I've helped you unpack, I'll go get you something. We'll do the rest of your paperwork later."

While helping Ginger unpack, Theresa ran across a letter from the health department, which showed that Ginger had contracted gonorrhea from a David Portugal, and the heat of anger rose up to her face, making her turn red. She took a deep breath to compose herself so that she wouldn't scream out loud. She didn't really know how to begin a discussion about it, so after she brought Ginger's food up to her, she began to recount her own previous life as an actor.

Cora managed to sneak into her own bedroom before Theresa caught her, but returned to listen outside Ginger's door as soon as Theresa brought the tray of food back. Theresa continued to help Ginger get organized and inconspicuously slipped David Portugal's name in when it was convenient to see if Ginger would respond, but she didn't. Theresa decided she would continue her discussion with Ginger another time, since she didn't seem ready to talk about it. Cora thought that Theresa had handled the situation perfectly and smiled. She continued to listen secretly.

"So, Ginger, how old are you?"

"I just turned eighteen."

"You look much younger."

"That's what everyone says. Some like it that way."

Theresa knew exactly what Ginger meant. She had to leave or risk blowing up. She smiled. "You're all settled in and you've eaten. There's no need for me to hang around your room."

"You really know David Portugal?"

Theresa clenched her teeth the way she always did whenever she heard his name. She answered as if his name didn't faze her. "Yes. I do, Ginger. I've been in many of his plays. Why do you ask?"

"He's a pig. Don't trust him."

"Yeah, Ginger, I know."

"You know about him?"

"Yeah. That's why I'm here. Well, that's what brought me here. He did a lot of junk to me that I can't forgive him for."

Cora thought it was good that Theresa had opened up first to Ginger.

"If I told you what he did to me, you could," said Ginger.

"I don't think so, Ginger. It couldn't be worse than what he did to me."

Ginger dropped her head, and her hands fell

in her lap. "He talked and kinda forced me into having sex with him and another man."

Theresa wasn't surprised to hear that but managed to keep a straight face so that she wouldn't discourage Ginger from talking.

Cora was happy when Theresa didn't lose control.

Theresa crossed her arms to control her body language. "What made him do something like that?"

"I don't know, but that wasn't the first time someone had taken advantage of me like that. My mother's gay—"

"You were abused by your mother?"

Cora was thinking to herself, *Let her talk, Theresa. Just let her talk.*

"Nooo! She had a girlfriend, and I was embarrassed by it, so I gave her and her friend lots of mouth and trouble because of it. One New Year's Eve, when my mother and her friend went out, I had to stay with a friend of my mother's friend. She looked like a nice old lady with grandchildren, and she was nice to me, too. But when she ran my bathwater and wouldn't leave after I got in the tub and started washing me up, I thought it was strange. I was old enough to take my own bath, but I didn't say nothin'. I've always respected older people, no matter what. My mother did teach me that, so I just kept quiet and thought it was because she was one of them older ladies who always had to do everything for a kid, but she wasn't. She kept on washing me all over and breathing hard. I got scared of her then, so I told her my skin was burning. She told me okay in that high-pitched voice and asked me to stand up so that she could dry me off. Instead, she did something dirty to me, and I went crazy. I'd seen my mother do that stuff with that bitch—"

"Ginger, you won't be using that type of language around here, no matter what happens. Do you understand me?" Ginger's language made Theresa understand why Cora had been so firm with her.

Ginger responded quickly. "Yes, Theresa. Yes, ma'am." She was just trying to see what she could get away with. She had had very little parenting and was still practically on her own.

Cora was still listening, applauding Theresa's ability to remain firm, but not be too forceful. Ginger needed to feel comfortable enough to talk about herself and clear her head.

Ginger began again. "I started punching her in the head, Theresa, and I pulled on that old scraggly hair of hers until that bun fell down. She took me by my throat and pushed me up against the shower wall and told me I'd better be quiet, or she would kill me. Then she finished what she was doing to me, even though I squealed and begged. Then she made me go to bed."

"How old were you then?"

"I was fifteen. She thought I was ten, 'cause I was so little and looked so young. While I was fighting her, I was telling her that I wasn't some baby she could just take advantage of, but she didn't listen. She was just anxious. And she looked different when she got anxious, and that bun came down. Everything about her did."

Cora was still outside Ginger's door, listening and remembering her own encounter.

Before she became too consumed in her own thoughts, Theresa asked Ginger, "Do you feel gay or something?"

"Why? Do you?"

It was hard for Theresa to hold back the snicker, and Cora, too.

When Ginger thought about it, she smiled and tried to give a better response. "Oh! I see what you mean. No, I don't feel gay. I don't have an attraction to women."

Cora put her hand on her chest and let out a silent breath, relieved that Ginger hadn't been led into a lifestyle by false feelings.

Theresa was astonished by how well adjusted Ginger was, and proceeded to ask more questions. "So, did you tell your mom what happened to you?"

"Yeah, but she didn't believe me. But her friend did, because she'd set me up. When my mother left me alone with her, she told me that was why she'd told me that I was going to have a special New Year's Eve. And that's why she told me, 'Enjoy, Gin-Gin, enjoy,' because by the time they got back, I'd be all snapped up."

"So what does all this have to do with David Portugal?"

"My mother's girlfriend worked at one of the after-school centers David visited. He was one of the people who came to the center, trying to recruit young actors. I would go there after school, and she introduced me to him. He chose me the first day. My mother took me out of school so I could start taking lessons with him. She had to give consent since I was only fifteen."

Theresa looked at her, trying to see if she fit his profile, and she did. She was pretty, with flawless skin, shiny hair, and an exceptional figure for her age. "Yeah, Ginger, I can see why he picked you."

"Yeah, well, it wasn't just for some old play. If I had been smarter, I would have caught on to him when he was letting me drive that red sports car of his with the black convertible top, and giving me weed, alcohol, and other junk, and getting me into some of the dirtiest bars in town, knowing I was much too young to do any of that junk. That's where it all started. In one of those dirty bars. He was drunk out of his mind and asked me to be his designated driver. He had me drive to one of those sleazy spots and was about to go in when I told him I wasn't going in with him. He walked around to my door, dragged me inside, and nobody said a thing. Nobody tried to stop him. Okay, so now, I'm really scared, right. But he takes my hand and leads me to a front-row table. Theresa, they give live shows there, and I was right up front. My face turned so red, it must have lit up the room. Dave couldn't help but see how embarrassed I was, but instead of getting me outta there, he leaned closer to me and put his hand under my skirt. I tried to push his hand away and started screaming out of control. Then he told me to come on.

"I was really mad, but I didn't say anything to him, because I thought we were leaving. Instead, he led me to a different part of the bar and slid me into a booth. Then he went under the table and did the same thing that old lady did to me, and I cried again. There was an older white man sitting at another table, having a drink, smoking a cigarette, who kept watching us. I was so upset and embarrassed when it was over. I just sat there waiting for Dave to tell me when we were leaving. He got up and went to the bathroom. He told me we were leaving as soon as he came out. While he was gone, the old man brought his drink over to our table and slid in next to me. He asked me if I was okay. He said he knew I was underage, that he'd seen Dave bring me into the club and what he'd done to me. He told me, if I wanted him to, he could take me home or to the police station to turn Dave in. I was afraid of him, too. He'd sat there watching all of what Dave had done to me. Why hadn't he stopped him or called the police then?

"Anyway, I told him no, and he got insulted and started saying stuff to me, ugly stuff. Like he asked me how I could be afraid of him and not the nigger, and whether I thought the nigger was better than him. He went on and on. I tried to get out the other side of the booth, but he snatched me by the arm so hard, I fell back and hit my head on the seat. Then he started touching me. By that time Dave had come out of the bathroom and had seen us. He snatched the guy up and asked him if he'd paid for that, meaning me. The guy was telling him no in a shaky voice. Dave told him that he didn't have a right to be touching me, then. The man pulled Dave to the side, and they began to talk. I thought about running while they talked, but there are so many perverts around that area, I felt my chances of getting home alive by myself were slim.

"When Dave and the guy finished their conversation, Dave walked away, and the man came back to the booth with me. I pretended Dave was my boyfriend and said, 'Didn't you hear what my boyfriend just said to you? Now get away from me!' He just stared and grinned at me with those rotten teeth. I kept telling him to leave, until he told me to shut up. Then I started crying. He asked me who'd bought me the sexy little black skirt with the split on the side. I didn't want to answer him, but he yelled out the question, and I immediately told him Dave had bought it. He said, 'And that's the one you call your boyfriend, right?' I nodded yes. Then he told me, 'Well, your boyfriend says that you can either do what I tell ya so that he can get paid, or you can find your way home the best way you can.'

"I cried some more. He put his hand on my shoulder and said, 'The longer you cry, the longer it's going to take me to get what I'm here for, honey.' By that time I was trembling all over. He said, 'Calm down. All I want is what you did with your so-called boyfriend, baby. That's all they'll let us do in here, and that's all I want, and you can go. Come on now, baby. You don't want to try walking home with all these perverts around, now do you?' He knew I was too young to be in that bar, but he took advantage of me, and when he finished, he offered me a drink. I held my head down in shame and wondered if I could get cancer from the stinging of his liquor and nicotine mouth. When I didn't answer him, he asked

me again. I shook my head from side to side to let
him know that I didn't want a drink, and he got
up and left.

"When I looked up, I saw him giving Dave
quite a few bills. I believe they were hundreds.
Dave sat down in the booth with me again. He
said, 'Ginger, I love you so much. That's why I
did those things to you tonight in front of all
these people. But what you just did to help me
out made me love you even more. You're the
best friend I have, Ginger. No one else would
have done something so nice for me. How did
you know I needed money to pay for my apartment? I know what you did took a lot. Thanks for
helping me out. Most black women would have
never helped me to that extent.' That made me
feel proud and wish that I had tried to enjoy the
situation, but now that I see how sleazy it was, it
makes me feel stupid and dirty."

Cora was still listening outside Ginger's door.
She had heard many stories, but this one upset
her to the point of tears.

Theresa remembered the skirt Dave had bought
her and told her to wear the night he'd done
almost the exact same things to her, and the lies
he'd told after he'd done them. She almost lost
her temper. She asked Ginger, "Is that how you got
involved with two men?"

"No. I really believed Dave when he said that
I was being a friend to him. One day he told me
to come up to his apartment. He specifically
wanted me to take the bus there, and I did.
When I got there, he had plenty of beer and
hashish, because he knew I liked both. When I

was high enough, he asked me if he could touch me the way he had in the bar that night, and I refused. He said, 'Ginger, I know I said we're only friends, but I also told you that I love you, and I really do. I'm so in love with you, it makes me crazy. You're too young for me to have natural sex with, but we can still be lovers. Don't you love me, too?' I'd gained some affection for Dave, well, actually, a lot of affection for him, after being around him so much, but I didn't want to admit it, so through drugged and drunken, slanted eyes, I timidly nodded yes, that I loved him, too.

Then he said, 'Then prove how much you love me. I need to be able to touch you somehow, so that me and you can stay together. A man needs some satisfaction from the woman he loves. Come on, Ginger. Let Daddy have his way with his baby.' And I let him have his way with me right there in his living room. He gave me another beer and some more smoke, then tried to lead me upstairs. I pretended to pull back and told him I thought all he wanted to do was what he'd asked for. He told me he had but had changed his mind. He said he also needed to see what it would be like with me in a bed, and I went with him. When I got to the door of the bedroom, there was another man lying there, totally exposed and erect, if I can say that word." Ginger didn't want to offend Theresa again.

"Sure, Ginger, that's fine. Just no bad words, okay?"

"Okay. Well, that's when I realized that what Dave had done to me downstairs was for the benefit of the man upstairs. I tried to run, but Dave grabbed my arm and said, 'I thought you were supposed to love me. Are you just pretending to love me and to be my friend, Ginger? Are you just using me to get what you can out of me, or are you really my friend?'" Ginger sniffled. "I told him that I was really his friend, and he told me to prove it by being with him and his friend.

"The other man talked like a girl or something and was complaining about not being able to stay ready. Dave talked to me some more, and when he helped me undress, kissed me, and sat me down on his lap, I got weak. What topped that off was him pushing that weird guy away from us when he came too close while Dave was holding me and trying to soothe me, and I let Dave have his way. It felt good holding his neck while making love, but when we were done, it was the other man's turn. But he wanted me in a different way, and Dave let him have me.

"After he was done, Dave started kissing me and touching my body with his lips. The other man got jealous and cussed Dave out, telling him he did that only because I was a young white girl, that touching breasts and female sex were never a part of their agreement. To prove that I didn't mean anything to him, Dave performed oral sex on the guy right next to me on the bed, and then they did it again to each other. When they were done, Dave's friend wanted him to take me way out someplace and leave me or kill me, just because Dave had broken their agreement. Dave told him that wouldn't be necessary, that he had me under control, and told me to get dressed. When we got downstairs, he had sex with me again. By then I was aching. I trembled and moaned until he was done. I didn't want to lose him.

"When I started missing my period, I told Dave. He went to my mom and told her that I'd gotten pregnant because she'd been neglecting me too much, and that I should come and live with him until the baby came. That way she'd have a chance to think out her relationship with me, and with her friend. I never had that baby. Dave was so sexually abusive, I lost it. The doctor thought it was because I was too young, but Dave and I both knew the truth."

Theresa could relate again. She remembered that Dave's abuse had almost destroyed her.

"He went to my mother again to explain that she wouldn't be a grandmother, how my young, fragile body couldn't support the baby full term, and how remorseful he was about the loss, and she bought it. By the time I turned eighteen, I was Dave's prostitute. He'd shown me how to do all the things he'd done to me, and I did them because he'd told me that I'd never be anything more than white trash. I was pregnant four times by only God knows who, not including the one I lost by Dave the first time, and he was responsible for making me lose all of them. He'd make me have unprotected sex with men to get more money, whether I was expecting or not, and he'd have all sorts of unprotected sex with me himself.

"And whenever he wanted, him and that guy, or his boyfriend, the one he'd conned me into sleeping with the first time, Julian Montgomery, shared me constantly, and Dave would always continue when he'd take me back to my room.

He never made the mistake of having vaginal sex or touching my breasts in front of Julian again. He'd always make sure that Julian wasn't around before he made that move, and that continued until I finally got up enough nerve to come here."

Theresa knew who Julian Montgomery was, but kept a straight face, ignoring the name and changing the subject. "You came here on your own, Ginger?"

"Well, yeah, sort of. One of the older black women in one of his plays gave me this pamphlet, told me I looked like I needed it. Said that back in her day she couldn't even look mistreated, or she'd be accused of doing something wrong. Your house was at the top of the list."

"Does your mother know you're here?"

"No. And I'd appreciate it if you didn't call or tell her. I don't want to have nothin' ever again to do with that old, no-good woman."

"Do you think that your mother's no good because she's gay?"

"No. I think that she's no good because if she had paid closer attention to me, I wouldn't be sitting here at eighteen, pregnant for the sixth time."

"You're pregnant now?"

"Yeah."

"Is it David's?"

"I don't know whose it is, but it ain't gonna be mine. I'm scheduled for an abortion. I scheduled it before I left David."

"We can't make you change you mind, but we have to recommend that you have it and let us help you raise it or put it up for adoption."

"Nice try. But I don't wanna have that baby, or even look at what might be inside of me."

Theresa dropped her head. She wished to God she could have felt that way, but she loved her baby and still felt the pain of losing her.

CHAPTER 47

Ginger made good on her threat to abort her baby and didn't blink twice after doing so. Theresa and Cora had no choice but to support her decision.

Cora spent most of her time at the clinic's front desk, trying to talk with the head nurse regarding Ginger's situation, but got nowhere fast.

"It's done now. She's gotten rid of the baby." The no-nonsense nurse looked over her glasses at Cora. "I'll tell her to call you as soon as she wakes, if you want to go home. There's nothing more you can do here tonight, anyway."

Cora was disappointed in the nurse's lack of compassion. Couldn't she see Ginger was only a child? "Nurse, maybe you see this side of these girls every day. Maybe that's why you're so abrasive. But I see them before they come here, and I get to hear all about their nightmares, so forgive me if I seem to care too much. But if this girl was my daughter, I'd want someone like me to care about her if I weren't around, and I'm hoping that if she was yours, you'd feel the same way." Cora picked up her sweater and purse and headed back to Ginger's room.

"Miss, miss! I'm sorry!" The nurse now had a slight smile on her face. "If you want answers about Ginger, I'll have her doctor come in and see you."

"Thank you. I'd really appreciate that." Cora smiled politely, turned with ease, and went to Ginger's room. When she got there, Ginger was awake and lying in bed, crying.

"What's the matter, Ginger? There's nothing to worry about. You can go home in a few hours," Cora told her.

"I know."

"Then what's wrong, sweetheart?"

"It was his. My baby was David's. As soon as they sedated me, I knew it. I just knew it."

"Do you still love him?"

"I don't know."

"But you said he mistreated you."

"He did, Auntie Cora, but he still treated me better than my mother."

"Your mother never made you sell yourself, never forced you into sodomy, and never knowingly let other men have you."

"She might as well have, Auntie Cora. She let that old woman take advantage of me, and didn't do nothin' about it even after I told her. That could have made me gay, and she didn't believe me."

"Ginger, nothing can make you gay but you."

"Tell that to all the people who have been abused and think differently."

"Ginger, my only concern right now is you.

You need to think about what you really want for yourself."

"But I don't know what I want."

"What about school? Do you want to finish school?"

"Yes, but I wouldn't fit in. I feel as if I'm too old now . . . older than everybody."

"It's natural, Ginger. When this type of thing happens, most feel that their life is over, but when you get things back into perspective, and time goes on, you'll feel a change. You'll realize that none of what happened to you was your fault. And once we put David Portugal in jail, that should relieve even more of your guilt."

"You're going to have him arrested? You're going to have him put in jail? But I don't want him to go to jail, Auntie Cora."

"I'm sorry, Ginger, but that's one thing you don't have control over. I'm obligated to report what I feel is abuse."

"You didn't report Theresa's. I knew I shouldn't have come here."

"You did the right thing by coming to us, Ginger. You need help. And Theresa was of legal age when the abuse started, and her story wasn't as strong as yours."

"I won't testify against him, Auntie Cora. I swear, I won't."

"You don't have to. We can test your fetus."

"Suppose it's not his?"

"Ginger, we cannot allow David Portugal to keep on ruining young girls' lives. Don't you want to do something to stop him?"

Ginger didn't know what else to say. She knew

Dave liked to mess with girls, girls who were young and innocent, but just like with Theresa, the things he'd done to her were beginning to register differently, confusing her and getting her hooked. She couldn't distinguish the bad feelings from the good and didn't want to lose him, if he really loved her.

"But he still loves me, too, Auntie Cora."

"Then where is he?"

"He doesn't know where I am, or he'd be here."

"Okay. Then when we get home, we'll call him. If he promises to come get you and marry you, we won't tell on him. If he doesn't, then the police will pick him up before you can hang up the phone. Is that a deal, Ginger?"

Ginger was slow to answer.

"Ginger, is that a deal?"

"Yes, Auntie Cora, it's a deal."

Cora extended her hand to shake on it. She wanted Ginger to know just how serious she was about the gamble.

Ginger looked at her in confusion for a moment before realizing why Cora had her hand extended. "Oh! You're really going to shake on it and everything, Auntie Cora?"

"Yep! My word is always my bond. I hope yours is, too."

Cora knew she didn't really have a leg to stand on, but she was still determined to get Dave one way or another.

CHAPTER 48

Ginger was positive Dave loved her and would have never let her leave if he'd known she was pregnant. She immediately called him when she felt better, and Cora listened in on the extension.

"Dave, it's me. Ginger."

Dave pretended not to know who she was. "Ginger who?"

"Ginger Moore."

"Baby, the only Ginger Moore I know ran off on me when I needed her most."

Ginger became real quiet.

Cora kept listening, waiting for Dave's proposal and begging to start.

Dave spoke again, refusing to call Ginger by name. "Hey! You! You still there?"

Ginger was embarrassed but put on the best front she could. "Yeah, yeah, I'm still here."

"Good. Then are you finished playing on the phone, little girl?"

"Dave, you know who I am. Why are you doing

this to me? Why are you treating me this way? You said you loved me."

"Look! If you wanna be with me, you gotta act like it! You didn't! You got up in the middle of the night and left me! I don't know you!"

"But you were mistreating me and making me lose my babies, Dave."

"Are you telling me that some unborn babies are more important than our love?"

"Dave! Those were my babies, and s-s-s-some of them were yours. Y-y-you didn't care about them or me."

"A man buys you nice things, pleases you in a public place, at times other men wouldn't, and he doesn't care about you?"

"Dave, you turned me into your prostitute."

"And that hurt me more than it hurt you, Ginger. Do you know what it's like for a man to watch his woman having and performing all kinds of sex with other men and not be able to get it himself? That damn near killed me!"

"So did the gonorrhea you gave me, Dave. I'd never even had sex before, let alone gonorrhea. So you'd been messin' with dirty people, and I didn't say nothin' about you sleepin' with that asshole, Julian."

"You watch your mouth. Oh, wait a minute. That's your best feature." Dave kept silent for a moment, to make the comment even colder. "Why are you so quiet, slut? You run out of brilliant things to say?"

Now Ginger was really embarrassed and began to cry.

Cora was listening to every insult, and Dave just would not shut up.

"Now, you just listen to me. If you want me, you come back here right now, or it's over. Do you know how much money I'm losing because of your idiocy? Then there are the nights that I need you, Ginger! Do you know what those are like for me? If you had been there for me when we first got together, you wouldn't have gotten gonorrhea, because I wouldn't have had to sleep with anyone else! You, Ginger, you made that happen, because you neglected your man! Ginger! You're to blame! You made me do that, so don't try to blame those neglectful ways that you inherited from your mother on me!"

Cora couldn't believe the way this full-grown man was talking to such a beautiful, young girl. She wanted to intervene, but she knew that wouldn't be the remedy to Ginger's affection for Dave. She had to let Dave exhaust her patience, since interference only made fake passion worse. Tears ran down Cora's face, but she still kept silent.

Dave went on. "I need you here, Ginger. I need you to do the things for me that I've taught you to do. When should we expect you?"

Ginger knew what "we" meant and was crying with every emotion she had. "I'm not coming back there to let you and him rape me again."

"What do you mean, rape? We're all mates, baby."

Ginger didn't want him to finish explaining the relationship; she didn't want Cora to know the details about them being mates.

"We've all slept in the same bed many nights, and

many of those nights you initiated the behavior. Why are you acting so perfect now?" said Dave.

Ginger just stood there, holding the phone and crying.

Cora came into the room where Ginger was, took the phone out of her hand, hung it up, and hugged her. Ginger threw her arms around Cora's waist and cried until she felt empty.

"Are you ready to deal with him now, Ginger?"

"Yeah, I'm ready. He's filthy, isn't he, Auntie Cora?"

"Yeah, he's filthy, but we'll deal with him. You'll be the last baby he takes advantage of for a long time."

CHAPTER 49

Dave had been waiting for Julian to show up for over an hour. He had become frustrated and decided to call him.

"Julian! I thought you were coming right over? I have another girl for us, and everything's all set up, even dinner, and your portion's getting cold as we speak."

"Dave, I told you I can't come right now. My cousin's here."

"What cousin? You've never mentioned your cousin to me."

"That's because he showed up out of the blue, man. I can't send him on his way right now. I'll have to see you later, okay?"

"Well, yeah, I guess it's gotta be okay. If you can't make it, you can't make it!"

Before Dave could hang up the phone, an innocent, concerned voice echoed from the living room. "Dave, is everything okay?"

Dave slowly put the receiver down on the cradle

and walked toward the voice. "Everything's just fine, Dionne, just fine. Are you okay?"

"Yeah, I'm just a little sleepy, that's all. Probably the delicious food and wine put together. I'd better be getting home."

"No, no, no, Dionne. That's nonsense. We're friends. You can stay here tonight."

"Are you sure?"

"Of course. Here, take this stuff and go on upstairs. Take the largest guest bedroom. I'm going to turn in myself."

Dave was irritated with Julian, but he wasn't going to let that stop him. He had been planning to make his move on Dionne even before he'd known Carlette, but Carlette had been so beautiful and interesting to him, he had decided to get her before she got away.

Dionne was snoring when Dave reached the top of the stairs. The bedroom light was still on. She had always been afraid of the dark and had been sleeping with a night-light since she was a child.

He turned off the light and tiptoed over to her bedside, but she didn't stir. He wanted her to be somewhat awake during the attack and undressed her in a rough manner. When he finally got the nightshirt off that he'd given her to sleep in, she flopped back down on the bed, on her back.

"Uh-uh-uh! What's up? What's going on? Dave, is that you?"

Dionne was too groggy to know who was in the room with her or what was going on, and Dave never answered.

Dionne was making the sounds of agony that Dave had learned to recognize, so he decided not to cuff her. He began to fondle her while she continued making the sounds. When he thought of Julian, he became more aggressive, making her moan in pain.

Dionne tried to swing her arms to fight him off, but they felt so heavy, she could only flail them. Dave became angry and jerked her by her legs, making her long body slide down to the end of the bed. He used his moist lips to send her into a sexual convulsion.

"No!" Dionne screamed.

Dave did it again, then penetrated her. After she passed out again, he cleaned her up, dressed her, turned the light back on, and left the room. When he got back to his room, he couldn't sleep. He kept thinking about Julian and his excuse for not being able to make his planned event.

Dave got up, got dressed, and drove over to Julian's apartment. He became furious when he tried the key Julian had given him and it no longer worked. He went around the building and walked up the flight of steps that led to the sliding-glass door located in Julian's bedroom. He gently pushed. Julian had forgotten to lock it.

Dave slid the door open and stepped inside the room. The only light he had was from the streetlamps. He could see two figures lying in the bed, asleep, naked, and intertwined. He just knew that wasn't Julian. He must have let his cousin and his friend take his room, and slept in another part of the apartment.

Dave took a step closer to get a better look. Sure enough, it was Julian in bed with a white male.

Julian woke up, stroked and kissed the other figure's head, making him sigh, then slid downward, indicating to Dave that Julian was obviously cheating on him.

Dave shouted out, "Oh, hell no!"

The bedside lamp went on as if it had a mind of its own. Julian was shocked and trembling. He blurted out, "Dave! What the hell are you doing here?"

Dave didn't answer. He went over to the bed and pulled Julian out of it.

While Julian tried to pry Dave's arm from around his neck, his partner jumped up, grabbed what he could of his clothing, and ran. Dave was so enraged, he never noticed the man leaving, nor did he seem to care about him. His main concern was to punish Julian for betraying him.

"Let go of me, Dave! Let me go!" Julian was frantic.

"You really want me to let you go, Julian? Do you? Huh? Do you?"

"Yeah, Dave! Just let me go!"

Dave released his grip on Julian's neck. "What the hell were you trying to prove here tonight, Julian?"

Julian turned to address Dave's comment, but before he could answer, Dave punched him square in the face, and the two began to fight like two dogs after the same bone. But Julian was no match for Dave's muscular body. Dave beat Julian and wrestled him to the floor, causing him to land facedown with a thud, with Dave on top of him.

Julian begged Dave to let him up. "Come on now, man! You've won! You've whupped me! Let me up! I need to see a doctor!"

Dave wouldn't respond.

"Come on, Dave! Let's talk about it! Let's talk!"

Dave growled, "What's there to talk about, Julian? I've been bustin' my ass to keep you pleased all kinds of ways. You got on me about that white girl. Then I catch you all laid up here with a white man."

"Give me a break! You're the one who's always layin' up with them women and claiming it's because you hate 'em or that you want me or you to use 'em to get even! Even for what, Dave? Even for what? I don't be wantin' those women! I do that stuff for you! My preference is strictly dickly! And don't think for a minute that I don't know that you screwed that white girl again when you got her downstairs that day! And all them other times you pretended to take her back to her bedroom to calm her down! I heard her cryin' and tellin' you no many times, Dave! Many, many times! I heard it all, Dave! I heard every nasty word! But you did what I needed before you touched her again, so I let it slide!"

Dave still spoke in a low, angry tone. "Oh, so you let me slide, huh? Well, guess what? You don't get to let me slide. I do what I want, when I want, and how I want. I'm the one in control of this relationship and all the others. If you want me to do something, you talk to me about it, and if I feel that I want to stop, I do, and if I don't, I don't. But you don't ever, ever try to get back at me or take advantage of me. Do you hear me, Julian? Now, turn over!"

"I can't, man! You're lyin' on top of me!"

Dave eased his body up so that Julian could turn over and they could lie face-to-face. Julian could smell the weed and alcohol on Dave's breath.

"You know what, nigga? I should kill you."

"Dave—"

"Shut up, Julian! And if I have to say shut up again, I *will* kill you!"

Dave began assaulting Julian, and Julian's head began to spin.

"This ain't clean, David!" Julian cried out. He started gagging and threw up on his bedroom carpet.

"That's what makes this so wonderful, Julian. The freakiness of it. I'll be the last feeling you remember."

Julian grabbed his stomach. He was disgusted and could smell the vomit on the carpet.

Dave turned Julian over so that he could complete what he had started.

Julian tried to rise. "Please, Dave, please don't do this." He felt trapped and helpless.

"Do you still love me, Julian? Do you still love me?" Dave began kissing Julian. He knew this would get him going.

No answer.

"Come on, now. You know you love me."

Still, no answer.

Dave yanked his head and began kissing him on the lips. Julian could no longer hold back the effect the kissing was having on him. As sick as it was, the kissing was driving him crazy.

"I love you, Dave. I love you!"

Dave knew the kissing would work. Julian had always begged Dave for kisses, but Dave had always handed them out sparingly. Kissing men was for gay people and making up to lovers. He wasn't gay; he had sex with men from time to time, but mostly with Julian, when he needed different love. Different love didn't make a man gay; it made him more virile. Women just weren't enough for a man like him, who needed a man's love and body to fulfill him. Women sometimes left him empty, and he had no choice but to go to a man when that happened so that he could be filled.

Dave became more aggressive after his steroids and libido enhancers kicked in. When the ordeal was over, Julian lay on the floor, crying in a hoarse voice from pain and the embarrassment of telling his attacker how much he loved him.

"Do you want me to take you to the hospital, Julian?"

"Just go away and leave me alone, Dave."

"What's that supposed to mean?"

"I don't want to see you anymore. I just can't take the way you are."

That was an insult to Dave. It made him feel so insecure, he wanted to try and force Julian to want to be with him, but he put up a front and tried to look and sound as if he didn't care and was still in control.

"And how am I, Julian? Huh? How am I?"

"You just don't care. You saw how I was just layin' up here with that white man, and you did all the stuff to me—"

"What!" Dave refused to let Julian complete

what he was saying. He straddled him and slapped him with his rough, coarse hands, which reminded Dave of his father's farm, a place he hated and had vowed never to return to. As hard as Dave had worked for his father, his father had turned against him when Dave tried telling him that his best friend had sexually abused him early one morning in their main house, while his father, mother, and older brothers and sisters did the chores. He watched his hands as he slapped Julian harder and harder, first seeing his childhood attacker, then his father.

"Dave, please! Dave, please! You're going to kill me!"

Dave came out of his trance and stopped hitting Julian. He could see that he'd had enough. Julian's face and eyes were swollen, and he was bleeding. He walked over to the bedroom door but was afraid that he might be seen going out the front door, so he left by the sliding-glass door through which he'd entered the apartment, saying to Julian, "Go ahead. Have your white boy, that's if you're still any good. I've drained you. You won't be any good for a long, long time. Did he give you any money, Julian?"

Julian didn't answer.

"I asked you a question! Did he give you any money?"

"Yeah, Dave, yeah."

"Where is it?"

"It's on my nightstand."

"You just stay put, Julian, and don't you dare move."

Dave went to the nightstand, removed the

money, and counted it. "Two thousand dollars? He gave all of this to you for one night?"

"Yeah, Dave, yeah. Just take it—"

"As if you have to tell me that. You're just like my worthless father, weak and no good. You turn your back on those who help you most and love those who don't give a damn about you or your family. I should have had you turnin' tricks for me, instead of those women you complained so much about." He kneeled down and whispered in Julian's ear, "I should mess with you some more, but you know what? You can have your white boy. I'll just keep his money. I should burn down your apartment building, the way I burned down my father's barn." Dave laughed psychotically. "You know I smiled deviously as I watched him cry over his precious barn. Thinking of it still makes me laugh. Sometimes I even laugh out loud. Yeah, I should burn you out. That would teach you a lesson you'll never forget, just like it taught my dad."

The man is insane. Julian kept his face to the floor. He didn't want Dave to know what he was thinking. Dave was in an irrational state, one that could easily cause him to murder if the situation wasn't handled properly.

Dave stepped across Julian as he moved away from him to make his exit. As soon as David slid the glass door shut, Julian tried to jump up and lock it, but became dizzy. He crawled over to the bed to use it as support. As soon as he pulled himself up, he noticed he was bleeding and called the ambulance.

When the EMTs arrived and saw Julian's

condition, they questioned him about what had happened, but he wouldn't comment. Instead, he asked one of them to lock his sliding-glass door before taking him to the hospital. During the blurry, agonizing ride, Julian thought about what had happened, the things he'd been involved in with Dave, how Dave had turned on him, and how embarrassed it made him feel. Then he blacked out.

CHAPTER 50

It was early morning by the time Dave returned home. As he entered his apartment, Dionne met him on her way out the door, with a puzzled look on her face. Dave had forgotten that he'd left her there while he went on his personal mission.

"Dionne! Hey!"

Dionne stared down at the floor.

Dave lifted her chin. "Hey, Dionne, D-D-Dionne. What's the matter?"

Dionne just shook her head sheepishly as if nothing was wrong.

"Come on now, Dionne. Tell me the truth. Is something wrong?"

Dionne was still hesitant.

Dave liked hearing the dirty details of his "sex thievery." "Come on, Dionne, tell me."

"How long have you been gone, Dave?"

"I left last night, after you went to bed. Why?"

"Is there someone else in your house, Dave?"

"No, Dionne. Why?"

"Something happened to me after I fell asleep last night that I don't understand."

"What, Dionne? What happened?" David kept the confused look on his face.

"A man came into my room and raped me."

"What? If I find one of my no-good friends in this house!" Dave took a step like he was going to search the apartment.

Dionne grabbed his arm. "I already checked, Dave. No one else is here."

"But who could have done that, Dionne? We were the only two in the apartment last night, and when I left, I made sure the door was locked."

"I don't know, Dave. I don't know."

"Maybe if you'd talk to me about it . . . What did the man do to you? I mean, tell me something that will help me to help you." Dave wanted only to hear the dirty details. He wasn't the least bit concerned about Dionne's rape.

Dionne decided to talk, but not the way Dave wanted her to.

"It must have been a dream." Dionne could tell that Dave had been in some sort of struggle. "Ooh, Dave, what happened to you?"

"I got into a fight with a guy over some stupid girl. You think I look bad? You should see him."

Dionne smiled.

"That's the face I'm used to seeing, Dionne, the one with the smile on it."

"Yeah, I know. But that nightmare was awful. I even woke up sore."

Dave almost burst into laughter but managed a sincere smile before responding, "Dionne, it seems as though we both had a rough night."

As Dionne walked to her car, Dave smiled and licked his lips. *She was good, but not as good as my beautiful Carlette or my perfect Julian. She's one I won't waste any more Three Hour on.*

Dave shut his door, pulled the money he had taken from Julian's nightstand out of his pocket, licked his thumb, and proceeded to count it as he headed to his upstairs shower.

CHAPTER 51

Dave vowed never to be with Julian again, and he didn't want Dionne, either. They were both busters, as far as he was concerned. This would be one of the few times in his life he would be settling into bed alone. In his mind this was a definite no-no for a man so virile, important, charming, and gorgeous. A stud like himself should always have options.

After a couple of days of coming home alone, Dave decided to visit an old friend, Sajoy Trooner, for some much-needed attention. Sajoy was African American and Asian, with long, dark, wavy hair, a beautiful face, and as usual, an almost perfect figure. The kind Dave looked for. A traveler by trade, she bought and sold merchandise for many companies all over the world, and she had an eight-year-old daughter named Tooginee, who could have been her twin, and who traveled with her but at times was left with a nanny. Dave had courted Sajoy on and off.

She was headed out of town when he stopped

by. Dave and Sajoy talked for a while. He offered to babysit Tooginee while Sajoy was out of town. If he babysat her daughter, Sajoy would have no choice but to come to his house when she returned from her trip, and he was sure he would get compensation for it. After a short visit, he headed home with Tooginee.

When they arrived home, like he had done many times before, he placed the eight-year-old in a room with a large-screen television and a Game Boy. When she tired of that, there was the fully loaded recreation room. Tooginee had spent hours alone in that room, playing and calling all her friends.

It was 3:00 a.m. by the time Dave began preparing for bed. As he stepped out of the shower, there was a knock on his door, then a pound. Dave was angry about the intrusion and refused to be polite, no matter who it was at such an ungodly hour. "Who is it? Who the hell is it?" he yelled.

"It's the police!"

Dave knew something was terribly wrong. As he threw on his robe, he wondered if Julian had pressed charges and prepared to lie. Dave was an upper-class person. No one as insignificant as Julian would ever be able to win against him, no matter how many political people he had lain with. And Julian was good about sleeping with people of stature.

He took a deep breath and opened the door. There stood two officers and what looked like a detective. He began to breathe heavily.

The officers could tell that he had just recently

been drinking. The detective frowned from the smell, then spoke. "Are you David Portugal?"

"Yes, sir, I am." Dave was trembling uncontrollably.

"We're here to arrest you for the rape, assault, and prostitution of Ginger Moore," said the one that looked like a detective.

"But I don't even know her," Dave lied.

"Mr. Portugal, it would be in your best interest to wait until after we've read you your rights before you speak. Read him his rights, Officer Lester," the detective said as he placed Dave's hands behind his back.

The officer read Dave his rights. Dave asked if he could get dressed before going downtown and requested that a lawyer be present before he talked to anyone. He was granted his request.

Dave headed for his bedroom. One of the police officers followed him.

"Hey! Wait a minute! You don't have a search warrant! Why are you following me to my bedroom?"

"We have to keep an eye on you, Mr. Portugal," replied the officer.

"For what? I'm not going anywhere."

"You might have a weapon in your bedroom, sir."

Dave tried to slam the bedroom door on the officer, but the force of the officer's forearm and foot would not allow the door to close.

"Mr. Portugal! That was unnecessary!" The officer stepped inside the bedroom to continue his chastisement and was stunned when he caught sight of the little girl that slept in Dave's bed, through the commotion, without stirring.

Beads of sweat were popping out on Dave's forehead. "She's my niece."

The officer called the detective and the other officer into the room.

"She's my niece! I told you! She's my niece, man!" Dave bellowed.

The officer shook the little girl. She would not wake up. He shook her again, and she moved slightly. He could smell the scent of alcohol coming from the child, indicating that she was in an intoxicated sleep. He immediately called an ambulance, while the other two cuffed Dave without allowing him to get fully dressed.

Poor Dave. The idiot had left an open beer, which he had been sipping to calm his nerves, on the nightstand, and Tooginee had finished it for him. Having such a young minor in his bed, drunk, was going to cost him extra punishment, although he hadn't touched her or planned to.

As Dave was being cuffed, he thought about the cuffs he had used on some of his victims and the drugs he had used on all of them. If the police had had a search warrant, they would've found the drugs, and he would've been in a whole lot more trouble. If they were to dig into Ginger's past, he and her mother would probably get a lot of time for abusing her.

Before he could complete his thoughts, he was jerked around and forcefully pushed into the hard, cold backseat of the police car, while his neighbors gawked.

This made Dave think about the day he'd gone

over to Theresa's apartment building and stood in her doorway, coaxing her to do what he knew she really wanted to do. Theresa had actually invited him there, then had started a fight, to heighten her emotions that day. She had wanted Dave to be forceful, and as usual he had come through.

Dave whispered under his breath, "Do these people have police scanners in their houses or something? No matter what time the police come to someone's house, the whole neighborhood is up, watching."

When he arrived at the station, he was treated like scum, as the officers ridiculed, mocked, and controlled him. He was strip-searched. They even searched his buttocks for drugs, which he thought was totally uncalled for, and touched and groped him for no reason.

The questioning took the rest of his dignity. One officer pretended to be his friend, while the other yelled at and badgered him. He felt defenseless and wondered if he'd ever see the outside world again.

CHAPTER 52

Standing at Julian's bedside, Dave gently stroked his forehead, then tenderly kissed his lips. "Don't hate me for what I did."

Julian turned his head away and grunted. "I didn't tell on you. There's no need to pretend you care."

"But I do care, Julian. You know that I have hit you only a few times before, only when you've made me angry, and the other night was the first time you made me do what I did that time. Be honest, Julian. You are mostly at fault for being in here. You know you're mine. You know how I feel about you, how obsessed and possessive I am with you."

"That's why I bailed you out, Dave. I felt partially responsible for what happened between us. I should have told you about him. Maybe you wouldn't have gone looking for one of them to please you and gotten caught up in such a mess."

The flashback of Julian and the stranger made Dave squint evilly, and Julian telling him why he had lain with another man almost sent him into another rage.

Dave was trying to control Julian with his reasoning again. He forced a smile and the right words to come out of his mouth. "Nonsense. You had every right to do what you did to me—to cheat. I had no business flaunting those freaky whores around you, knowing how we felt about each other."

"You mean you did love me?" Julian tried sitting up.

Dave gently helped him to relax. "What do you mean, did, Julian? I love you still."

"Then what did we need with women?"

"Julian, in my rambling I said things about my father that are true, and my mother didn't listen, either. She took that man's side, no matter what he did or how foolish his decisions were. I figure all women are the same. They'll take the abuse, and we can have fun with them while we're doing it." The glazed look returned to Dave's face. "That way we kill two birds with one stone. We get back at those uppity tramps who try to use us for our money, and we send a message that they don't deserve respect, because they leave it all up to us men to decide if they should have it." Dave turned away and laughed wickedly.

Julian swallowed loudly.

Dave spun around. "You okay?"

"Yeah, my throat is just a little dry."

Dave quickly poured Julian a cup of water and helped him to drink it. "Oh, baby, things are going to be so different when you get out of here. Only the best for you from now on. Only the best for my man, and I mean every word."

Dave kissed Julian long and hard, the same way he had the night he attacked him. Julian reached up and held Dave's head. Dave's breathing became intense. He searched for Julian's tongue with his.

The kiss lasted much longer than anticipated. Julian loosened his embrace, indicating that it was enough. He needed to relax, to ease the stress on his battered body. What if a staff member was to catch them? What would they think, of him especially? He would be there alone when Dave left. Maybe they would refuse to care for him because of what they had seen. Suddenly Julian realized he wasn't as bold with his sexuality as he'd thought.

Dave had no concerns and pulled him closer, causing Julian to lose his breath. Dave burrowed his tongue deeper. He traveled Julian's body with his hands, then followed the same trail with his lips.

Julian struggled slightly, to indicate to Dave that what was happening in his hospital room shouldn't be.

Dave massaged Julian's trembling thighs. "Relax, babe, relax. We belong to each other. Nothing will come between us. I won't let it."

"But Dave—"

A hand covered Julian's mouth, and Julian arched his back, one of his unwilling hands embracing the back of David's head, the other his bed railing. *He's crazy. He's really crazy! Carrying on like this in a hospital. What was the matter with me, and why didn't I take heed when I first saw it? The man beat me, then took advantage of me. I should have seen this coming. It was a mistake. Getting David Portugal released was a big, fat mistake! The man's brain is definitely damaged. But there's no way I'll try to fight him off or call for help and embarrass myself further. They would all find out that I lied to get my white boyfriend, I mean Avery, to bail out my attacker while I lay here in my sickbed and waited. But I felt so guilty. And when he said he loved me just a little while ago, I even thought about going back to his place after I was released. No, I won't tell or scream or fight. I'll just lie here quietly and suffer because of my miscalculation.*

Julian saw Dave's head coming toward his face and remained still and quiet. *I shouldn't have answered my cell phone when I saw that number I didn't recognize. Why did I accept the call? Why didn't I just tell him to kiss off when I found out he was the caller and was calling me from jail? Why did his voice alone make me so stupid that I was almost climbing the walls? It had me jumping through hoops. It made me call Avery and lie about Dave exposing the two of us if he remained locked away. I knew Avery would run down and pay Dave's bail. He's too rich and his family is too uppity to want what happened mentioned in any tabloid. I knew he would come running with that bail money and use my identification so I could claim it later. But how did his voice alone get me so excited, although it made me remember what he had done to me? Why did it make me think more about the great sex we had the night he put me here more than the reason why I am here? God, I need help. I need help. If there is a God, like my grandmother says— and even if you don't like my lifestyle—if you're out there, please, God, please, help me to get away from this lunatic. Give me a way out.*

Dave lowered his lips to Julian's. Julian relaxed as he breathed through his nose and slowly released the bed railing. He would have to embrace Dave, or he might not leave the hospital alive. He closed his eyes. The tears hidden under his lids slid down his face.

Dave stood up, and Julian opened his eyes and stared helplessly as he watched Dave begin to unzip his pants.

"If you're really good to me, I'll see about staying with you overnight," Dave whispered.

Julian closed his eyes tightly and lay quietly as he waited for Dave's next move.

Although Dave had forced himself on Julian the night he ended up in the hospital, Dave saw it as a sexual favor. Julian owed him and knew he was crazy enough to carry out the rest of his plan right there in his hospital room.

"How are you gentlemen getting along?" said a female voice from the doorway.

"Great! Just great!" Dave quickly adjusted his clothing, spun around, and looked at the nurse sheepishly. He relaxed a little when he saw her looking down at the pad she was writing on.

"Well, we're going to take your friend here down for some more X-rays. He'll be gone awhile. You might want to come back later," said the nurse.

"How long will the X-rays take?" asked Dave.

The nurse looked up from her pad suspiciously. "More than an hour, hon."

"Nurse, can I spend the night?" asked Dave.

The nurse glanced over at Julian, a smile on her face. She saw pleading in his eyes. "No. Mr. Montgomery was almost assigned to intensive care when he came in. He needs to be alone for a while to get some rest so that he can heal. We still haven't found out all that is wrong with him." The nurse crossed her arms. She was almost positive that the visitor had something to do with her patient's condition. "Maybe he can have someone call you later if he's up to it, sir, but right now he has to have some tests run, and we don't know how long that will take." The nurse smiled politely.

Frustration caused Dave to run his hand over his head vigorously. Surprising Julian by climbing into bed with him later so that they could cuddle and make love the way Julian liked it had been a part of his plan before the nurse walked in. He had to think about that one. He had gone more than a day without a fix. "Okay, but please call me later. I'm really concerned about him," he replied.

The nurse almost chuckled as she proceeded to prepare Julian to be taken to X-ray. *As they say, I might have been born at day, but not yesterday, at night, but not last night,* she thought to herself as she rolled the bed toward the door, then looked back. "Okay, sir. Mr. Montgomery will see you later." Her smug look went unnoticed.

Dave ran his hand over his head again. He needed relief. "Can I use his bathroom?"

"No, sir, it's against our hospital policy. There's a public restroom down the hall." The nurse pushed Julian out of the room. "Is he the reason you're in here?" she asked him in a hushed tone.

Julian whispered back, "No, he's not the one, but I don't want him here. He wants me back, but we broke up aeons ago." He burst into tears. "And now I'm more than clear on why I stayed so long and put up with so much from him—history, sex, and his money. It all had my reasoning altered, until he showed up today out of the blue." Julian tossed his head from side to side. "And now I know all I did was waste my time. It just wasn't worth it, and neither was he."

The nurse smiled.

Julian's thoughts went back to his plea. *There is a God. He sent this nurse to my rescue.*

Dave ignored the nurse's orders. No woman could tell him anything. As a matter of fact, if he could get her alone, he would prove it by taking her down where she belonged and putting her in her place.

He stepped into the large, clean bathroom, shut the door, and proceeded with his plan. He left relieved, refreshed, and smiling like the lunatic Julian had portrayed him to be. He thought, *Why do they call pleasing yourself a sin, when it's so satisfying?* He had once heard a pastor preach about it, stating that it was unnatural and wrong. The preacher had had the nerve to say that masturbation was a form of having a same-sex partner and encouraged homosexuality. *If that were true, I wouldn't still want women every now and then, now would I?* Dave asked himself.

That stupid sermon had made Dave so angry, he took one of the pastor's supposedly most devout, goody-two-shoes female parishioners home with him the same day and had some fun with her, to prove the pastor wrong. Dave laughed. "So much for him telling me that I'm gay because of my sexual preferences, and her telling me how she's saving herself for marriage. My Three Hour told another story and allowed me pleasures with her that I learned to use on Julian." He cleared his throat. *Wonder what happened to that fine woman. She had one of them big, tight, hot behinds, which my big, bad friend couldn't say no to.*

Dave suddenly remembered that she'd called him, talking about this erotic dream she had had about him. He'd talked dirty to her, told her what he wanted to do with all that fine wagon she was draggin', and she'd hung up on him and never called again. *You would think she would have figured out what me and Three Hour had done, and wouldn't have wanted anything else to do with me, but she didn't. She was strictly an airhead, and there ain't nothing but one thing I want from one of them. Good riddance to that holy garbage!*

Dave walked down the hall, laughing loudly, causing everyone at the nurses' station to stop what they were doing and stare at him until he was out of sight.

CHAPTER 53

Dave Portugal sat in the courtroom, looking simple and powerless as he waited for his paradoxical views to be challenged by experts. Where had his perfect little setup gone wrong? He had given out so much good loving, there was no way he should be sitting in a courtroom filled with so many people he had pleased and who were now willing to testify against him, and with such viciousness. His lawyer had shown him the gut-wrenching statements.

What he hadn't known about was Cora's scheme to get Ginger to see him for what he really was, so that she would press charges, and how that scheme had worked and caused a domino effect. Ginger, Carlette, and Theresa, all victims of David's abuse and all in the same house, were godsends. From there, the discussion had snowballed. Everyone who had been traumatized by Dave began making calls. Many of his victims were too ashamed and afraid to show up to testify because of his previous threats. Maybe he would win and come after them again. Maybe they had been foolish for allowing themselves to be put in such a predicament.

The testimony against David Portugal was overwhelming. First, Ginger took the stand and described in detail what he'd done to her. The defense tried to confuse her, but she knew what she had been through with Dave. Her story never changed.

Cora's testimony supported Ginger's statements. She told the court about the conversation between Dave and Ginger that she had heard over the phone at the house.

Theresa spoke next. Her story was similar to Ginger's, and she also talked about her conversations with Ginger regarding Dave's abuse, and the conversations she'd had with him regarding his abuse of other people.

Carlette told how he'd drugged her and taken advantage of her.

Surprisingly, Dionne showed up and told the same story. Cora had found her after going to Dave's theater hall and asking the actors if they knew anything about him and his abuse of women. Dionne had called Cora later and told her about her visit to Dave's apartment and her suspicions that someone had broken into his apartment that night and raped her.

After hearing what had happened to the girls that had gone to Cora's house, Dionne knew that her assault hadn't been a dream, as she'd originally thought. Dave had actually drugged and raped her.

More surprising, Julian testified against him, too. The police had taken a report of Dave's abuse at the hospital. At first Julian didn't really want

Dave arrested. He wanted money. He wanted to be compensated for his pain and suffering, and for the time he'd missed from his modeling and acting career because of Dave's abuse, and for Dave not really loving him and only him when he thought he needed Dave to.

Without shame, Julian told the court about being taken by ambulance to the emergency room after Dave broke into his apartment through his second-story sliding-glass door, beat him, then forced him to have sex several ways. Julian told them that it happened because Dave became jealous and enraged over a lover he'd caught in his bed that night and that Dave had had no right to be there, let alone put his hands on him. He told them that Dave had lined up many young women for them to have sex with, but that he had always thought that these women were willing and that he hadn't really wanted to have sex with any of them because he was gay. He said that he was so afraid of Dave that he'd just do what Dave said to please his sexual freakiness. To back up his story of fear, Julian produced pictures of his beating for the court. He even had a backup who could attest to Dave being in his hospital room after the attack, if it came up. He was going to say that Dave had forced his way in and raped him again.

Tugging on his tie, Dave cleared his throat as he sat on the stand. "They were willing. They all wanted my money—to use me. If I *had* taken advantage of them without their consent, they would have deserved it. They were all acting like greedy whores and needed to be taught a lesson."

Dave's lawyer grabbed his face with his hand and gripped his writing instrument tight.

The prosecuting attorney looked David Portugal in the eyes with a cold stare. "What taints them taints you. Do you have such little respect for your manhood that you use it to punish others?"

Dave frowned. "Yes. I mean, no. I was only getting compensated for what they promised me. Why should I have to give and not get? Why is it, when I ask them for something and get it, it's called rape, but when they ask me, it's called an okay thing to do? Is it because they are my lovers and they should get it, and I shouldn't expect anything in return, just because I am a man who doesn't refuse to love whoever wants to be loved? Even married people compensate each other, Counselor."

"Mr. Portugal, that might be so, but most couples don't drug each other so that they can be compensated."

Dave lost his poise and growled, "Maybe men should. They wouldn't have to listen to their whining bitches while they got pleased."

Some of the courtroom spectators laughed, causing the judge to beat his gavel on the sounding block. "Order! Or we will clear the courtroom!"

The prosecuting attorney continued. "Is that why you drugged your lovers, Mr. Portugal? So that you wouldn't have to listen to the whining?"

"I never drugged anyone, at least not without their consent!" Dave pointed around the room at all his victims. "Yes, I had sex with all of them, but we were all willing, and we all took libido enhancers together to make the sex more interesting, and to give us more feeling."

"So you're telling this court that all these people are pretending to be victims? That they are all lying and enjoyed being unconscious and raped, that being out cold stimulated them, gave them more feeling, as you put it?"

"They were conscious."

"Mr. Portugal, we have established that Three Hour allows you a certain window to have sex with a partner while they are weak and in a hallucinogenic state, before they totally pass out. Now, tell me, how did your partners enjoy you while they were unconscious from Three Hour?"

"I don't know what you're talking about." Dave swallowed hard. "What is Three Hour?"

The prosecuting attorney stepped away from Dave and picked up an exhibit from the table. "Do you recognize this drawer, Mr. Portugal?"

Dave squirmed. He looked at his lawyer for help, but he didn't respond.

"Your Honor, will you direct the defendant to answer the question?"

"Answer the question, Mr. Portugal," ordered the judge.

"It looks familiar. It's a drawer," said Dave.

"Do you know where this drawer came from?"

"No, sir, I do not."

The prosecuting attorney stepped over to his projector. "Mr. Portugal, this is a picture of one of your guest rooms." He zoomed in on the missing drawer. "There's a drawer missing. This is it."

"So?" Dave tried to hide his concern because he knew what this was leading to.

The prosecuting attorney turned to the judge. "Your Honor, I present to you Exhibit A. This drawer was confiscated from one of the defendant's dressers. As you can see, it contains the Three Hour drug as well as other drugs."

Dave's attorney stood up. "Objection! That was not placed into evidence!"

"Your Honor, if you will check our list, you will see that we requested that all containers, including dresser drawers and their contents, be part of our evidence," said the prosecuting attorney.

The judge raised his brow as he looked at the list. "Objection overruled. Continue, Counselor."

As the prosecuting attorney was about to speak, Dave cried out, "I use them on myself during nights I can't sleep!"

"No more questions for the defendant." The prosecuting attorney went back to his seat.

Wiping the perspiration from his brow, Julian breathed a silent sigh of relief. This case really had him nervous and on edge.

After the judge had dismissed the court for the day and everyone had filed out of the courtroom, Dave argued with his lawyer about not doing more.

The lawyer told him, "It's not over, but if we're going to win this case, I need you to maintain a cool head." Dave's lawyer also informed him that Julian's lover was the person who had bailed him out. The two could say that Dave had threatened them. If their testimony was found viable, it would mean a harsher sentence for Dave.

Still feeling restless and insecure even after David Portugal left the courthouse, Julian wiped more sweat from his forehead as he headed home for the day.

CHAPTER 54

The trial lasted several weeks. To Dave, it seemed like forever, like the questioning would never end. As time passed, he got less and less rest and was unable to keep up his pristine appearance. He decided to grow his hair and his beard. That way he could just trim the hair on his face and put his mane in a ponytail.

Everyone involved showed up faithfully and brought their A game with them, ready to make sure that their offender received the harshest sentence possible. Angry, ready, and fired up, if they could have thought of a cheer, they would have gathered together and chanted it.

Toward the end, Julian thought about not going back to the courtroom and just dropping his complaint. To him, Dave looked good with his new Hollywood-talent-scout makeover. He would often daydream about Dave and wonder how he could look so good with all that hair growing everywhere. Then there were the times when Julian would come back to his senses and think about what would happen between him and Dave if Dave was found not guilty. *No! The man needs to be punished.* This would be the last round of questioning before Dave's sentencing, and if the victims were to have justice and peace, Julian had to stick to his guns and do his part.

Although Dave hadn't molested Tooginee, the court wanted to question her separately, but Sajoy would not allow it. She hoped that her baby would just forget all about David Portugal and denied the court permission to interview her child. She was just happy that her little girl hadn't been harmed.

The jury's decision came swiftly.

Dave was convicted on all charges and given the harshest sentence possible. As he was being carted away, Dave, his eyes tear filled, looked over at Julian. Julian's brain went into overdrive. He had to get Dave out of this mess without him doing too much time. There was no denying he still had feelings for the man. Dave just needed a little cooling-off period to acknowledge his wrongs.

Outside the courtroom, all the women, except Ginger, hugged Julian and each other, and thanked Julian for his testimony. They felt that the pictures of his abuse were among the most damaging and incriminating things placed into evidence.

Ginger walked away from the celebration, not wanting to have anything to do with Julian. She knew he'd lied about not knowing that the girls hadn't been willing. He had had her perform oral sex on him and had had anal sex with her many times. When she heard his testimony about what Dave had done to him and saw the pictures of the abuse, she was happy that Dave had almost killed him and wished Dave had. Julian would have been another unpleasant memory out of her way, one less nightmare to remember.

As she continued down the seemingly unending corridor, there was a tug on her arm. It was Julian. She immediately snatched her arm away from him and ordered him to get away from her.

Julian was determined to get her attention and took her arm again. "Ginger, wait a minute. I'm sorry, real sorry."

Ginger just stared at him, hate in her eyes.

"Ginger, I know you hate me, but what I said in the courtroom was true. I didn't want to sleep with you or any other woman. Dave would make me angry with you. He'd tell me that you'd said different things about me. He would tell me all sorts of things to upset me and would make it seem as if you'd done or said what he'd tell me."

"Julian, the way I see it, you sent me to the hospital, and he sent you to the hospital. Now we're almost even." Ginger stared him dead in the eyes. "You can't blame everything you did on Dave. You have a mind of your own. So do me a favor, Julian. Pray to God that you remain what you think you are and that you never have any children, 'cause I know your punishment ain't over yet."

While Julian stood there, looking defeated, Ginger looked through him and called out to the women. "I'll be in the van, waiting!" She walked away from Julian without looking back.

Julian clenched his teeth and fists. He had helped to sentence his lover to almost thirty years, and this was the thanks he got? Didn't Ginger know that he knew people who knew people? He had slept with judges, governors, lawyers, and policemen. When the time was right, he would talk to someone about Dave. Even sell his body to get Dave another trial if he had to. All he had to say was that he and Dave had fought and Dave had won, that the sex had been consensual, but that he hadn't wanted to enjoy it, because he was still angry. He would make Ginger look like the biggest whore that had ever lived.

Julian narrowed his eyes and smiled wickedly. Ginger would be sorry for talking to him like he was nothing.

CHAPTER 55

Ginger felt relieved that the trial was over and pleased with the judge's sentencing. She was happy and grateful that Cora, Theresa, and Ricky Jr. had been there for her and had saved her from that monster that had taken her innocence. She had been vindicated of the sins he'd led her into and given a second chance before he'd totally consumed her. That was much better than what he'd received. He wouldn't be out for a long time, which gave her relief to the point of real happiness.

As she walked through the court building, she saw a little girl of about ten or so looking up and smiling at a handsome suited man. He was also smiling and had his hand under the little girl's chin. He reached down for her hand, as if he was going to escort her someplace. Ginger was determined to stop what she thought might be a bad situation. She didn't want the little girl to go through the hell she had been introduced to, knowing it would take a lifetime to erase the trauma her mind and body would endure.

As Ginger approached them, she seemed to be walking in slow motion. Then she heard the child say, "Daddy! Daddy! Happy birthday, Daddy! Mommy's waiting for us outside! We're going someplace special!"

Then she saw the man pick the little girl up, and they gave each other a big hug. That shocked her. She had never been hugged by a man, not even her father. She didn't know her father. She had no idea that a man could be so caring. She could only stare at them in wonder as she tried to put herself in the little girl's place. Then she heard a deep voice.

"May I help you, young lady?"

It was him, the man that the little girl had called Daddy. He had called her a young lady. Did he mean that? Couldn't he see what she really was? Ginger continued to stare.

The man spoke again. "Young lady? Are you lost?"

Ginger could barely speak. "N-n-n-no, no, sir."

"Are you okay, sweetheart?" The man was very pleasant. "Are you okay?"

Sweetheart? Am I okay? Ginger couldn't believe it, but it felt good that a stranger was truly concerned about her welfare, and she responded respectfully. "Yes. I was on my way out of the building. I thought I knew you two. I guess I made a mistake."

"That's okay, sweetheart. It's been said that everyone has a twin." The man put his daughter down, took her hand, and they headed for the door.

As Ginger exited the building, she realized the display she had just witnessed between the father and child meant that not all men treated women and little girls the way she had been treated by the men she had encountered. They could be gentle, loving, caring, and thoughtful. Some could even act like they were supposed to and be real fathers. That made her determined to work harder on herself mentally and physically. She wanted to leave the negative behind and be prepared to meet a man like the one in the courthouse corridor, who had seemed to love the little girl so much that even on his birthday she was still his favorite gift.

By the time Ginger reached the courthouse steps, Julian caught up to her again. He grabbed her arm and whispered in her ear.

Ginger was trembling and pale when she got into the van. Her lips were tight, and her jaws were slightly puffed with air. She saw Julian smirk and then casually hop into a cab and ride off, as if the events of the day had never occurred.

"What's wrong, honey?" Cora cupped Ginger's hands with hers.

"He's going to have him released." Ginger tried blinking back her tears, but they flowed down her cheeks.

Cora frowned. "Who?"

"Julian is going to have David released."

"He can't do that. The judge's decision is final," Cora replied.

"Auntie Cora, you just don't know these people. Julian has friends in high places. I know them. Julian introduced some of them to me and Dave, and I sold myself to them willingly.

And I said it was to please Dave, but when I saw all that money, I was willing to do whatever they wanted, and I did." Ginger pulled her hands out of Cora's. She wrung them as she sat zombie-like and stared at nothing. "They were big friends of Julian's, not Dave's, and they can find ways to get Julian whatever he wants." She swallowed hard. "And when I left, they wanted me, Auntie Cora. That's why Dave was so furious. Those people wanted me, and he wanted their money."

The other women were staring at Ginger with sadness in their eyes, their cheerful victory celebration blunted by the disturbing news.

"Would you like to go away, Ginger?" asked Cora.

"Where would I go, Auntie Cora? I have no one other than you who cares about me."

"I have other friends in other places, with houses, and caring people just like my unit. You can go to one of them if you'd like."

Ginger dropped her head, then lifted it. "I'll go. Maybe it's better that I do."

"Then it's settled. You will leave when and if you decide you are ready."

"Julian's a monster."

"He seemed shifty from day one to me, Ginger. The way he sweated when David was on the stand. He seemed to be afraid that something would be exposed, something he didn't want anyone else but the two of them to know."

Ginger lowered her head. She knew about the secret. It was the fights. Julian loved the way Dave handled him when they ended, but most of all, he loved the way Dave had slammed the door in Ginger's face to keep her out. What Julian didn't know was that Dave had always found a way for her to watch, which he had demanded she do in Julian's absence.

After Cora and the women celebrated their victory in court, Cora and Mr. Williams headed to Las Vegas and got married.

Genevee headed out there to meet them, with Frank in tow. They had gone for years without speaking after the day she had accused him of wanting to be with her niece Carlette. Genevee had eventually apologized for her immaturity and confessed that she had been in love with Frank since the day she met him. They had made up and planned a date on the same day Carlette had shown up for her visit. At the time, Genevee hadn't been ready to tell Carlette that Frank was the reason her hair was looking extra nice. But now her secret was out, they were married, and Frank could admire her plump bottom as much as he wanted.

Chapter 56

Cora's house was now Ricky Jr.'s and Theresa's responsibility.

Ricky ran his hand over his wife's stomach as they sat on the bed, talking. "This baby will make it and have more than we did. You won't go without, either, Theresa. I have never loved anyone the way I love you. Y'all mean everything to me. Hope you're not too disappointed that we didn't have a big wedding. We should have—"

"It doesn't matter. I feel the same way. Bigger don't mean better or more special. What we have couldn't be any better or more special to me. I have a man who cares not only about me, but about other people, who is going to be here for his family's needs. I love you so much, Ricky. I don't know how I lived without you for so long." Theresa laid her head on Ricky's chest.

Ricky cupped her head with his hand. "You'll always be my sweet, sweet Theresa. No other woman will be able to fill your shoes."

CHAPTER 57

As they lay on the beach, celebrating their second honeymoon, Ricky Sr. leaned up on one elbow, placed his hand under his head, and allowed his eyes to roam his beautiful wife's body.

"God must have put us together. I can't believe we are a family again, and I can't wait for our son, daughter-in-law, and grandchild to visit us." Ricky Sr. sat up straight. He ran his hands down his thighs to brush off the sand. "You know what else I can't believe?"

Carlette remained lying on her stomach, her eyes closed, enjoying the sun. "What, baby? What can't you believe?"

"How beautiful you are, and that you belong to me. And even though you are beautiful, your sweetness overpowers it all. No other woman will be able to take your place. You will always be my beautiful, beautiful Carlette in every way."

Carlette turned over onto her back and looked into her husband's eyes. "Kiss me, Ricky. Kiss me the way you did the first time our lips ever touched."

Ricky Sr. didn't waste time. He lifted Carlette off the ground as he stood, and kept his lips to hers as they headed back to the hotel. He looked at her. "This will be a celebration more special than the first."

"Ricky, nothing can replace the first celebration. It was the beginning of something magical, the love we found in each other and the special way we changed each other's lives for the better. Nothing on this earth will ever change that or the love I have for you."

"I feel the same, Carlette. I feel the same. And we will never be separated again, no matter what I have to do to prevent it."

Ricky kissed Carlette passionately again as they slowly strolled across the warm sand, entered the hotel, then the elevator, and then their room.

"God, how I love the way my husband kisses me. Your kisses fill me to a point where lovemaking is almost unnecessary." Carlette rolled her eyes upward under her closed eyelids. "I said *almost*, God, *almost* unnecessary. Don't you dare let this moment pass. I mean, can you please help this moment to be even more special?"

Carlette wanted to giggle at her silliness, but her husband's passionate kiss overpowered her. There was no way she wanted to interrupt the lovemaking, which would take her to a place from which she would never want to return.

As Ricky laid Carlette on the bed, she thought, *Not many women own this kind of love, and if I ever lose my husband, I will probably never find it again. He makes me feel so special that I'm prepared to please him in every way so that nothing will ever come between*

*us again. Not even the pretentious behavior I displayed
in the past so that he wouldn't think any less of me.*

*Oh, God! Oh, God! I missed him so much all those
years we were apart, and I tried so hard after we found
each other again. Soon we will be holding each other so
close, we'll become one, and now I'm ready to show my
wonderful husband how much I love him and want us
to be that way. I'm now willing to give all the passion
from my heart that our unity deserves. I want to be sure
that he will keep his promise to never let me go again.
Our life together is like a passionate dream that I never
want to wake up from, and from now on, I am going to
do all that I can to make sure my dream never ends.*

Carlette whispered in her husband's ear, "I
love you, Ricky, with all my heart." Then she
thought to herself, *And so that I never forget what I
went through to get here with you, I will be sure to enter
it in my journal as a reminder, if I ever think about sep-
arating from the man I love again.*